"Sheehan's writing is lively and vivid and her feel for historical detail is fine."
—*The New York Times*

"Sheehan uses her skills as both a psychologist and a writer to create a solid, insightful story that will leave fans eagerly awaiting another visit from the strong heroine, her dog and her friends."
—*Kirkus Reviews*

"A searing tale of love and desperate acts set against a backdrop of surreal beauty and unspeakable cruelty . . . Enthralling, exhilarating, *The Center of the World* is a cinematic tale whose characters and their difficult choices will stay with you long after you've closed the book."
—Suzanne Chazin, Award-Winning Author of *Land of Careful Shadows*

"Jacqueline Sheehan's riveting novel fuses family anguish, political drama and page-turning storytelling. *The Center of the World* is a deeply satisfying read of the heroics and viciousness we rarely hear of—and choices we hope to never face. I loved this book."
—Randy Susan Meyers, National Bestselling Author of *Accidents of Marriage*

"An epic story of war and peace, love and fear, family and friendship . . . In turns heartbreaking and heartwarming, *The Center of the World* is the perfect book club selection—intelligent, thought provoking, and utterly captivating."
—Lori Nelson Spielman, International Bestselling Author of *The Life List*

"The day I discovered novelist Jacqueline Sheehan marked a great moment in my reading life. In *The Center of the World,* her best book yet, Kate Malloy truly has a heart that is a compass, holding fast to true north. Sheehan finds new ways to prove to the world that mothers are the strongest people on earth."
—Jo-Ann Mapson, *Los Angeles Times* Bestselling Author of
Solomon's Oak, Finding Casey, and *Owen's Daughter*

"Jacqueline Sheehan's striking new novel, *The Center of the World,* is a sure-handed exploration of grief and transcendence. I found these characters memorable, the story compelling, the author's ability to make a place come alive on the page a rare gift. Sheehan is a writer with a large heart."
—Steve Yarbrough, author of *The Realm of Last Chances*

Also by Jacqueline Sheehan

Picture This

Now & Then

Lost & Found

The Comet's Tale

THE CENTER OF THE WORLD

JACQUELINE SHEEHAN

KENSINGTON BOOKS
www.kensingtonbooks.com

This book is a work of fiction. Names, characters, places, and incidents either are products of the author's imagination or are used fictitiously. Any resemblance to actual persons, living or dead, events, or locales is entirely coincidental.

KENSINGTON BOOKS are published by

Kensington Publishing Corp.
119 West 40th Street
New York, NY 10018

All Kensington titles, imprints, and distributed lines are available at special quantity discounts for bulk purchases for sales promotion, premiums, fund-raising, educational, or institutional use.

Special book excerpts or customized printings can also be created to fit specific needs. For details, write or phone the office of the Kensington Sales Manager: Kensington Publishing Corp., 119 West 40th Street, New York, NY 10018. Attn. Sales Department. Phone: 1-800-221-2647.

eISBN-13: 978-1-61773-897-5
eISBN-10: 1-61773-897-2
First Kensington Electronic Edition: January 2016

ISBN-13: 978-1-61773-896-8
ISBN-10: 1-61773-896-4
First Kensington Trade Paperback Printing: January 2016

10 9 8 7 6 5 4 3 2 1

Printed in the United States of America

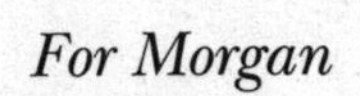

For Morgan

THE CENTER OF THE WORLD

Part One

2003

Massachusetts

CHAPTER 1

Sofia dropped her gym bag in the entryway and one soccer shoe fell out, streaked with a bright green grass stain from sliding past a defensive player. She had just returned from soccer practice and the late afternoon sun cut a warm slant of light through the kitchen window. She had run hard for two hours, one of the few things that felt good these days. The red message light on the answering machine blinked on the tiled counter. Probably a message from her mother. She hit the button.

The message was from her grandfather.

"I have a letter for you from your stepdad. It just arrived. I think it would be better for you to come down to the post office when it closes. Can you do that?"

How could her grandfather have information from her stepdad? The dead didn't send letters.

Sofia and her mother, Kate, were still reeling from the accident that had killed her stepdad, Martin. A student from UMass, who was set to graduate and start his life as an accountant for the city of Houston, had looked down for one instant to answer his phone while driving to his afternoon class. He said later that he'd been up all night studying for finals and swore that he never saw the guy on the bike in the intersection.

Martin had been biking home from his job at the middle school where he taught art. Sofia could picture her stepdad glancing up at the trees, smiling at something that he saw, something he'd tell his students about the next day, and they'd all try to paint the way afternoon sun glittered through the trees.

Sofia had been afraid that her mother's ribs would crack from crying. She'd never seen her mother cry the way that she did after coming back from the hospital in Northampton with her grandfather, the way something uncoiled from deep inside her. Sofia and her mother had slept together for the first month after Martin died, each one waking after a few hours of sleep from dreams where he was still alive, then realizing the horror of reality.

The small post office was an easy two-mile ride. Of course she could do that, now that her mother no longer forbade her from riding her bike and she had regained her ease of riding, the still-warm October wind on her face. Her grandfather had said, "Kate, it was an accident. Don't stop Sofia from living. Martin would never want that." Riding the light blue Schwinn Hybrid was as natural to Sofia as breathing. She parked behind her grandfather's office, looping a chain and a lock around the wheels.

The post office was officially closed but Grandpa would be finishing up.

She pushed open the door. "Grandpa? Where are you?"

She knew every inch of the back room, the heavy sacks of mail, the rows of small cubicles for private mailboxes, and her own childhood drawings plastered above the coat hooks. Even the sound was familiar for this time of day, the rattle of the mop bucket from the utility closet after he had cleaned the front room where customers lined up from nine in the morning until three in the afternoon.

Grandpa flipped up the counter gate that separated workers

from customers. He smiled the second he saw Sofia, but the fold between his eyebrows did not unfurl, and Sofia's stomach tightened up. Sam was tall, "Six foot two and eyes of blue," he liked to say, and he still looked like a mountain. She stepped easily into his arms and his late-day stubble rubbed her cheek. He smelled uniquely grandfatherly; a mix of spearmint gum, cinnamon, and perspiration that had just turned the corner from fresh.

"Come sit down, sweetie," he said, taking her small brown hand in his pale hand, which had recently sprouted a few dark age spots. He dragged two metal folding chairs near the back entrance.

Sofia pulled her straight black hair into a ponytail.

"Just tell me, what is it?"

Her grandfather handed her a letter. The white envelope didn't have an address or a stamp on it, and it hadn't been sealed. Sofia pulled out the letter and unfolded it, quickly thumbing the top corner to see that it contained three pages. Her stepdad left her a three-page typed letter?

"Martin left this letter with a lawyer who just gave it to me today. After you read it, I'm going to call Kate. In fact, I should have called her first, but this is how Martin wanted it done, although for the life of me, I don't understand why Martin would have done this."

Sofia began to read the first page.

If you are reading this, it means I have died. My sweet, wonderful girl, I am so sorry not to be with you and Kate. The day that I met you two was the start of my life, the start of me learning to be a father and a husband, and my life was full in a way that I had never imagined it could be.

I am sorry that I won't be there for the rest of your life. I always had a funny feeling that my life was so rich, sort of condensed, that I might not get the full ride. I come from a line of people, both adopted and biological, who veer toward catastrophic events. That's why I left this letter with the lawyer. Well, that's one reason.

We were both adopted, but you know that. My parents always told me that they didn't know anything about my birth mother, or where I came from. I learned the truth when my mother was dying. Don't start smoking, Sofia. Lung cancer is a useless reason to die.

She finally told me that my birth mother was a teenager and had been raped. My birth mother made the choice to give me up and seal the records. My mother didn't want me to know that I was conceived in violence. But she was wrong, and the lie carved out a distance between us that I never could put words to, but I felt it.

I promised your mother that I would not tell you about your background as long as I was alive. In death, there is a kind of freedom from lies. And it also means that you aren't eighteen yet, because I had decided that when you were legally an adult, I would tell you in person. If you were old enough to vote, you were old enough to be told about your birth parents. Even now, whenever now is, you have your mother and grandpa for support, and I am counting on them to help you.

Here goes, and I hope that I'm right about doing this. You are Guatemalan. Your mother took you illegally from your home and, at great cost to her, obtained documents that listed you as a child of Mexico, lawfully adopted.

Sofia stopped reading. Her grandfather sat across from her on one of the few chairs; postal clerks were meant to stand, not sit. He tapped his fingers on his legs, waiting.

"Have you read this?" she asked.

"Yes, honey, I read it. Martin wrote the document and hired a lawyer to take possession of it with very precise instructions. Kate doesn't know yet that he wrote it. I'm going to call her now that you've read it. Maybe I should have called her first, but Martin went to great lengths to get this letter to you and he must have had a reason."

Sofia was fifteen and in her second year of high school. It wasn't right that she kept getting her legs kicked out from under her. Wasn't it enough that her stepdad had died? Did something else have to upend her life? Had her mother done something wrong?

"My birth family is from Guatemala?"

"Yes. That's what the letter says, but if this is true, I have never heard a word of it until today. It would be better if you read the whole thing. He explains a lot, as much as he knew. It's your mother who really knows all the details."

"What's all the hush-hush?" she asked. She thumbed through the three-page document. Words like *civil war* and *massacre* leapt up at her as if they were illuminated.

"What do civil wars and massacres have to do with me? Why didn't they want to tell me that I was born in Guatemala instead of Mexico?"

"It looks like it was your mom's choice. If this is true, your documents of identity and adoption are falsified. Technically, you are undocumented." He cleared his throat.

Sofia leaned forward. "You've got to be kidding. I grew up in Leverett. I was a Girl Scout. I'm on the varsity soccer team. What does this mean? Can I be sent away from you and Mom?"

Sofia's skin was golden, the color of light brown sugar. Her hands looked small pressed against the white paper. She had always referred to herself as "a person of some color," which had pleasantly confused her teachers.

"First, let's find out if this is true. Martin is gone, but Kate can answer everything."

Sam pushed up from his chair and stood up. "You probably have other questions; I know I do. Your stepdad went on to say that Kate has lived with a daily terror that you would be deported or that some other harm would come to you. According to this, she refused to allow him to disclose any of this to you. He also said your mother was the bravest person he'd ever known."

She loved how soft her grandfather's hair was, how gray, how predictable.

"Can I keep this?"

"Of course. It's yours. I have a copy," he said.

"Am I going to be deported? This is my home," she said. Sofia had the sense that the floor was shifting and everything she knew was slipping away.

"You are my granddaughter and this is your home. I swear to you that I didn't know any of this, not since the first day I saw you standing with your mother at Logan Airport."

"I want to talk to Mom first. Alone. Do you think that my father could have done this as a joke? He was a funny guy. He once dressed up as the tooth fairy, with a tutu and everything, and showed up in my bedroom when I woke up. . . ."

She had never seen her grandfather so serious. "There is always the possibility that someone isn't telling the truth or that their version of the truth might not jibe with a videotaped version of an event. But I don't believe your stepdad would tell you anything but the truth. He loved you and Kate more than anything else in the world." Sam leaned forward and reached for Sofia's hands, covering them in his paper-roughened palms.

"There must be a good reason that Martin did this. I loved him like a son," said Sam, his eyes shutting for a moment.

"The lawyer said that Martin instructed that this letter be given to me no sooner than six months after his death with the hope that this news would be more tolerable to you. Martin wanted me to give you this letter because he knew that Kate wouldn't. Or couldn't. He didn't want to hurt you, but he believed that you deserved the truth. I'm trying to understand that this was complicated and difficult for him."

Her mother had taken her out of Guatemala illegally? Why? And if so, why had she lied to her?

"I have to go home now," she said, giving her grandpa's hands a squeeze.

She started to get up and her legs refused to cooperate. Sofia was an athlete, a soccer player who had already been contacted by a college recruiter. Unless she was injured, which she had been on numerous occasions in the course of her soccer career, her body was the surest thing in life. It never occurred to her that her body wouldn't obey a command to stand up. She put her hands on the arms of the chair and pushed. She got halfway up and fell back again.

"Hang on, Sweet Pea. You were probably holding your

breath and you didn't know it. People do that with shocking news. Breathe deeply. I'll get you some water."

He got up and left the room. She heard the sound of a fridge opening and the rubber-sealed closing. Something squeaked in his shoes, otherwise she never would have heard him coming back. He handed her a plastic bottle of water. She twisted off the cap and took a sip.

"Tap water," she said in a whisper.

"What?"

"This is just tap water in a fancy bottle. Don't waste your money or the plastic."

"You sound like your mother," he said.

She wanted to get out of the post office with its heavy scent of paper and glue, to breathe outside air.

"Maybe this isn't true," she said, feeling her legs again.

"Maybe," he said. "The lawyer said he was going to call your mother. I'll try to get to her first."

He plucked a business card from the envelope and peered at it as if the thing could speak. He pinched it between thumb and forefinger.

"We are family and I don't care what a piece of paper says. Do you understand me? Nothing has changed."

But everything had changed. Sofia hugged her grandfather and pressed her face into his large chest.

"Tell Mom I'm riding home," she said, pushing away from the safety of his chest.

Outside, she unlocked the Schwinn and hopped on. But as soon as she grabbed the handlebars, she shook with sudden tears that she had held back while reading the letter. Her stepdad helped her buy the bike, promising trail rides in the summer. Every time she touched the bike, she thought of him, smiling, riding next to her. But why had he done something as weird as this? Did she really know him at all?

CHAPTER 2

Kate got the call while she was at work. The worst thing about being promoted in the Fish and Wildlife Department was that she spent two days of the week at the central office. Being indoors that much sent her happiness level below the tolerable line. Where it hovered until she could get back in the government-issued 4WD Ford pickup and head for the maze of dirt roads that skirted the Connecticut River. Or whatever was left of her happiness level, more like a blanket of cold, wet wool wrapped around her since Martin died.

For people who claimed to love the outdoors, those who worked for Fish and Wildlife had created terrible interior settings. When other workplaces had long ago upgraded from the old-fashioned flickering fluorescent tube lighting, their office maintained it. All the cracked Naugahyde furniture of the world had been shipped directly to their address.

Kate spent three days of the week along the wide river, which she loved more than anything, with the exception of her daughter, Sofia. And Martin, she had loved him. She never imagined that someone like Martin would come into her life, especially after Guatemala. Sofia had been eight when they married, after Kate had softened to the sweet unexpectedness of him. "Martin is a goodness generator," Sofia announced when she was eight, speaking with the unsullied clarity of a child.

Sometimes Kate felt Martin riding next to her in the truck, cracking jokes about the gearshift with electrical tape wrapped around it. His dark hair would have needed a haircut. As soon as she left the main roads, she parked the truck along the earth berms that flanked the river and talked to him, telling him about the university coaches who were recruiting Sofia.

"Martin, I want to be sure they care about Sofia, not just her crazy shots on goal. Please, could you tell me the best thing to do?"

Today she was headed to the Oxbow of the Connecticut River. The wide river was blessedly quiet on Wednesday afternoon, free of the weekend boaters with their roaring motors. The October light glittered off the maples with their Crayola-orange leaves. Martin would have loved this kind of day. He might have slipped a note into her lunch bag that said *Remember to see how many kinds of orange are in the hills. I love you.* Today, there had been nothing in her paper bag except a cheese sandwich, which she was unable to eat.

Kate pulled off the road and drove down the steep dirt road to the Oxbow, missing some of the ruts but hitting a big one that shook everything in the truck.

Her phone vibrated in the passenger seat. Fish and Wildlife had just equipped all the staff with cell phones. She wished that they had spent the money on better lighting in the office. Kate looked at the caller ID and saw that it was Martin's lawyer. She hadn't spoken with him since the last time they looked at the life insurance policies that Martin had put in place. Had she forgotten to sign something? She flipped open the cell phone.

"Hi, Vincent," she said, turning off the truck engine.

"Hello, Katherine," he said. "Sorry to call you at work, but this is important."

Kate realized that she didn't know much about Vincent, that

every time she was in his office, the air was tinged with death, pockmarked with the deepest sorrow. But he had a family; photos on his green walls offered glimpses of two preadolescent girls with teeth that looked too large for their mouths.

"How are the girls?" she asked, desperate to slow down whatever train of bad news Vincent had.

"The girls are good; one is at a swim meet and the other is talking her mother into getting her ears pierced at the mall. I don't understand body piercing," he said.

Did he wish that he could say more about malls and daughters? Kate felt a twinge of sympathy for him with his earpiercing daughter.

"I have just carried out instructions from Martin, something that he put in place about six years ago. It has nothing to do with his will. This is a separate document."

A dragonfly landed on her windshield. It was a Violet Dancer with a slender purple abdomen, resting briefly on her wiper blades. Whoever named dragonflies must have been a poet.

"Are you still there?" he said.

Kate took a breath. "I'm here. You're using your bad news voice, so I'm going to walk down to the river before you tell me that Martin had two other wives or something like that."

Kate opened the door of the Ford cab, left the keys under the mat, and walked twenty yards to the quiet curve of the boat launch. Her work boots rested in two inches of water; tiny waves rippled near the eyelets of the laces. Maybe she could hear bad news if the river held her.

"Okay, go ahead," she said.

She heard Vincent shuffle paper. "Martin left instructions for me to give your father a document that tells Sofia about the origins of her birth. I have just carried out his instructions. Martin left a three-page letter describing what he knew. Sam said Sofia was coming to the post office to look at the letter. We're going to need to talk."

"What do you mean, origins of her birth?" Black dots swam past her eyes.

"He told me everything that he knew, everything that you

had told him. He told me about Guatemala and the forged papers. That the adoption was technically illegal."

Kate stepped out of the river. "You gave this to my father?"

She tried to picture Sam reading about everything that Kate had hidden for the past twelve years. How could she ever begin to explain to him about the horror of the massacre, picking up Sofia and running?

"Yes. This letter may be very alarming to Sofia, which is why Martin insisted on giving it to Sam first. And Kate, this is a very big problem. I'm not a specialist in immigration law, but I'll do some checking. Call me when you're ready."

Kate was sure that Sofia would go straight home and wait for her. She knew her daughter.

Her phone rang again. It was her father. "I know," she said. "I'm on my way home."

Sofia saw her mother after the lie erupted. Kate was in the green work truck, heading north on Long Plain Road, and the late-afternoon sun lit up her tan skin, her golden hair. Sofia squeezed the brakes on her bike and pulled onto the sandy shoulder. She twisted around and saw that her mother had stopped; the truck sat shuddering on the berm with its turn signal blinking.

Her mother turned around and pulled past her. With odd slow motion clarity, Sofia saw her mom's tight hands gripping the steering wheel, her face crumbling, and braced for trouble. Her grandpa must have called her, or maybe it had been Vinnie the lawyer.

Sodowski's Farm Stand, closed for the season, was within sight. They had gone there hundreds of times for ice cream, hot dogs, or the special Polish Plate. Her stepdad always said, "Give me the multiple meat special," which made her feign gagging each time.

Sofia pulled back onto the asphalt and followed her mother, turning in as she approached the farm stand. She didn't know if she should lean her bike next to her mother's truck as she would have always done.

Sofia dropped the Schwinn on the ground and one wheel kept spinning. Her mother opened the door of the truck and stood with a hand on the door frame.

"So who am I?" Sofia said. Her voice shook. "Mom, what's going on? Where am I from?"

The two women, the green truck, and the bike formed a planet, a universe tilting on the gravel parking lot.

"You are my daughter. I picked you. You've always known that," said Kate, gripping the door.

"That's not going to work anymore. I'm not six. I just read the letter from Dad. I've got it here," Sofia said, pulling the envelope from her back pocket.

"I know. The lawyer called me this afternoon. Then Grandpa called a minute ago."

"Why did you create this big story? What difference did it make if I came from Guatemala or Mexico? We all knew I was adopted."

Sofia had on her blue nylon soccer pants with a white stripe up the side. She was ready to charge at Kate, ready to pass and run, corner kick, take a header and smash it into the goal. Her muscles were so charged that she might incinerate on the spot.

"Martin didn't know everything. Remember, he came later, after we had been here for years. By then, there were some things that had settled far back into a space that I couldn't easily reach. I was afraid . . ." Kate stopped. "How could Martin do this to us? I thought he understood."

Sofia wanted him to be here so that she could rage at him too. If he had known, why didn't he tell her? And why didn't her mother tell her?

Kate took off her sunglasses. "I made your father promise. Don't blame him for not telling you. I was wrong. He knew keeping this from you was wrong and he agonized over keeping the secret."

"What else is a lie? Is everything that you've told me made up?"

Kate closed the door to the truck and it made a solid, defining sound.

"You're from the Mayan highlands of Guatemala. You are not from Mexico."

"Who are my biological parents? What happened to them? Why didn't they want me?"

Her mom had a fleck of spittle on her lower lip, something that Sofia would normally tell her about. She might even reach over and dab it with her own finger. But not now.

"They aren't alive. It wasn't about them not wanting you. They loved you. They were killed, all of them."

Sofia balled the letter into her palm. A breeze grabbed a strand of her smooth black hair and whipped it across her dark eyes. She felt the muscles in her face quiver and she fought them, refusing to give in.

"Who in my family was killed?" she whispered.

"Your parents. Your grandparents had died earlier. And others in the village." The words sounded old and damaged with dry rot, like a box of papers confined to the dark recesses of a basement, all stuck to each other with the adhesive of decay. "And your brother."

The blood left Sofia's hands and feet and retreated to her torso for the upcoming disaster. She held her body in a new way; all the existing bits of her re-organizing along with the truth, changing even her skeleton. The new parts fell into place along her arms. Her feet had already widened, so they could hug a steeply terraced hillside along the mountains of Guatemala.

"Let's go home and let this settle in. I know this is a shock. I'll tell you everything," said Kate.

Could her mother tell the truth after so long? More than anything Sofia wanted to sink into her mother's embrace. If only she'd step one foot, just one foot forward, she would feel the warm touch of her mother's arms.

Sofia stepped back, out of reach. "You aren't my mother," she said.

From the mouth of an adopted child one would think this would be expected from time to time, but Sofia had never said these words, even in anger, even when grounded for a week, even when Kate had refused to let her attend a party where the parents were openly absent when she had been fourteen. The razor-like quality of the words visibly struck Kate. Her mother bent at the waist with her hands over her face and then sank to the ground, knees landing without mercy.

Hurting her mother was new and Sofia was unaccustomed to the power and the pain of it. She picked up her bike with so much strength, so much anger, that she could have tossed it over the row of trees on the edge of the parking lot. She spun the bike around and rode away from home, as far away as she could imagine. She leaned into her handlebars, standing, pedaling as though her life depended on it. A bank of clouds slid over the last of the sun, and dusk settled into the river valley.

CHAPTER 3

Kate sat on the gravel parking lot, paralyzed. This is what the worst day of her life felt like, far worse than she had imagined for twelve years. Was this worse than the day the hospital called for her when Martin was killed? The pileup of worsts threatened to bury her.

As she pulled her knees in closer and rested her arms and head on them, the wind blew in from the east. When the wind blew easterly, sweeping across the Atlantic, nothing was right, like a north wind ruffling the waters of Lake Atitlán in Guatemala. Kate drove to Leverett and the black asphalt dragged at the wheels of her truck, sucking with a deep, slow gravity that made her sweat. Her daughter needed time to ride out the fury of betrayal. But she expected to see Sofia's bike in the driveway when she pulled in.

The urgency that drilled up Kate's spine pulsed red with crackling heat. The house was empty, untouched since their usual morning ritual of *Are you going to practice, what time will you be home, will you start rice for dinner? Yes, Grandpa is coming over, yes he's sick of chicken too but that's what we're having, good-bye, love you.*

They had almost reached a wonderful mundaneness after Martin's death. Almost.

She tried to keep the panic out of her voice when she called Sofia's friends. She could not reach her daughter anywhere. Her friends had not heard from her.

In her daughter's bedroom, the scent of Sofia's shampoo mingled with stale pizza hit her like a bomb.

She rang her father, knowing that he'd be home by now. "Dad, she's gone, I mean she hasn't come home. Is she there?" She gripped the cordless phone in Sofia's room.

"What in God's name were you thinking? Please tell me that our girl wasn't taken illegally out of Guatemala. Please tell me the truth, and no, she's not here," he said.

This was the price she would pay, like a criminal who had murdered someone and held on to the secret for years. Finally, without the mitigating forces of a good-intentioned confession, the past was exposed, laid naked and guilty before those she cared about more than her own life.

Her husband had reached from the grave, freed from his unwilling promise to her, and set an avalanche in motion. She wanted to scream at Martin, pound him senseless.

"Kate! Say something," her father said.

She wanted her own mother with the same unbearable longing that erupted at times of celebration and sorrow. Would Kate have been a better mother if her own hadn't died when she was fifteen?

"Stay there. She'll come to your house before she comes here. But call me the minute she gets there. I just need to know that she's okay," she said.

What mattered now was finding Sofia so that she could explain how it had happened. The awful wound was lanced. Kate wanted to keep the flow of deceit pouring out of her body, disposing of it like sewage. She longed to say the words *I lied to save you, to protect you, and I had to make you believe it.* But she'd have to find her first.

Why would Martin have done this? They had nearly split up

over the disagreement of telling Sofia about her parents. Once Martin had discovered the deception, they had been married for a year, and he had looked at Kate as if he had never seen her before, this woman who would lie to her child about the most elemental essence. She had begged him, made him swear that he wouldn't tell. In exchange, she told him everything about Guatemala. And almost everything about Will. She had loved Martin and felt the sureness of his love for her, but the injury of this disagreement had lodged into them.

Four hours later, she heard a car pull into the driveway. She was at the front door before the silver and blue police cruiser fully stopped.

No, not Sofia too, not killed, not hit by an unaware driver, a drunk or distracted motorist, not mangled on her bike, not like Martin, not because of Kate.

As the officer opened his door, the interior light of the cruiser illuminated Sofia's face, her head turned to the side.

"Sofia?"

"Usually I call parents to pick up their kids when they're intoxicated, but Sofia is on my daughter's soccer team, so . . ." He turned his palms up and his uniformed shoulders rose slightly.

Kate searched his face for some feature of familiarity. Had he been among the lawn-chair parents, cheering the girls on from the grassy sidelines? She didn't recognize him. Sofia was on the varsity team for the first time this year and she was one of the younger and certainly smaller players.

"Is she okay?" Her chest was shredded by hours of fear.

He opened the back door to the cruiser. As he did, it struck Kate that Sofia had been confined, unable to get out of the car if she had tried. He held out his hand to Sofia, blocking Kate with his wide backside.

"Here, take my arm," he said.

The smell of beer and vomit hit Kate like a solid wall.

"This was your solution?" Kate said, louder than she had intended, a shriller tone than she had ever used with Sofia. Now that the secret life was exposed, what new voice would emerge, rusted over, oxidized down to the primer?

Sofia stood up, head pulled back and bobbling. Her eyelids were swollen, her eyes bloodshot from crying. Kate wanted to hug her and choke her simultaneously. She was alive, this is always what mattered, the core of it, that Sofia would survive, and it had all been worth it. Now Sofia had to survive with the truth and with Kate's betrayal. Betrayal; too strong a word. Not strong enough.

A quick appraisal showed nothing broken, just a disheveled fifteen-year-old sodden with drink for the first time. "Where is your bike?" asked Kate. She had not been able to bear the sight of Martin's mangled bike, bits of his shirt somehow tangled in the wheels. She had asked her father to have it taken away.

Headlights caught the three of them, then a car pulled into the driveway behind Kate's. It was Sam in his Jeep Cherokee. Kate reached out to touch her daughter, pull her back into how they had been before, how they had always been. Sofia recoiled and turned her head as her grandfather approached—long legs, deep furrowed brow, brown Carhartt jacket with frayed cuffs.

Sofia ran to him in a sloppy, childlike gait, the alcohol robbing her agility. He folded his arms around her, nearly carrying her. "My bike," she said between sobs, "it's gone, everything's gone."

Kate started toward her, but Sam held up one hand and said, "I might be very good at just two things—delivering the mail and sobering up teenage girls. You remember, don't you, Kate?"

Sam tucked Sofia under one arm, keeping her upright until they made it to the front step, and then opened the door with one arm and went inside.

"She'll be okay. I'm sorry about your husband," said the cop.

Kate pressed her lips together and nodded at him as he left. She made it to the porch before she slid to the floor, exhausted.

Kate had been a freshman in high school when her mother and father told her about the cancer. Every cell in Kate's body had been fully occupied with negotiating high school. She didn't have enough space left over for her mother's cancer.

She had to figure out who to be friends with, where to sit at lunch, what expression to put on her face as she walked the halls from one class to another, what to wear, what to say, should she raise her hand in class or engage in passive resistance like some of the other kids? Should she take the school bus or walk home?

"Will you have to go to the hospital?" asked Kate. Her parents looked concave, leaning against each other on the brown plaid couch. She thought her mother might be sick for a few months.

"Yes, I'll have treatments there," said her mother, reaching for a slight tear in her jeans, slipping her pointer finger into it. Her mother found a soft thread and plucked at it, like a bird searching for twigs to build a nest.

Her father still wore his mailman uniform. At least it wasn't summer. With his long legs and knobby knees, he looked ridiculous in uniform shorts.

"We'll get through this," he said.

But they hadn't. Kate's mother transformed into being sick with such ferocity that for several years after her death, her illness blotted out any memories of her before the cancer. All she had left was the rapid descent, the Olympic luge ride with no stops, through surgeries, chemo, to a hospital bed at home and a parade of home health care people, then hospice, then gone. The luge had dumped her out.

Kate had been alone in the house when the phone call came from the man who made the headstones. The difference between life before her mother's death and after fell hard, like a lead wall. Kate was fifteen. *I'm too young for this, too young,* she had raged.

"I need to double-check on the spelling of the deceased's name." His voice was old, but Kate was becoming older by the second, losing every sweet morsel of childhood.

"You want to know how to spell Elizabeth?" she asked. Who

doesn't know this, how hard could this be? They had cremated her body, but still her father had wanted a headstone. They had picked pink marble, no, her father had chosen pink marble; she had hated it.

"E-L-I-Z-A-B-E-T-H."

"Thank you," he said. "There are many ways to spell names these days. You can't imagine."

Kate felt herself sliding through the phone lines into the mire of cemeteries. She struggled to gain a foothold in the kitchen that had once been so warm, so delicious.

"And the short phrase that you and your father selected, may I check that also?"

Whatever life she had before, shopping with her mother, the canoe trip on the Connecticut River where they had argued over the merits of the J stroke and then both fallen asleep on a sand bar after lunch—all of this fell away, beyond her reach. What was she now?

She swallowed hard again and again to get past the clot in her throat. She and her father had labored over what to say on the gravestone. Nothing was enough or right. How did they find words for her? Or were the words about them and not her at all?

"She rode on the river with her face to the sun," said Kate.

"Yes, that's what I thought. I can do this in two lines or three. Three looks better to the eye," he said.

"Three," she whispered, impaled by the number. There used to be three of them.

When she hung up, she opened the fridge and took out a beer, one of her father's Dos Equis, the bottle with the red and gold label. She slid open the silverware drawer and found the opener in the green plastic divider. She yanked off the metal cap.

Her parents had allowed her sips of beer or wine before and she had taken half-hearted slugs of beer on overnights with her girlfriends. But this was the first beer of her new life without a mother and she drank it with determination, then relief, as it poked holes in the sorrowful blockage in her throat.

She drank another—now she was filled with amber carbonation that soothed her and woke up the frozen places. She left the two bottles on the counter. Her father had stopped buying food, no one did the laundry, and he had forgotten to sign her report card. Would he notice his missing beer? Would he notice the empties right in front of him?

Trent's house was half a mile away if she took the road, closer if she walked the trail behind their houses. It was Thursday and he would be home. He was older, a senior, who had begged her to say yes, to let him push his hand into her pants, even in the midst of her mother's rapid-fire dissolve.

Trent's rottweiler, Jasmine, thundered off the front deck and announced Kate's arrival, wagging the stump of her dark tail. Trent came to the door and she walked to him, tossing back her hair, slipping her hands along his waist.

"I've been drinking beer," she teased, "and I'd like another. Do you have any more?"

He pulled her into the house, where the hours of parent-free time opened up for them. They had until six, when his parents came home from the university.

They went into his bedroom and closed the door. She took off her clothes and when the air first hit her skin, she was shy, but only for a moment. Trent dropped his nylon track shorts and kicked them aside, pulled off his T-shirt with one hand and then hooked a thumb under the waistband of his white underwear and slid them off, hindered only by the obstacle of his already hard penis.

Kate climbed on the bed, lay back, and said, "Do you know how this goes?"

He clambered on the bed, on his hands and knees over Kate. "Yes. Are you sure about this, Kate?"

She reached up and felt the cool firmness of his flank, a strip of gooseflesh along part of his butt, and fell into a space that opened ever wider for her, with all its jagged edges of broken glass and welcome comfort. Kate wanted to blot out the wet grief with sex, and Trent obliged her.

For one full year her father went fallow. He went to work

every day at the post office, stamping, weighing, packaging, selling boxes and envelopes. When he came home he fell into his recliner with a beer or two or three as if he had only been pretending all day at work. Even at fifteen she could see that what he wanted more than anything was to turn away from everyone, including her.

Her parents had never had to tell her to do her homework or even ask her if she had any. Back when she had been in junior high, the three of them settled in on a routine after supper. Her mother graded papers from her biology classes at the high school, her father cleaned up the dishes, and Kate spread out her homework on the kitchen table. Three people in a home make a family, but two made a crippled atom, as if her mother's death left them in nuclear decay.

When she came home from Trent's house, the scratchy drone of the television led Kate to the man who had been her father. He was a deflated version of her old dad, the one who built the tree house with her, showed her how to fix the tires on her bike, and claimed ownership of all things grilled. He had dissolved into the brown recliner, with three cans of beer lined up in front of him. Three beers in one hour; that had to be a new record. He had been in the war in Vietnam and said drinking wasn't good for him.

"What are you watching, Dad?" She was a little afraid of the new dad, as if he was half dead, quasi-zombie.

"I'm waiting for the local news," he said, without saying hello. The Phil Donahue Show was on.

"What's for dinner?" she asked, just in case they were going to have dinner, just in case they could go back to how their lives had been before.

She was afraid that her father was not enough, that whatever constitutes a family unit was beyond his ability now.

In the spring of her sophomore year, just days after turning sixteen, Kate felt old, gutted by her mother's death, stripped of who she had been before.

In May her father forgot her birthday. Trent was not home,

but Kate found a bottle of vodka in his house. She mixed it with orange juice and drank it in two large glasses while the rottweiler sat at her feet. After dark she walked to the high school. A cop had found her walking, stumbling really, in the parking lot. She had fallen to one knee and was trying her best to act as if she had dropped something. She was not able to get up without his assistance.

"I can drive you to the police station over in Amherst, or I can drive you home," he said.

She chose home, because in either event the cop would talk to her dad. Kate held on to the pitching sea of her stomach as she rode in the backseat of the cruiser. She didn't know where her backpack was. Her mother had been dead for almost a year and she didn't know if she could go on.

At the simple Cape Cod home on Meadow Road the cop got out of his car and walked to the front door. He knocked and stood back. It was hard for Kate to focus that far away. Her father, backlit from the living room lamp, appeared at the door. He put one hand on the doorframe, head tilted down, as he listened to the details of her debacle. The two men walked side by side to the police car. The cop opened the back door to the cruiser.

"Get out of the car, Kate," said her father. Even drunk, she felt his sadness and tried to pull away as soon as her feet touched the driveway. He put a firm arm around her, squeezing hard on her shoulder.

The porch light was not kind to faces, and it created deep gouges of shadows and dark hollows around the eyes. Kate and her father watched the cruiser pull away. When she turned back to her father, expecting the husk of the man who now lived in their house, she was startled to see him fitting back together like puzzle pieces magnetically forming a whole picture. He opened the door and moths that battered the porch light surged inside.

"Let's go in," he said. Even his voice was finding its way home again.

Kate stepped inside. She did not deserve the house, the father (or what was left of him); she had become a criminal. The entire center of her body heaved. "Daddy, I'm going to throw up."

They stumbled together to the half bath on the first floor. This was something that her mother would have helped her with: a sickness of any kind, anything to do with the bathroom. She couldn't remember being in the bathroom with her father in years. Kate knelt in front of the toilet, raised the seat, and puked hard.

"I'm sorry, Kate," he said. In between heaves, his warm beer scent surrounded her. They were both drunk; this is what they had become together.

He gave her a wet washcloth for her face, then a drink of water to swish out her mouth.

"Have you ever been so drunk that you threw up?" she asked him. She closed the seat and sat on the toilet. She was a little less drunk; the walls weren't swirling as much. The bathroom was small; only a toilet and a sink. A border of roses ran along the wall. They had not been this close since the funeral.

"In the army," he said. "We weren't exactly social drinkers in Nam. We drank to get annihilated. The body can only take so much alcohol. I'm familiar with bowing before the porcelain god."

He leaned against the wall, taking up most of the space in the room.

"You need to go to bed now. We'll talk tomorrow."

She left her bedroom door open for the first time in months. The soft light from downstairs filtered into her bedroom, the way it had when she was nine or ten and she went to sleep listening to her parents' voices murmuring below her.

Daylight streamed into her room through windows that had gone unwashed since before her mother got sick. Kate's eyes were swollen, her head was encased in a metal helmet too small for her skull, and her breath could have melted steel girders. She sat up. Through the toxic haze of last night's alcohol, she smelled bacon, coffee, and a third thing that she couldn't identify at first. Eggs. When was the last time anyone had cooked eggs?

Her father was making breakfast. She splashed water on her face and went downstairs to the kitchen.

"Dad, why aren't you at work?" she asked, more alarmed than she wanted to be.

"I called in sick. You and I are going to the cemetery today."

At the graveyard, they talked of everyday things like the kind of cereal her mother had eaten, where to buy shampoo, where to get a haircut, how long milk lasted in the fridge. They inched their way back to life. Sam stopped stocking the fridge with beer.

Now it was Kate's daughter, drunk for the first time in her life, who had been escorted home by the local police.

CHAPTER 4

After Sofia repeatedly vomited and was tucked in for the night, Sam said he was going to sleep on the couch. Kate read Martin's letter, which Sofia crumpled into a ball, then curled into a hard tortoise shell on her bed, listening to the others sleep. At four a.m., still not able to sleep, she got up and made coffee.

Kate called in sick at work and then called the high school to verify Sofia's absence. Sam, who had not used a sick day since the bad year after his wife died, caused the biggest to-do when he called in and reached his work partner at the post office, Jane.

"No, it's nothing serious, I'm just feeling . . ." Here he paused, not having banked metaphors for illness. "Queasy, sick to my stomach. I ate out in Sunderland last night. What? No, no need for you to look in on me after work. Yes, I know that nausea can be a symptom of a heart attack. On a scale of one to ten, how nauseated am I?" Sam considered, as if he truly was sick, which in some ways he was but not in the way that he told Jane. "I'm a good solid five-point-five. I'll let you know about tomorrow."

After the calls were made that excused all of them from the outer world, Sofia headed for the shower. Sam opened the cabinet over the coffeemaker, reaching for a mug. The cabinet door squeaked. He opened and closed it four times, pouring his entire attention into the sound. From beneath the sink, he pulled out a can of WD-40, then aimed a precise spray of liquid at the top and bottom hinges and swung the door back and forth again.

"Stop it. You're being good and fixing things. I appreciate the thought, but it's not helping," said Kate.

He put the tiny red cap back on the can. "You and I went through hell and back after your mother died. I thought we were past lying about anything. Why did you lie about Sofia? I don't know if anything you told us was true since the minute you showed up at Logan Airport with her, years ago."

The water pipes clanged as Sofia turned off the upstairs shower. The walls and floors of the house seemed to fade away and Kate could picture her daughter standing in the tub, wringing her black hair, water slipping along her soft brown skin. Kate wanted to reach her, wrap her in soft woven cloth, a cocoon of safety, and put her hands over her daughter's ears.

"She was a war orphan," said Kate, each word hard as a breech birth.

Sam poured coffee into a blue mug. "We live in a cruel world and war orphans are nothing new. Vietnam was filled with kids roaming the streets." Sam rubbed his temples with his long fingers. Her mother had told her that it was his way of trying to erase the images that still erupted unexpectedly.

"I didn't plan to take her. The last thing that I imagined was to go to Guatemala to find a war orphan. You know what I was like back then—it was all about losing Mom, like I was hemorrhaging. And then I found the graduate program and research about water. It was like Mom was with me." This wasn't what he asked her. Kate felt the distance in the room grow alarmingly large, a gulf between her father and her.

They both turned at the sound of Sofia's feet on the stairs. Other fifteen-year-old girls would have blown their wet hair to perfection, which in 2003 meant straight, very straight. Sofia's hair was still wet; black sheets fell in the latitude between her collarbone and her small breasts.

"I knew I had a brother. I always knew. How could you have lied to me about something like this, about a part of me?" Droplets of water fell around her feet.

Sofia was turning into a Mayan warrior, her feet spread wider, elbows in close, part jaguar, ready to pounce. But if she was becoming a jaguar, Kate wanted to reach out and save her from extinction, from the forces that threatened to rip through her young skin.

"He was your twin. At least I think he was. Your biological mother tried to tell me but she didn't know the Spanish word for *twins* and neither did I. Kaqchikel was her first language. Your first language."

Sofia visibly reeled from the words, like rocks ricocheting off a mountain, an assaultive mudslide.

Sam stood behind the kitchen island, protected by the barricade from the waist down.

"Oh Jaysus, Katie," he said. There was a hint of Irish brogue in his voice, dredged up from his childhood, from his grandfather, as if he had put out an SOS to his ancestors.

"What happened to him?" said Sofia. Kate had never seen her daughter's eyes in such unblinking intensity before. She had turned part interrogator, part prisoner of war.

Kate took a few steps toward her and Sofia stepped back. A new territory was born yesterday, a new distance that was already breaking Kate's heart.

CHAPTER 5

Sofia

By the time she was seven, she no longer told her mother when she dreamt of her brother. She used to tell her but her mother said, "No, you were the only one when I searched for a child to adopt and I picked you. There was no brother. Dreams are different from waking life. They are like a story."

But still, he came. And he came because she asked him to come. Here is how the brother dreams came. First, Sofia brought a glass of water to the porch and set it beside, never in, the geraniums. This was the summer plan; in the winter, she brought the geraniums into the kitchen. She put one hand on each clay pot, with the glass of water in the middle. She scratched each pot with her fingernails, scritch, scratch as if her fingers were running. Her fingers were legs running like little puppets.

Once, she thought her mother had seen the way she called the brother. Sofia turned around and there she was in the doorway of the porch, watching. It seemed for a minute that she knew Sofia was conjuring the twin, because Mom was so smart and she saw everything. Then Mom had smiled and said, "Sofia, are you listening to those plants?" That's how her mother was. She worked for Fish and Wildlife and she was on the river all the time, looking at plants and birds. When Sofia was little she used to call it Wild Fish Life, but later, when she was bigger, she understood the real title.

She said, "Yes, I'm drumming a song to the geraniums." The drumming song was really for her brother, not the geraniums, and she thought for sure her mother would see through this. Maybe the flowers heard the running of her fingers as a song, but it was a side effect, just like Grandpa had a side effect to taking Tylenol PM, which was that he had bad nightmares.

Back to her secret brother. After she did the geranium thing it was time to go to bed, after saying goodnight to Mommy and Martin. She took the blanket off the bed and turned it over. She had discovered all these steps through something called trial and error. Her mother told her that when scientists want to see if something is true or not, they keep trying different ways until they get it right; it was a scientific thing.

The science review:

Step one: Put the glass of water between the two pots of geraniums.

Step two: Stand with one hand on each pot. Her fingers turned into legs and they ran and ran on the pots.

Step three: Turn the blanket over so that it's the flip side up.

Step four: Do the same thing with the pillowcase; turn it inside out and put it back on. Then she put her head on the pillow and closed her eyes.

Here was the most important step. Sofia wished and wished for her brother. It was a smoke signal, a laser beam, or a horn, honk, honk. She made space for him in her dreams. And sometimes, he came.

Sometimes when she dreamt of him, she couldn't see all of him, but she still knew it was him even though she could only see his feet. His feet were brown like hers and shaped like hers too, broad from big toe to little toe. Sometimes she heard a sound and it was his voice, braided into her voice, vibrating in her chest.

But now her mother had told her that he had existed; he was dead, killed, not listening to her call. It was as if her mother had reached into her dreams and stolen him.

CHAPTER 6

The very hint of Sofia pulling away from her, seeing the hurt in her dark eyes, was worse than the imagined loss of Sofia being taken away. Kate could not have pictured this. What had her own mother feared when she had been dying of cancer, leaving Kate and her father behind? Had it felt anything like this, like her core wrenched out?

How much could she tell Sofia and her father without annihilating them? All of it? Part of it? The kitchen floor beneath her feet was cold and her toes gripped it hard to steady her.

"I know this will be horrible to hear. Your brother was killed. People in the village had marched to the army garrison demanding the bodies of . . ." Kate stopped. She was bludgeoning her daughter with every word. The massacre had crept forward in time and slammed into her kitchen. Everything she fought to keep out of their lives came streaming in through the windows, the vent over the microwave, and the cracks in the basement floor.

"The people of the village demanded the bodies of your father and another man who had been shot by the soldiers."

"If he was my twin, he was just a baby, like me. They shot a little boy? Wait, they shot my father?"

Kate was losing her footing on the tile floor. If she unhinged her focus, she saw her sandaled feet stepping over bodies.

"They shot everyone in the village square," said Kate.

"I've seen him in my dreams. He looked like me, didn't he?" Sofia clenched her fists.

Every part of the unveiling would go like this, raw, abrasive, chinking away at Sofia. If only Kate could absorb all the pain of hearing this, not Sofia. She would volunteer to take Sofia's place. That was the true pain of parenthood that no one tells you about, that you want to be the stand-in for a daughter's pain, but you can't. This was not what Kate wanted for her daughter. Sofia was her daughter, she was.

"He was your fraternal twin. You were both so small, but yes, he had a smile so much like yours." From his station behind the island counter, Sam exhaled and ran his hands along his face.

"I know the difference between fraternal and identical. Don't talk down to me. Martin wouldn't have talked down to me."

Sofia now wavered between calling Martin her stepdad, Dad, or just Martin.

"Believe me, talking down to you in any way has just gone off the table. And I wish Martin was here too. More than you know," said Kate. The kitchen clock, a silly Mickey Mouse replica that was plugged into the wall, ticked like a metronome. "You were the only one alive. Your mother's body saved you."

"My mother? You knew her? Tell me her name!" A wisp of beer and vomit pulsed off Sofia, despite her efforts at cleaning up.

"Manuela," said Kate, letting the name of her friend fall from her lips. The soft music of her name expanded, at last, into Kate's kitchen. Sofia's torso collapsed and then hardened.

"That's enough for now," said Sam, nearly forgotten in his role as witness.

Sofia whirled her head and drops of water flew off in a spray as if she was a sea creature, caught and breathless in the unnatural confines of a house. "No! That is not enough! I want to know everything."

Kate's stomach curdled. Teenagers did run away and it always ended badly. Not that Sofia had said the words, but something in the electrified air of the kitchen hinted at it.

"I'll tell you as much as I can. There are other people who could tell you more. Some of them are gone, some are still in Guatemala and I don't know what has become of them. I can only tell what I know."

And what Will had told her.

CHAPTER 7

Sofia

Growing up, there had always been a double take when strangers looked at Sofia and her mother, back and forth, trying to figure them out. She didn't match her mother. Her brown skin against her mother's pinkish complexion told a story and it was well woven in her for as long as she could remember. She was adopted and she'd always known it.

When she was seven, she noticed that her best friend Emma and her mother matched. When she watched Sesame Street, Elmo asked her to find the two shapes that matched, the two fruits, the colors that matched. If the puppets had asked her to find the mother and daughter who matched, she would have picked Emma and her mother. They both had wheat-colored hair, the dried part of the wheat. And their eyes were blue with flecks of green.

"Why are you two the same?" Sofia asked Emma's mother one night after a sleepover. She didn't want to sound stupid, but she didn't know how to exactly ask something more complicated. They had cereal bowls in front of them and they were kicking their feet in the breakfast alcove.

Emma's mother stood a bit straighter as if it helped her think better. "Because Emma is my birth child. She shares the same genes that her father and I have. Things like light hair and blue eyes are recessive genes, which means they aren't the normal, dominant qualities. That makes us the masters of the recessives."

Emma's mother was a professor at Smith College.

Emma rolled her eyes. "Mom, we don't have any idea what you just said. Sofia, you are adopted."

"I know that," said Sofia. She dipped her spoon into the cold cereal.

"My mom's stuff in her body poured into my body. I have my dad's ears. Some of him poured into me too. That's why we match," said Emma.

"My mom and I both like the double swirl cone at Dairy Queen. We match," said Sofia.

"Yes, you match your mother perfectly in that way," said Emma's mother with some eagerness.

Later, curled up on the couch together, Sofia told her mother about matching and not matching. Her mother said, "You've always known you were adopted. Genetically speaking, you are from a man and a woman in Mexico. I've shown you where Mexico is on the puzzle map. Something went wrong and your mom had to give you to people who could take care of you. Remember, I told you how sick she was? But I was searching for you for a long time and it was magic that a birth mother who could not take care of her baby happened along just as I was searching for you."

Sofia pictured her mother's white arms plucking her from a sea of babies and scooping her up. As soon as Sofia landed in Kate's arms, she got on an airplane and flew to the airport in Boston where Grandpa was waiting for them. But she must have learned some things from the people in Mexico, like how to sit up, crawl, and stand, before her mother Kate found her. Had they taught her anything else?

Sometimes she remembered another self, a mirror image with the same hands, feet, and legs covered with dust, and below, cobblestones, round and wet.

"I remember the cobblestones," said Sofia.

"No," said her mother. "There were no cobblestones in Chiapas. You are adding memories from other places, memories after I found you and when I brought you home. There are cobblestones in Boston and we have been to Boston several times."

A sliver of a muscle twitched along her mother's nose that meant sadness. Sofia hadn't been able to tell why the cobblestones would make her mother sad. After that, she didn't try to tell her mother about her brother anymore.

When they found the cat, she could tell the cat all about the boy in her dreams and the cat listened. She also understood being small, like Sofia.

If anyone was to ask her about soccer, she would have to say that she learned it from the small cat that they took in when she was five years old. She and her mother bought a used washing machine from someone who was moving. As they considered the white appliance, a small black cat jumped on her mother's shoulders and meowed a long story. Not just meow, meow, meow, but a long cat saga, with vowels and short urgent high notes.

The guy selling the washing machine said, "We can't take the cat with us. We're moving to Vermont. We'll have to put her down if no one takes her."

Sofia hadn't been sure what *put down* meant but knew it wasn't good. Just to check she asked her mother, who had turned her head to look at the cat on her shoulder.

"It means they will have the cat destroyed," said her mother.

Sofia was stunned. Every part of her body melted with a huge sadness about the world, but mostly about this cat. Her mother knelt down on one knee next to Sofia with the cat still in place on her shoulder. The cat kept her claws retracted and touched Kate's face with one paw while still telling her desperate tale.

"But that won't happen because we're going to take her home with us." Her mother looked up at the man. "We'll take the cat and the washing machine. I'll have to come back with a truck for the washer, but we'll take the cat now."

Sofia felt her body come back together. She inhaled the power and sureness of her mother. She liked this part of her mom, who was unlike the other moms. She could count on her to tell the truth, even if it hurt.

The cat kept her given name, Bear Cat, although there were other names: Little Bear, Black Bear, and Bear. She was small, like Sofia. The vet always said, "She's one of the smaller cats that have come through here. She's a beauty, though. I'd say she's about eight years old."

When Sofia went to their pediatrician, Dr. Dumont usually said something about percentiles and how Sofia was in the 60th percentile for height and weight. Small like Bear Cat. And fast.

She missed her stepdad fiercely. What had stopped him from telling her the truth, even if her mom hadn't wanted him to? If he were here right now, they'd get in his truck and drive and talk until they got to their special place, The Blue Bonnet Diner, across the river in Northampton, and they'd have their special breakfast, eggs and bacon and toast. They had gone to The Blue Bonnet Diner after Bear had died right after Sofia had graduated from junior high. The small black cat had politely waited for Sofia to emerge into the light of high school.

It felt like the wattage in all the lightbulbs had dimmed since Martin died.

Sofia found Martin for her mother while they were washing clothes at the Laundromat. When the second washing machine broke, Sofia saw a man with pillowcases bursting with laundry. He whistled a song as he plucked the stuffed sacks out of the back of his bright red truck, tossing them like cotton balls on the sidewalk. The tune that he whistled pulled at Sofia's chest; it sounded like a bird song that she had heard long ago but she couldn't think where.

It had been midsummer and scorching hot. His T-shirt had sweat marks under his arms; dark red smiles. He looked up at Sofia and her mom, who stood in the doorway, and he said, "You two are the prettiest matched set I've ever seen. The way you both smile, the way the light catches in your hair."

Sofia looked up at her mother, who raised an eyebrow at the man, as if to say, *Oh, come on now.*

"No, really. Here, let me show you." He pulled out a drawing pad the size of a book and faster than Sofia knew was possible, he drew a picture of the two of them like they were right out of a storybook, a mother and daughter on a summer day with a big sack of laundry. Soon the three of them sat together on the broad granite step to the steaming Laundromat, looking at the drawing, sipping ice tea.

"I'm Martin," he said. "I'm the new art teacher in Amherst."

Sofia knew right away he was the one for them. Not because he was an art teacher, but because he saw them as magical storybook people, really saw them and drew them on paper. And because of the way her mother leaned back against the door frame and laughed. She must have heard the bird song also.

When she learned later that Martin was adopted too, she knew he was the perfect future stepdad. He would understand Sofia and maybe someday she would tell him about the brother in her dreams. But she never had.

She wanted Martin to be there with them when her mom told them about Guatemala. He might have said, "Come here, Sweet Pea, and sit next to me." She knew just where she would have sat, on the blue and white rug that they bought at the Christmas Tree Shop, her back up against the couch, her shoulder pressed against his leg. He would have anchored her.

Part Two

1990

Santiago Atitlán, Guatemala

CHAPTER 8

Kate put her notebook, pens, and envelopes in her small L.L. Bean day pack. She had two things to do today and one of them would determine if she could stay in Guatemala for one more term. The letter she was going to write to Dr. Clemson, her graduate adviser, had to be compelling. She pulled her hair back with a clip, grabbed the key to the room, and stepped out onto the inner balcony of the Monja Blanca Hotel.

In her first letter to her father four months ago, she had written, "Monja Blanca means *White Nun.* Pretty funny, huh? It's also the most revered orchid of Guatemala." Was there finally enough distance from the bad teenage years that her father would find the humor in white nun? The weekly rate for her room was $23—surely he would find that astounding.

In the inner courtyard, Pedro, the owner of the hotel, shook out his hammock. Scorpions loved dark places like pillows and blankets. Rule number one: Always shake out shoes and clothes before putting them on. Kate waved at Pedro as she came down the stairs and headed for the front door.

This morning she imagined her mother's voice saying, *If you don't ask, you'll never get what you want.* Instead of collecting water samples before the English class that she taught, she'd write the letter, making the case for an extension for one more semester. She couldn't possibly finish her project in four months. Teaching the English class was the second thing on her list today.

One of the problems with staying for another term was that she'd have to pay tuition at UC Davis in order to stay enrolled, and she didn't have it. Her father would help if she asked him, but she wanted him to see that she was taking care of herself. She knew that people in the upper echelons of academia worked off grants, and in a first flush of professionalism, she'd ask her adviser to use his grant money to pay her tuition as well as living costs in Guatemala.

Her mother would have been proud of her.

Her father was not expecting her home for Christmas. Since her mother's death, the holidays had been a painful reminder of what they'd lost. Maybe being apart would be less agonizing for both of them.

Tomorrow she would take the hour long boat ride across the lake to Panajachel and leave the letter at the Chisme Café, the main gringo hangout. The first traveler going north would be commissioned to take the letter and post it when he or she crossed the border into the States.

Phoning was so complicated that Kate didn't even contemplate it. There was one phone in Pana and its availability was sporadic. It was difficult to remember that this was nearly 1991, that people chattered away on phones in the U.S., and that the United States Postal system ran smoothly and inexpensively.

Santiago Atitlán was the largest village on Lake Atitlán in the Mayan Highlands of Guatemala. It was a center of Mayan commerce, as opposed to Panajachel, which even in the midst of the long civil war was still drawing backpackers from North America, Australia, and Germany. Kate had been in Guatemala just long enough to be startled when she saw another North American ambling in unmistakable bravado. She was here to study water, not to stay stoned all day, smoking marijuana. She stayed high enough on the crystalline beauty of the lake, ringed by bougainvillea, banana trees, and wild orchids.

She walked along Calle Principal and turned right along the cobbled street that led to the central plaza. Two Mayan women walked by her, carrying an impossible load of firewood on their backs, supported by a strap around their foreheads. The firewood had to account for half of their body weight. The Mayan people were small, making Kate feel like a giraffe. She winced as the women walked by, imagining carrying the load on her own back.

The women of Santiago wore long red skirts, one solid piece of fabric wrapped around their waists, held in place by a woven belt. The men wore thick cotton pants that stopped abruptly a few inches from their ankles. Kate tried not to romanticize the indigenous people. She knew that beneath their colorful clothing, they struggled with crushing poverty.

The day would soon warm up. December in the Mayan Highlands of Guatemala was their coldest month, but by noon, Kate could peel off her thick sweater as the temperatures hit the seventies.

Kate stopped walking; something was wrong. Santiago was a hub of Mayan commerce, and yet the town was silent. What was going on? People walked the streets, Mayan women carried massive firewood bundles on their backs, men carried huge sacks of avocados from their dugout canoes, but they were all silent. Even the small children spoke in muffled tones. She was sure it had to do with the swaggering soldiers in their camouflage pants, but she wondered if something larger was going on.

Kate felt a kind of static electricity prickling her skin, and the sensation made her shiver. She constantly double-checked her perceptions in Guatemala. Was she colliding into culture shock once again, reacting with a gut-inverting spasm, or was this merely another day? Who knew what was normal or what was not? Was it a special date on the Mayan calendar, a 260-day system with religious holidays floating unrestrained by repetition, or was it a standard and unremarkable day? Their calendar had its own way to divine the Earth's revolution around the sun and did not entirely correlate with the Gregorian calendar.

By the time Kate had walked several blocks from Monja Blanca, to the center of the town, she saw that it was not the mutable idea of time that had her on edge today; it truly was the presence of the militia.

She hated that the soldiers were so young, even younger than she was at twenty-four. She'd been in Guatemala for four months and the sight of a seventeen-year-old soldier with an automatic weapon was as terrifying to her in December as it had been in August when she had arrived. But she was an American researcher, a graduate student, and while the politics of Guatemala were reprehensible, she felt a sense of immunity as long as she kept her head down and worked.

The plaza was quiet this morning, only the sounds of chickens coming from courtyards. The cedar trees in the plaza looked out of place next to the palm trees. Perhaps the tortilla lady would be here today and Kate could get fresh tortillas before she went to the restaurant for *café con leche* and serious letter writing.

Kate had grown fond of the tortillas that were cooked every morning by the same woman in the central *mercado.* Women sold stacks of cloth, bananas, avocados, and dried corn in the small stalls the size of a broom closet. Each woman staked out an area under the verandas that lined the buildings. This morning, the soft clucking sound of chickens was as loud as the soft murmur of the women.

She made sure to pass by the tortilla lady each day. The anticipation of the palm-sized tortillas, still warm from the pan, was her primary thought when she came to a corner and bumped into four men dressed in alligator-green fatigues and black boots that came just shy of their knees. The boots looked hard, like they could bite. They wore sunglasses and carried guns with ammo slung diagonally across their torsos. One gun touched her, its oiled menace grazing her chest.

Kate stopped and jumped back, and a gasp escaped from her

mouth. Being white had offered a degree of protection. But a reporter from *Newsweek* had been killed near the border with Mexico and the word on the street was that the military were to blame. Not like it could be proven, but that's what everyone said.

She did not want to be mistaken for a journalist, not like VJ Kirkland (who hated being called VJ), the foreign correspondent from the *San Francisco Chronicle* who was somewhere in the country. Kate had met her several times before, when she was still in California. They had talked about her research in Guatemala, and Kirkland said that the newspaper was thinking of increasing her assignment to Guatemala.

Here in the village, Kate made a huge point of telling people that she was a teacher (not exactly true) and that she was studying water, just water. To cement her teacher status, she agreed to teach English one day per week. She was due to meet her students before noon today, at the church.

The militia had carte blanche and everyone knew it. They could do anything they wanted. They had guns, an inequitable source of power. One of the soldiers smiled. The other three looked like they had stopped smiling a long time ago.

"*Lo siento,*" she said. *Sorry for what?* Sorry that right now everyone on the street was watching and trying hard not to look like they're watching. Everyone is wondering, will this be the day that even the protection of white skin falls away? Had things just ratcheted up a notch?

One of the skinny, unsmiling soldiers placed the butt of his gun dead center on her left breast, and used it to push her aside. She had on a thick sweater, but still, it felt like he had placed his hand on her and she was suddenly naked. Kate stumbled from the broad flat stones of the walkway and tripped into the street. The soldiers had never touched her before. Kate wanted to go back to the hotel and take a shower.

The four men walked past her and the sound of their boots was sharp and crisp. Something larger must be happening and, as usual, she didn't know what it was. The air crackled around the soldiers, sputtering and fuming as if they formed a clattering engine that had to be fed. She had to shake it off. Kate refused to turn around to look at the men, even when she heard them laugh. Her body was ready to run, but she forced herself to walk, head up, until she got to the tortilla lady. The warmth from the small stove pulsed out to her.

The woman was a foot shorter than Kate, who at five foot five was no giant. The sides of her brown face caved in where she had lost teeth. Her entire frame was birdlike, her eyes deep and dark. Her black hair was partially covered by a red cloth wrapped around her head. And like all the women and girls, she wore a showstopping shirt, a *huipil,* with intricately woven designs against a blue background.

Kate's hands trembled as she reached into her pocket to retrieve some coins. Without speaking, the tiny woman gave her three tortillas instead of the usual two. As Kate tried to press the coins into her hand, the woman shook her head. She had seen everything with the soldiers. For the first time, Kate felt a door open and she stepped in. The price of entry in this case had been shared humiliation by the soldiers. Her nose filled with the scent of burning wood and singed tortillas. She smiled at the tortilla lady. The food tasted like a medicinal tonic, like it could obliterate the clatter of the militia.

Kate had time to get her coffee in the Tolimán Restaurant, named for the dormant volcano that loomed over the town, before she went to the church for the English lessons. She sat on the veranda of a café facing the plaza and pulled out her notebook. The letter flowed, all of her adrenaline fueling her argument for staying longer so that her research about the lake and water usage patterns could continue. That would settle her nerves, sitting at a table and asking Dr. Clemson for something that she wanted. As she sat in the December sun, the warmth of late morning gradually penetrated her bones.

There, she felt it again, something unsettling in the air. Of course, it had to be the soldiers. In her daily explorations, she had noticed insects skating across the lake without breaking the tension of the water, oblivious to what the deep, black waters held. She was just like them, skating across the village, never understanding the depth of life that brewed below her. When she took a boat to Pana, the gringo gossip center of Lake Atitlán, she'd find out if something was brewing.

Kate put her pen down and finished her sweet *café con leche.* This was how she imagined the air felt before a tornado: green and dangerous. Not that she'd ever seen a tornado in Massachusetts where she grew up, but she could imagine. She stuffed her letter and pen into her bag and glanced up and down the street. The persistent scent of wood-burning fires flavored the air, mingled with aromas of cooking black beans and tortillas from the confinement of courtyards.

She heard the faint rumble of a vehicle long before she saw it. Cars and trucks were not frequent and their entry into the town required notice. This was a military truck with two men hanging on to the sides with one-armed bravado and two men riding inside, rifles adorning each man. Now they had doubled the normal number of militia in town. Great. And this was Friday. She hoped they did not plan on staying for the entire weekend, keeping everyone on edge.

She wiped a spill of coffee from the small metal table with the edge of her sweater. Time to pack up and head for the church.

Kate cut through the center of the plaza. She brushed past a cedar tree and a palm tree on a stone path that zigzagged through the center, stepping over dog and bird droppings. Despite everything—the soldiers, the loneliness of being foreign—Kate had never felt as alive. She was not ready to leave the beautiful, crescent-shaped lake.

CHAPTER 9

Kate had been in her second year of graduate school at UC Davis when she learned that her adviser had been awarded a grant to study water usage in Central America. "Water," he said. "In the future, everything is going to be about water. The population growth of the Earth is unrestrained and every one of us needs water. We can live without shoes from Italy, cashmere sweaters, even toothbrushes. We cannot live without water."

He was a British transplant to California. He looked old to Kate, an ungracious fifty-something with freckles splattered on skin that should never have been in the midday sun. In what seemed to be out of character for an academic, he wore Italian shoes and, occasionally, a sweater that her grad school buddies swore was cashmere.

"Everyone studying water is doing research in California or the southwest," he said one day in class. Professor David Clemson was an excitable man, seemingly intent on dashing the stereotype of British propriety, and pounded the podium as he spoke to the class. "Don't follow the herd on this one and wander around the Colorado River. I've got a grant to study water usage in third world countries. We're going to need the most low-tech way to conserve water. Take one semester and see how it goes. What the hell else are you doing? Sitting in the classroom taking notes from old farts like me?"

The next time the class met, he introduced a guest speaker, VJ Kirkland, foreign correspondent to South and Central America. "Let's leave our small view of the world and listen to what she's been up to," he said.

VJ Kirkland had not overdressed for the event; she wore khaki pants that looked a bit too big for her and a long-sleeved T-shirt. She wrote for the *San Francisco Chronicle.* Her life was spent on buses in Colombia, living for weeks in small hotels in Chile, and now Guatemala, covering the economics of emerging countries. "We have been deeply involved in controlling the economies of countries in Central America for decades," she said, "and we are only now seeing the full damage of our interference."

Kate couldn't have been less interested in politics. But she was interested in the door that Kirkland had opened, the possibility of stepping past the national border into other countries as if they were Florida or Oklahoma.

Kate scheduled a meeting with Dr. Clemson. When she entered his office, he continued on with his monologue about water as if class was still in session.

"Look around, Miss Malloy. This campus is on the outer edge of the Sacramento Valley, which should be a desert. But we've pumped the bloody daylights out of the Sacramento River to create rice fields and expansive lawns for our campus with sprinklers that turn on once a day whether it's raining or not." He paused, as if forgetting why Kate was sitting in his office.

"I wanted to talk to you about your grant to study water." She was ready to step out into the world. She had grown up next to the Connecticut River in Massachusetts, watching great blue herons soar just inches above the water. Her mother had taught her how to handle a canoe by the time she was in second grade. She had never traveled out of the country, never taken a breath in any direction that deviated from being a student. The world beckoned her and she felt the breath of her mother blowing her forward. "That's it, Katie, keep going," she could hear her mother say.

"I want to talk with you about studying the impact of water on rural village life, you know, health and economics. I think there's a lot we can learn on the macro level from the microcosm of isolated villages and how they use water," Kate said. She hoped that she was hitting all the right tag words. He had to sign off on her research design, but first she had to convince him that she was smart enough, tough enough to do this. "I'd like this to be my dissertation. I could help you with your research."

"Where are you thinking about? What country?" he asked, leaning back in his chair. His was an interior office with no window. Kate would sooner be unemployed and living on the streets than teaching at a university where her office was a cinderblock bunker with refrigerated air blowing out of the ceiling vent.

"Guatemala. The Highlands area around Lake Atitlán has a lot of isolated villages. They're hard to get to and some of them don't have passable roads at all, only footpaths. Water usage patterns should be clear and distinct," said Kate. "The common link for all the villages is Lake Atitlán."

He raised his eyebrows and spread his palms open. "Political instability?"

She was prepared for this. "The unrest is confined to the more urban areas and the northern highlands that border Mexico. The villages around Lake Atitlán are relatively calm."

He drummed his fingers together. Kate imagined that he wished he were going on a research trip right now instead of sitting in his terrible office. She knew he would say yes, but that he was required to fuss first.

"I think this could work. But I'm not so keen on a young woman working alone in Guatemala. Well, times are different, aren't they? I want you to get a bit more information from that journalist. Kirkland."

One week later, she located the correspondent from the *San Francisco Chronicle.* The reporter was rarely in the office by all accounts. They spoke by phone and then agreed to meet at Judy's Place, a restaurant in Oakland, not far from where Kirkland lived. Kate spotted Kirkland at one of the red padded booths along the side.

Kirkland was tanned and beautiful in a dusty way, wearing sandals and jeans, her backpack fitted with cameras and airport stickers. Her rich auburn hair was pulled back and held with an elastic cinch. She was bone thin, and Kate noticed that a ring on her right hand hung two sizes too large. Kirkland caught her gaze.

She spun the ring around her finger. "Two months of amoebic dysentery this time. I lost eighteen pounds. Every time I return to the States I go on a diet of milkshakes and chocolate bars to beef up for the next round."

Kirkland's raw beauty and warrior determination clinched the decision for Kate. If she could choose to be like someone else, it would be Kirkland, flying off on dangerous missions, writing important stories, living on the edge. She wondered if Kirkland's mother had died also, if that was why she flitted around the world, attached by the thinnest filament, picking only the hardest places.

"So, you want to go to Guatemala to study low-tech ways of water management. You'd pretty much have the market cornered on that one. I've never heard of anyone studying water there. Bats, yes. Monkeys, yes. Guatemalan fabric, yes. Water, no."

"Dr. Clemson wants to find out if we're missing something with our technology, if there's something so simple that third world countries might know that we can't even see. The research could go the other way too. We might offer them water technology that benefits them. He's got a grant and he's willing to fund a trip for me for at least one semester," said Kate.

Kirkland sipped her beer. "Have you done much traveling in other countries?"

"None."

Kirkland raised a finger to get the bartender's attention. "Can I get a burger here?"

She turned back to Kate. "That's the other thing that I eat when I come home. Meat. There's nothing like starvation to cure my old vegetarian habits."

Kirkland doused her burger with ketchup. She was not a dainty eater. Kate pointed to her chin. "You've got food right there."

"Thanks. I don't clean up very well these days."

Kirkland ordered another beer. The woman ate and drank like it was her last day of life.

"So, you want to know what it's like in Guatemala. There are many Guatemalan stories. Which do you want?" She pushed her plate away.

Kate felt like she was being tested. But for what?

"Is it dangerous? I mean, is it too dangerous?"

"Here is one reality—you might never see any evidence of civil unrest. You will see the most beautiful countryside imaginable. There are parts of the country that are untouched. Besides, you are a gringo and no one is fighting with you." Kirkland flicked her glance toward the door.

"But another reality is that they have been in the midst of a civil war for the past thirty years. The military have waged a war against their own people. It's the same playbook that despots have used since the beginning of time. Big companies like United Fruit wanted more land and they bought off the military so that they could run indigenous people off their land and get it for free. Sound familiar?"

Kate shook her head. "I study water. I don't even follow politics in my hometown, never mind Guatemala."

Kirkland threw her mangled napkin on the table. "Nobody is stopping them and they are careful to make nice when tourists are around. Not that many tourists go to Guatemala. Mostly it's the pot-smoking still-hippie types who aren't taken all that seriously by the local governments. But it's their own military killing their own people. If you're a reporter, you are regarded with suspicion. By all means, make sure everyone knows that you are not a reporter."

If Kate were brash and courageous like Kirkland, would she still feel the tremor of being a motherless girl? Even now, the hollow place left by her mother's last days grew larger. Had she told her mother that she loved her? On those last days, when her mother looked so much like her old self, Kate begged to go to school, anywhere except her mother's bedside.

"For the most part, if you're white, you can go about your business, especially if you stay out of their politics. Stay out of Guatemala City and don't go to the far northern mountains near the Mexican border and you'll be okay. Amazing, isn't it?"

"So are you telling me that it's safe or not?" said Kate. She licked the last of the beer off her lips.

"If you're just going to float around in a little boat testing water for a few months, you'll be okay. If you stick your nose into the conflicts between the Maya and the army, be prepared to get in trouble."

Kate had followed up their meeting with several more phone calls about what clothes to bring, what kind of shoes, would there be electricity. Should she bring iodine tablets to purify the water? She had not wanted to sound afraid, but she could hear it in her voice.

Kirkland had softened somewhere along the third phone call. Laughing, she said, "Tell me where you live in Davis. I'm here for another week. I'll bring you some of my old stuff, maps and books. And remember, I told you to be careful, not petrified."

Kate had followed Kirkland's advice, until now.

CHAPTER 10

The church, built by Franciscans in the 1600s, was the most imposing building in Santiago. Kate crossed the large square, walked up the thirteen broad stone steps, and pulled open the thick doors to the church, making her way down the right side. Her sandals clapped on stone until she came to the doorway that led to the meeting room. Manuela was her only student again. Like all Mayan mothers, she had her children with her. Kate was surprised at how easily Manuela could manage the two toddlers and study English at the same time.

She had met Manuela at the marketplace where the young woman sold her handwoven fabric and belts several times per week. Often, Manuela set up her back-strap loom, attaching the threads to a post on one end, with the other end tied around her waist. She sat on the ground with her legs tucked beneath her and passed a wooden shuttle back and forth, creating a twelve-inch-wide length of fabric with designs particular to her village. Her motif was a deep red background with thin blue stripes running through it.

On other days she brought avocados to sell from her cloth

bag. The fruits were dark green orbs brimming with soft abundance and comfort that Kate bought ten for a dollar. She chose not to bargain with Manuela even though she knew this was the gringo price. When Kate's marginal Spanish grew, the two women had easily started up a twice-weekly conversation at the *mercado.*

"You are the one who studies the water?" Manuela had asked in Spanish, which was not her first language either. Manuela spoke Kaqchikel, one of the twenty-two dialects of Mayan languages. Her hair was pulled back into a long gleaming braid and wrapped around the crown of her head. Her lips were soft and her light brown face was unlined.

"Yes," said Kate. She had accepted that all her actions were noted by the local people, including her daily excursions to different parts of the lake, wading through the weeds, collecting samples, testing as much as she could.

"I want to learn everything about the lake," said Kate, disappointed again that her language deficit kept her from expressing her deepest thoughts. Living among the Maya had produced the odd sensation of feeling both much older and much younger. She had at first felt as if she possessed a massive warehouse of knowledge that the indigenous people did not.

In the first few weeks, she imagined all kinds of benefits that she could orchestrate for them with her vast knowledge and access to medicine, science, and water management. Kate felt the lure of superiority and fought it at every turn. Even her height made her feel like an adult in a world of children, or very small adults. Some of the men were as tall as she was but the women rarely topped five feet.

But after several months, she felt more and more like the clumsy one who had to be taught the most basic skills: how to make tortilla dough, which avocados were the best, how to negotiate the wild world of bargaining, and most intriguingly, how to tie the long handwoven fabric across her chest so that she could carry parcels.

"The lake is the center of everything. We call it the belly button of the world," said Manuela. Kate thought she recognized frustration on Manuela's face; the woman wanted to say more but her facility with Spanish was not that much greater than Kate's.

Manuela's dark eyebrows rose at the center. "Are you here to take our water?"

Kate lurched at the sudden turn in the conversation, the divide between them, centuries of different pathways, and the ever present cloak of wealth that every North American was assumed to have. Kate would never be anything but the colonial outsider here, despite her discomfort with the idea.

"No. I want to learn how to keep water from going away. We all need water." Kate was sure she sounded like a pure idiot. Of course the Maya would wonder if she was here as a scout, just one more invader who wanted to pillage their resources.

Kate struggled to ask Manuela the kind of questions that had any depth. Three languages had stood between them: Kaqchikel, Spanish, and English. She had waited for a breakthrough, when Kate could ask her, *What is it like to have your husband gone so often, are you lonely, do you miss him or do you want to throttle him when he comes home?*

Instead they had asked each other, *Do you have a sister, a brother, do you live in a house?* These were the short concise demographic questions that each of them could answer in a language that the other one would understand. Was Kate married? No. Manuela had frowned, her soft brown skin bunching between her eyebrows. *Estudiante.* Mayan kids went to school through sixth grade if they were extraordinarily fortunate. What did Manuela think of Kate, at twenty-four, still going to school?

Kate wanted to explain about water, how she grew up along the Connecticut River and how it was wide and beautiful, filled with wildlife along the sides and with more than a few great blue herons, just like the ones that flew low over Lake Atitlán each morning. How she studied water usage, how without it, none of them would be here. How the human body is mostly water, how much our brain loves water, how it soothes children when they swim in the lakes of New England. She'd wanted to tell Manuela all of this, but instead she braced for the question that she had known would follow. "Where is your mama?" asked Manuela in careful English.

There it was. It always seemed to hurt others when she started.

"My mother dies when I am fifteen. She has an illness, very bad. A cancer, a terrible cancer," said Kate in present tense, pointing generally to her torso. Would Manuela know this was the worst, the fastest, most dreaded cancer? Did the Maya suffer from pancreatic cancer?

Manuela's eyes had brimmed over and she said something for which Kate needed no translation. Manuela was telling her that the death of a mother is horrible beyond all else, a child must have a mother and we are all children. Kate knew all about this; she had been motherless for nine years.

Two small children stood at the bottom of Manuela's skirt, each one gripping the tightly woven fabric.

"Are they your children?" It was an obvious question, but one that Kate could splice together from nouns and verbs.

Manuela nodded. Kate did not know much about children, how they learned, what they ate, why they stood and stared at you as if you were a giant rodent. But she registered that these kids were about the same age. She didn't know the Spanish word for twins or how to pantomime it. She had to work around it.

"How old are they?"

Manuela paused. Kate knew she was calculating from her world into Spanish.

"Two years, more or less," said Manuela, shrugging her shoulders, moving her hands in front of her like moving water. Then she took a pencil and wrote two dots next to each other. This had to be the Mayan number for two.

"They are both the same?" This was the path that Kate was looking for.

"*Sí,*" said Manuela, smiling and patting her abdomen. "Two. Both the same, at the same time."

Manuela apparently didn't know the Spanish word for twins

either. Kate hadn't seen any evidence of twins anywhere in Guatemala.

"I'm teaching English classes at the church. Would you like to come? We can trade for your avocados."

The deal had worked for the last four weeks. But today Manuela was upset and Kate saw it immediately. Kate's present tense Spanish would have to do. English would be impossible in this case.

"Why are the soldiers here today?" she asked.

Manuela's face was remarkably smooth, broad along her cheekbones. The muscles near the inner corners of her eyes squeezed slightly as if the question had hurt her.

"They are here to eat and take what they want from us," she said.

Kate remembered that Manuela's husband, Jorge, should have been back from the terraced fields of the mountains by now. Manuela looked younger today, too young to be contemplating the recklessness of soldiers.

"Are you happy that Jorge is home?" asked Kate.

Manuela lived in Santa Teresa, a smaller village outside of Santiago. Kate had never met Jorge but Manuela had talked about him.

Manuela's eyes filled at the sound of his name. "He does not return from the mountains. He is gone three weeks and this is too long." Manuela opened her hands for the unsaid, the speculation that Manuela did not have words for. "I worry that the military accuse him of things he has not done. They accuse us of things we have never done."

The indigenous people who lived on a subsistence level of agriculture were suspected of endangering the entire militaristic government. Kirkland had hammered away at that point one night after she had delivered a few books and maps to Kate's apartment in Davis. Kate had never seen the Maya armed with more than a machete or a hoe. She tried to picture a political uprising with people armed completely with farming implements.

Kate knew that most of what she could offer Manuela would sound hollow. *Don't worry. Things will be all right. I'm sure Jorge will be back soon.*

"Will you teach me to wear the cloth that you tie around you to carry the children? The rebozo?" asked Kate. Distraction was all she had to offer. One of the hospice nurses had told her father that distraction was highly underrated. "Let your daughter do something normal," the hospice nurse had urged him.

Manuela tilted her head and smiled. Manuela looked to be a few years younger than Kate, perhaps twenty years old. But Kate could be incredibly off with ages.

"In Spanish or English?" asked Manuela.

"Both. We'll use all the words that we have today."

Manuela's lips spread wide into a smile. She reached for the fat knot in the red fabric, near her right collarbone, and began to untie it. As she did, she swung one child around to the front.

"Here is Sofia," she said. "She likes you. Let her sit on you while I show you how to tie the cloth. Then you will tie her to your back like a good woman."

Kate pulled the small girl to her lap and then put both hands to her face and pantomimed terrible fear. She had learned to improvise, using hand gestures, grimaces, enough exaggerated facial gestures to win a role in an Italian opera, making her eyes wide in surprise, tracing lines of tears to downturned lips if she was sad. Little Sofia reached up and patted Kate's face, offering the sweet benediction of a toddler. Manuela laughed at Kate's antics.

"You will learn today," said Manuela.

They spent the rest of the lesson time tying and untying the long handwoven fabric, putting one child and then the other into the snug place at the back where they were safe. Sofia wore a miniature *huipil,* tied around her waist with a cloth belt. The little boy, Mateo, found a stick in the corner of the room and had to be persuaded to continue with Kate's on-the-job training. Only one child at a time would fit there, with a small dark head peeking over Kate's shoulder.

Mateo's hair stuck up with a stubborn cowlick that Manuela tried to pat into obedience from time to time. He ducked his head after several tries.

Kate could remember only one song from childhood. "The Itsy-Bitsy Spider." Why not give it a go with Manuela's kids? She was sure that kids liked hand motions. Her college roommate one year was an early childhood ed major and she spent an inordinate amount of time cataloguing singsong tunes.

"Can I teach the children a song?" asked Kate. Manuela understood *teach* and *children,* but *song* was an English word that she didn't know. She gave the universal shrug for *I don't know.*

Kate sat down on the floor with the two kids. "The itsy-bitsy spider climbed up the water spout." Kate turned her fingers into spider legs climbing up.

"Down came the rain and washed the spider out." Her voice wavered in self-consciousness. Her fingers flitted through the air like rain, or leaves, or something falling. She made an exaggerated sad face to cue the brother and sister where this song was headed.

"Out came the sun and dried up all the rain." Kate opened her arms and tilted her head up to the sky. Both children looked up. What do kids think this is about? They spoke Kaqchikel with a smattering of Spanish.

"And the itsy-bitsy spider climbed up the spout again." Kate clapped to signify the end of the song.

The girl and her twin brother looked expectantly at Kate. "Manuela, *como se dice* spider in Kaqchikel?" Kate cupped her hand and ran her fingers, hopefully like a spider.

Manuela tipped her head to one side and suddenly she understood what the song was about. "Ahm," said Manuela, laughing, repeating it to the kids. Manuela stood up and said she was done for the day.

"I wait for my husband now," she said. She slung the girl onto her back and tied the fabric in a fraction of the time that Kate had taken. Kate watched the young mother walk out, one child on her back and one on her hip.

Kate placed her hand to her face and sniffed in the scent of the children. They smelled of smoke, lake water, and earth. She gathered her backpack and closed up the small side room of the church. The lake and all its mysteries called to her.

She hired a water taxi for the rest of the day and explored the opposite side of the massive lake, stopping in the small villages of Santa Cruz, San Marcos, and Santa Catarina.

CHAPTER 11

The room in the hotel had been her sanctuary for months. The table was covered with her papers. Her test results of the lake water were stacked in glass containers under the window. She wondered if she could write instead of sleep, but the pull to be outside overrode all else. It was Saturday. She could sleep in tomorrow.

Even in Guatemala, with its banana and avocado trees, its green arms reaching toward the equator, the December nights had grown longer. Darkness sank ever earlier on the back side of the volcanoes into the bottomless lake.

It had not been all that long since Kate had regained some traction in her life. Her father had offered her a lifeline when she was sixteen, yet the road had not been without turmoil. She went straight from her mother's death to a steady intake of beer, interspersed with pot, all held together with sex. The mix of all three had been her pharmaceutical remedy and giving up on any of them had been frightening.

UC Davis was three thousand miles away from home, and she had hoped that the West Coast would be a respite from her grief. It was not until she had taken her first biology and botany classes that a bright light turned on. Her mother had been a biology teacher at the high school. Everyone thought that she should love science because her mother taught it, so she had made a huge point of avoiding it.

Her mother used to say, "Katie, we're all made of the same stuff—the fish, crickets, coyotes, and us. It's all the same gooey, beautiful molecules. And we're mostly made of water."

In the science classes, she had felt her mother again. She sometimes caught the scent of her mother's hair, a combination of water, sunshine, and the artificial peach smell of her shampoo. Yes, they were all made of the same stuff. They all needed water, sunlight, and food. They all thrived if touched, even the tomato plants. Even Kate.

Now Kate was uneasy, rattled by the presence of the militia and even more so by Manuela's news that her husband had not returned home. Sleep would not take her.

Kate's job was to study the ways that the lake contributed to the life of the villagers, but there was no way to study the stories that the Maya swore were the biggest truths, that the lake was beyond measurement, like God. Everyone had a story about the lake, almost always starting with the claim that no person had ever reached the bottom. Scuba equipment, lights, gadgets, all the things available to outsiders had brought no one near the bottom. It remained elusive, a place that hung close to the center of the Earth. The other story that Kate had heard a half dozen times was that a river gushed far below the surface, leaving the bottom of the lake and traveling westerly, under the mountains, emerging in the flat lands of the Pacific coast.

It was near sunset on Saturday and the encounter with the soldiers still unsettled her. She pulled on a pair of cotton pants, white T-shirt, and sweater. Her restlessness drew her down the stairs, past a small black scorpion that clung to the stucco wall. It curled its tail into an aggressive circle. Kate's startle factor had dropped off dramatically when she saw scorpions, from three months ago, when she had run to the owner of the hotel shouting, "Scorpion!" Now she walked past the creatures with the same degree of notice that she might give to a bumblebee.

In California, she might not have opted for a stroll near nightfall, but here she had attained a feeling of life happening around, below, and above her, but not to her. The Maya observed her as they might observe a gazelle, and as an oddity, she had a certain distance from interpersonal danger. But most convincingly, Manuela had told her that she'd have no trouble with the Maya. Perhaps Manuela had put in a good word for her. But should she alter her habits with the increased presence of the militia?

Kate's hotel was not far from the church. A walk around the perimeter of the town center would calm the chattering fire in her head. She stopped once when she heard the kitten birds that normally sang their mewling songs in the morning. She hadn't learned the real name of the birds and had at first thought they were kittens, stuck in a tree. Now, something had disturbed them.

As she turned a corner, a steady churning of voices hit her like a wall. Most of the villagers stayed home after dark. Now she saw the flash of the men's clothing, the abrupt cut of the traditional Mayan pants for men that ended a few inches up from the ankles, and the silhouettes of women, their long hair wrapped in fabric tied around their heads in a woven halo. She caught a glint of red cloth. These Maya weren't from Santiago, they were from Santa Teresa, where Manuela lived. There was the bulge of a child tied in a sling around the back of one woman and one in her arms. Was that Manuela?

Past the crowd, the military truck and a glint of moonlight spun a reflection of metal, the automatic weapons that the military carried like umbrellas. Hunched in a doorway to her right was an old man. She crouched down next to him and asked in Spanish, "What is this?" Kate could not tell who understood Spanish or who had stuck to their native languages. She bent toward him and hoped.

"They pulled a man from his home in Santa Teresa this afternoon, and then another tonight. They shoot our men. They kill our two men in jail," he said in Spanish. He pointed to the people who marched to the military barracks.

Kate had a horrible feeling; a stab of dread. "Who were the men? What were their names?" she asked.

"Jorge and Miguel," said the man.

Kate had never been a protester of anything. Her generation existed in the dust of another that was notorious for political marches, and she did not want to be like them. At least not in that way. And yet here was a sudden swell of people who were headed straight for the police station.

"The soldiers can kill us and there is no one to stop them," said the old man. The skin on his face was star-clustered with the wrinkles of high altitude sun, his eyes as dark as lake water. He had a solid seriousness beyond even the normal stoicism of his people. Kate put her hands over her heart in what she hoped was a sign of commiseration.

Past the veranda a block away, she caught a flash of Kirkland's long-legged stride. What! Why was she here, of all places? How long had she been here? Longing to speak English with someone to understand what was happening, she stood up, leaning in the direction of Kirkland's sureness. The man grabbed her hand, an unheard of thing for a man in the village to do; their sense of propriety guided every touch and glance.

"No!" he said, pulling her down to the ground in a powerful tug. A rapid-fire popping of weapons filled the air, something like shattered marble rising above the crowd. Howls of outrage came from the street, shrieks, and the skittering of footsteps. Bullets hit over her head and chunks of adobe fell into her hair.

She was going to die, here in Guatemala. She thought of her father, how this would destroy him, how they only had each other and now he'd be alone. She felt like she had fallen from an airplane and hurtled to a certain death. She covered her head with her hands, crushed into the side of the old man.

When the sound of gunfire ended, he released her and she pulled her hand through her hair to take out the bits of clay.

There was no sound. Nothing. And now everyone in the square lay on the ground. How did they all fall down? No, they had not fallen at all. Kate struggled to regain her senses. A paralysis threatened to take over her limbs.

In the second before all the gunfire, Kate had seen Kirkland trotting along the village center looking like a giraffe compared to the short, compact Maya. Had the soldiers shot her too? Kate's heart pounded against the leg of the old man who had pulled her hard against him. She pushed up to a crouch. The air was infused with hard metal and the scent of mass terror, rising up, reaching for the night sky. The old man covered his face with his palms and groaned.

"Are you hurt?" Kate asked him. She could barely speak; terror choked her vocal cords.

"Forever, all of us are hurt," he said in a language that was failing him.

"Are you shot?" she insisted. Was she shot? Kate ran her hands along her torso and legs. No. But the soldiers were still there in the square. She wanted to hide, to run away.

He shook his head.

A sound rose up from the pile of fallen-down bodies, a strange muffled sound within a familiar child's voice. No one moved, no one was running into the center of things; the world was frozen in place. From across the square, she saw the four soldiers who had been in town all week with their guns. Her legs turned into logs, immobile with terror.

She needs you, Katie. Get up. You can do this. The unmistakable tone of her mother's voice, coming from deep beneath her collarbone, released her.

Do the unexpected. What would be the unexpected in the midst of bloodshed? She stood up and shook out her long blond hair. Kate wanted the soldiers to see her. She wasn't sure why or if it would work but she couldn't think of one thing else to do. They were going to shoot her anyhow, but before they did, she could reach the child who beckoned her.

Kate took off her sweater, tying it loosely around her waist so they could see her white T-shirt. She walked slowly, keeping her eyes on the four of them, following the only sound that existed, the sound of the child who had worked into a crying, hiccupping wail, echoing in the square. She waited for one of the soldiers to move, to aim his gun at her.

Kate stepped over two teenaged boys and the man who had rowed her out to the center of the lake yesterday. Dead. She stepped over José's younger brother, who had tried to sell her a dustpan that he had pounded out from a large soup can. Dead. She followed the voice of the child like a ship sailing through thick fog.

Kate had seen the silhouette of the woman with the one kid tied to her back and the other kid holding her hand, and she came upon her. This was Manuela, her friend, the young, beautiful mother who told her that the children were twins. Kate's throat constricted and she pinched her lips together to keep from crying out. Dear, sweet Manuela. She lay faceup with a coin-sized hole over her left eyebrow. Her eyes were open, the moonlight playing a final reflection. One child lay motionless, facedown beside her, spread-eagled and silent with a darkening puddle beneath him. Mateo, oh God, the boy. He wasn't moving. The crying sound came from underneath Manuela.

Kate knelt down and stole a glance at the men with guns. Were they as shocked as she was? Were they as frozen by what had happened? The four soldiers watched her and seemed to sway like snakes. She willed herself to be the snake charmer, offering them a mesmerizing tune. She nodded to them as if they had agreed on something. A whisper began in her brain, tiny but clear. Kate had to pick up the child, even if she didn't make it out of there, even if she had to die with the toddler in her arms. It was Sofia, Manuela's daughter, and she had to do this. Nothing else mattered but saving one child. Everything in the universe squeezed down to this moment.

Manuela's instruction from the class was fresh in Kate's mind. She untied the sturdy knot at the front of the shoulder and loosened the cloth. Her hands trembled and felt liquid. She rolled Manuela over to one side, her flesh warm. There was the girl, gasping for air. Kate pulled the cloth, unwrapping it from Manuela. Layers of smell rose to meet her, defecation, the high notes of urine, and the smell of blood that billowed out all around her. She picked up the child, loosely wrapped the red cloth over her, and held her to her chest.

One soldier broke free of his daze and pointed his gun at her, raised it to his chest. The sound of a bottle breaking on stone made him turn his head. The scream of breaking glass seemed to come from the direction of the old man. With a nod to the soldier next to him, he lowered his gun and walked toward the sound.

Was Kirkland among those on the ground? All the cloth on the ground was from Santa Teresa, brilliant, intricate thread woven by women like Manuela, like a bed of flowers. Kirkland's solid machine-made coat was not here. She made her way around the other bodies and walked past the four soldiers. Her breath came out in gasps, pumping. Kate turned down the first alley that led to her hotel and ran.

"Kate! Stop!"

Kate whirled around and there was Kirkland, eyes wide and terrified. Kirkland looked at the child in Kate's arms. They backed into the darkest part of the alley.

"Is this kid hurt? What are you doing?"

"I heard her crying. It's Sofia. She was tied to Manuela's back. Manuela . . ." Kate's body shook, first her hands, then her entire body.

"Is Manuela her mother? Is she dead?"

Kate pointed back to the square. "Yes. She's . . . on the ground."

"Jesus Christ. She's dead. This kid is a witness. You're a witness. Is the kid old enough to talk?" Apparently Kirkland knew less about children than Kate. But wait, could the child talk? Yes, in Kaqchikel. She had heard her singsong voice with the silly song that Kate had sung to her.

"Yes, some. I don't know. What if they try to kill her?"

Kirkland's rapid breath blew cold puffs of clouds into the dark alley.

Realizing that Kirkland was truly standing next to her, Kate said, "What are you doing here?"

"Purely coincidental, sort of. I was in Pana and I knew you were over here, so I came over this evening. I was going to find you tomorrow." Kirkland ran her hands along her face. "Okay, I'm a terrible liar. Your adviser called me when I was in Oakland and asked me to please check in with you if I was in the area. I was in the area."

The tendrils of Kate's life prior to blood and murder startled her. Why had she ever come here?

"You've got to get out of here before the goons realize what this means," Kirkland went on. "I will never in my life know why they let you walk across those bodies and out of there. Can you get yourself out of Santiago?"

The child wiggled in her arms and pressed her hands into Kate's chest. The alley was narrow, not more than six feet wide, with a well-worn dirt path down the center. She leaned against a wall of painted concrete blocks to steady the tremors in her legs.

"Where should I go?" Kate was hollowed out, her brain ticking slower and slower.

Kirkland grabbed her by the elbow and moved her along the alley, away from the carnage. "Get your passport, money, and whatever you can fit in a small pack. Do not, I repeat, do not make it look like you are moving out with luggage or whatever you have. Make your way across the lake. Go to one of the villages like San Marcos and head for the road to Sololá and get to Antigua. Ride in the back of a truck if you have to. Get the hell out of here. And the kid?" Kirkland was panting, as if she had just run a race.

The child was Manuela's daughter. She only meant to pull the child out of the line of fire. But what now? What does one do with a child who has been pulled out of a war zone?

Kate shifted Sofia to the other hip and the glint of mucus showed on her lips. Kate wiped Sofia's nose and lips with the rebozo. The child's eyes were so dark, nearly black, that she couldn't tell if she was focusing on Kate or not. Sofia no longer had a mother. She was a free-floating daughter, like Kate, untouched by gravity.

"She's coming with me, just to get her to a safe place." As soon as the words left her, she wondered where exactly that safe place might be.

Church bells rang out in alarm and birds who had thought they could snooze for the night in the tower exploded into the air, shooting off like buckshot into the moonlit night.

"Nothing like this has ever happened before. They're ringing the bells to gather people. Oh my God, have they lost their minds?"

Kate shifted the baby on her hip. Who knew children were so heavy? Every bit of Spanish was excised from her throat as fear gripped her by the shoulder blades. "Good baby, good girl, that's right, okay, okay." If the child cried out, what would she do?

"Kate, pay attention to me. Go back to your hotel, grab your essentials and leave. Do you understand me? If you are taking this child with you, then you need to do it now. I don't know what's going to happen next here."

Kate nodded. It was a relief to have someone give her directions. She wanted to be home, to feel her father's steady voice in the next room, to be ten years old again, paddling along the river with her mother. Her jaws shook, rattling her teeth together.

"I'm writing this story. I'm giving an eyewitness account to the *Chronicle*. They're not getting away with this. I want the world to know about them. . . ." Kirkland's voice caught on a swollen ledge. At the end of the alley, two Mayan men ran by.

"You're going back out to the square? What if they shoot you or drag you away and rape you, then shoot you? Come with me. I can't do this alone."

The church bells continued to ring.

"I have to stay. There's a café in Antigua that has a bookstore. I'll leave you a message if I've made it out of here. Otherwise, contact the newspaper and they'll take it from there." Kirkland rummaged in her pockets, pulled out a pen and small pad of paper, and wrote a number.

"What do you mean, they'll take it from there? They'll dig up your body?" Kate didn't care about justice or politics. She was terrified and she needed Kirkland to go with her.

Kirkland put her arm around Kate's shoulder and gave her an awkward hug. "Just shut up." She dug in her jacket and pulled out a wad of quetzals. "Take this money too. Get out of here and do whatever it is that you're going to do, but get going."

Kirkland turned and trotted off without looking back to Kate, going back the way they had come, straight back to the square where everyone was headed. The temperature in the alley dropped, wrapping a damp arm over her. Kate switched the girl, once again, to the other side, feeling the unfamiliar burn in her arms from holding a child, and headed to the hotel. She hugged the sides of the buildings. When she got to the doorway of her lodging, she dashed inside, up the stairs, past the small scorpion that still clung to the adobe wall, and used her key to get into her room.

Kate set the child down on the bed. Sofia's eyes were huge and a steady stream of tears rolled down her cheeks. She slid off the bed and walked to the door, keeping her eyes on Kate.

"*Mamá, mamá,*" she said.

"No, please, stay here. We're going in just a minute." The child backed away and then stood as still as a statue.

Kate grabbed her passport, money, a clutch of papers from her research, another pair of jeans, a jacket, and a few shirts and rammed them into the pack. She prayed that she could remember how to tie the child on her back in order to carry her.

"We're ready now," she said, forcing a smile. She picked up the girl and sat her on the bed. It took three tries to get it right, always hovering over the bed in case she dropped Sofia. With the girl tied to her back in a little marsupial pouch, she pulled her hair up into a slouchy sun hat. The water samples dotted the room like so many insects peering at her with academic insistence.

"Good-bye," she said to them.

By the time she got to the dock and talked a man into rowing her to San Marcos, she wished she had taken her running shoes. She would continue to regret this for the next two days.

CHAPTER 12

The fisherman spoke no Spanish or English, but he motioned for her to lie down in the narrow canoe. Instead of the traditional clothing, he wore jeans, cut off mid-calf, a length that worked better for the fishermen, less likely to wick up the water from the bottom of the boat. As Kate huddled on the roughly hewn wood, she wondered why he had been at the dock in the middle of the night. The gunfire of course; everyone was on full alert in the village.

The moon was brilliant, glittering over everything. Her outline would have stood out as odd and thus noteworthy. The girl curled to the front of Kate's body and they nestled on the bottom of the boat for the trip across the lake. Sofia was used to being held snug to her mother's body and at least this one act might be familiar to her, pressed against Kate. The cold from the water drove through the wood and into her body. Something acrid made its way up Kate's throat, bubbling up from a core of terror in her belly. What was she doing? She felt like she was running without a map of any kind. Was she hurting or helping Sofia?

With an engine, a boat could make the trip across this section of the lake in thirty minutes. In a *cayuco*, the heavy dugout canoe, how long would it take? Kate did not have her watch on, and although her own internal clock was reliable to within ten minutes, she had no idea how long the silent paddle across the lake lasted, only that as they approached San Marcos, she could hear music. People were still awake and the world had not yet ended.

The man pulled the boat into a thick forest of reeds and got out first, dragging it to shore so that Kate could jump out with only the lower inches of her pants getting wet. The man said something in Kaqchikel that she desperately wanted to understand. He pointed up the mountain and brushed his arm along as if to say *That way*. Kate knew if she took the road up the mountain, she would get to Sololá, and from there she could get to Antigua. But she had only ever taken a bus from Pana, never from San Marcos. Did she really want to be on a road tonight, vulnerable to soldiers who had been out drinking on a Saturday night, or others who would be screeching in to add to the trouble in Santiago? Were there animals that came out only at night that could hurt them?

Not far from the shore, hopelessly drunk people spilled out of a gringo bar. She needed to buy food and water. What would people think of her carrying a child? Would someone stop her and remark about the child? Kate suddenly understood a secondary purpose of tying a child to your back; the girl was swaddled so tightly that she was immobile with only her head and one arm poking out. Why wasn't the child crying? She tried to remember if she had seen any Mayan children wailing in protest and she could not.

Two men turned to look at her with hooded eyes, the way men would when a new woman walks into a bar. She bought two bottles of water and some tortillas. The air in the bar was thick with smoke: tobacco, marijuana, and the sweet smell of wood burning.

No one here knew of the killings. She could tell by the wild oblivion that she saw, the head-splitting decibels of the music, the sweat-drenched bodies that pumped and whirled, spilling out to the patio paved with terra-cotta tiles. Should she say something? Should she tell them about the shootings? She adjusted the fabric sling with Sofia.

Kirkland's words rang in her head. *You are a witness. The child is a witness.* She had heard that the CIA had undercover people keeping track of the alleged guerillas among the villagers. They called them *orejas,* ears. Were there ears in this bar? Kate had honestly thought those had been unfounded conspiracy theories by paranoid people who saw conspiracies everywhere. It hadn't mattered before.

Could one of these people dizzy with drugs and dancing actually be stone-cold sober and observing? Was it the man at the bar who turned to look at her, as he ordered another beer, his shirt soaked with sweat? Or the fair-haired, whirling dancer, her batik skirt wrapped low around her hips, beckoning? Unbelievably, someone had a CD of Whitney Houston's music. "So Emotional" wailed from the speakers. The last time Kate had heard this song had been in June, before she could have imagined the horror of sorting through dead bodies.

If the child had not been on her back, Kate might have grabbed the least intoxicated person and told them that all hell had just broken loose across the lake and it might happen here too. Instead, she slipped out of the bar and headed out of town, stopping by trees, waiting, listening. Was anyone following her? No, she was sure that she left without notice.

The outline of the mountain loomed against the night sky. If she didn't let fear overpower her, she might be able to do this. But the truth was, it was not just an abstract, internal fear that nipped at her heels. It was blood, murder, and soldiers. It was Manuela and her villagers from Santa Teresa dead. She wasn't cut out for this, she wasn't brave enough. She knew about science and water; she knew nothing about running from the military in a third world country. But she knew about motherless children, she knew that they needed watching, that the world could feel cruel to them. And she could get Sofia to a place where people might know how to help her.

She would stay slightly off the road, but keep it in sight so she wouldn't get lost. She'd be there by dawn and catch a chicken bus to Antigua. Two thick clouds moved across the moon, slicing it in half. She kept twenty, thirty yards to the side of the dirt road, wincing with each step, fearing scorpions and snakes. Clouds moved across the sky, obliterating the moon. The darkness was so complete that she could not see the ground beneath her feet. The deep breathing from Sofia meant that the girl had mercifully fallen asleep. For hours, she moved slower and slower until she stopped, her breath shuddering.

Put one foot in front of the other. Think of anything except the carnage in Santiago, except the high altitude tug on her lungs. Do not let panic pull you down. What had she ever done to prepare for this?

Kate had a string of boyfriends in college. Not a string, but three. One from the ranch lands of Montana, another from southern California, and the last, Greg, from Davis, a homegrown guy who lived just down the road from the university. But when she imagined any whiff of them leaving her, growing disinterested, she broke up with them, citing any difference that could be amplified enough to justify a breakup.

The idea of them leaving her was intolerable. She did not want to be the one left behind, abandoned. When she had phoned her father to tell him about breaking up with Greg, he said, "Don't let this become the echo of your life." She had been shocked and at first, angered by his comment. Would the fear of being abandoned truly be the echo of her life?

Carrying the child in the rebozo made her shoulders scream in protest, yanking her back. When the breeze blew the large fronds of the banana trees, it sounded like rain. She had often been tricked by the sound, expecting rain where there was none. In Davis, she had longed for rain in the dry foothills. She had convinced Greg to go camping near the coast, to feel the welcome moisture on her skin. He had teased her, called her "Boston" when in fact she had rarely gone to the seaport city. As she plodded along in the dark, she thought of sleeping together in their warm sleeping bags along the coast of California. Anything to keep her brain sharp right now, anything to keep her attention on something other than the extra effort that it took to hike at this altitude carrying a child.

How did she lose the road? Was it when the first rustle of leaves announced an unlikely wind from the north? The Maya didn't trust a north wind; it was an indicator of trouble or disturbance that could take any form: weather, illness, domestic unhappiness. They paid respectful attention to the wind that poured across the lake and in the final analysis, the lake was annoyed by a north wind and it ruffled in irritation. Did she lose the road when the dark clouds rolled across the sky in military formation, or when the first rain began to fall, a light mist, then torrential within the hour?

Water poured off her hat. Kate pulled the child around to the front to offer her more protection. She stopped near the base of a broad-leafed tree and pulled out what remained of her research papers. She stuffed them around the girl for insulation. She could no longer see the glint of the moon in the child's eyes, so she patted her face and murmured to her in Spanish, "*Bueno,* Sofia, *bueno.*" The child had not spoken since the hotel and the silence rattled Kate almost as much as the darkness. Had the shock of the gunfire blotted out the memory for the child, or would it be etched in stone?

Her feet were the coldest part of her body. She pictured her Nikes back at the hotel, warm and snug, a likely home for the scorpion by this time. She wore the sandals from Chichicastenango, the ones that had been fitted to her feet by the shoemaker in his stall. The soles were made from old tire treads and the top was rich leather with bands crisscrossing over her feet. They had been so perfect until this night.

What if the soldiers came looking for her? What if someone at the gringo bar said that they had seen the woman and the child? Every step she took crackled and exploded with noise; they could be following her and she'd never hear them. She had to keep going, to put as much distance as possible between her and the lake.

The rain fell harder still, as impossible as that seemed. The sound of so much water crashing on the dense vegetation was deafening. Every surface in the mountain jungle pinged from the rain, clattered, shook in a collectively deafening roar. If she was not soaked by the torrents that fell from the sky, she was splashed by rain that splattered off the ground, seeking any dry spot on her. It was now impossible to see any remnants of the trail and the dirt moved like marbles beneath her feet. Mudslides were a constant danger in the rainy season. Entire villages had been buried in mud, the land resculpted. But this was not the rainy season and surely the ground could absorb the runoff.

She formed a mantra and repeated it from beginning to end for hours.

I have to survive. I have to bring this little girl to safety. It's just too bad if you're terrified. You have to suck it up.

She never had to be brave before, not in this way. Her mother's death had not made her brave. It had scattered her into pieces. She had seen her mother's bravery though, the quiet power and determination to stay alive, the iron will that had startled even the doctors. Had Kate been brave when she left Massachusetts and her father for the West Coast? No, that was something else, an attempt at a geographic balm.

The terrain was unbearably steep and she had never carried a child before. Her center of balance was thrown off and the weight of the child threatened to pull her off her feet, ricocheting from the mountain. Kate had long since lost sight of the lights from San Marcos and if music still boomed from the gringo bar, it was muffled by the rain.

Her foot smashed into a stump, then another. The Maya must have been clearing trees in this area for the smoky woodstoves in each house. Kate very nearly crashed into a lean-to shelter, left by the men who had been working here. Her face brushed against the palm thatch roof. Good enough for tonight, good enough to keep the rain off them. One entire side was open but three sides were loosely covered with something, she couldn't see what. Water gushed through the shelter along the ground.

Kate couldn't put the child down so she kicked a series of short logs into a corner until she had enough to squat on. She untied the drenched knot of fabric and put the child on the island so that she could grab several more pieces as well as an abandoned piece of palm thatch.

This was impossible. What had she been thinking? A blanket of despair fell over her, as wet and dark as the night. The adrenaline that had been pushing her forward abandoned her, leaving her slumped in a heap. She felt small, a dot of a human crushed between mountain and sky.

Through the night Kate sat huddled in the corner with the girl in her arms. They both drank from the plastic bottles. She leaned into the corner of the shelter and for brief moments fell precipitously into dreams where she held on to a slippery raft on an endless lake with angry waves.

CHAPTER 13

The rain lasted well into the next day. They drank the rest of one bottle of water and ate some of the tortillas that had stayed miraculously dry. By midday, the clouds rushed along on a new path to the east and the sun broke through. Kate took off her pants and hung them on a bush outside the shelter. Her spare pants retained some dry places; the seat was dry but the legs were drenched in water that found its way into the bottom of the pack, possibly through the seams that Kate had not bothered to seal.

Sofia was awake and wide-eyed, watching every move that Kate made, including the pee squat not far from the front of the shelter. Kate unwrapped her to see how wet she was and what needed to be dried out. Manuela had said her kids were about two years old, more or less. So the girl could be as old as two and a half, maybe. Or she could be less than two years old.

Kate had no idea. She had never been a babysitter, and she was an only child. Her entire knowledge of young children was based on an elective psych course on child development and on the babblings of one of her professors in grad school who had a new baby at home and continually complained of sleep deprivation.

As soon as Kate unwrapped her, the girl stood and looked straight at Kate, eyes unblinking and warm. A sweet gust of wind bringing dry air blew past, rustled the palms. Something fluttered in her breasts, a tightening that she couldn't account for scientifically, but she knew what it could be, having heard it enough from her own mother. How the nearness of a child can cause a chemical change in adults, an evolutionary mandate to care for babies and young children. She wanted only to get Sofia to safety, to protect the child against retaliation. She held out her small brown arms to be picked up. Kate bent over and enveloped the girl, carrying her on her hip.

"Let's get you out of the wet things and into my beautiful T-shirt so that we can dry everything." The decision to speak English to the child came as a surprise. Yes, she would speak English to the girl. Certainly Sofia had heard her mother and Kate conversing in English. On the surface, it was the worst possible idea, obliterating her most familiar language and Spanish. But if the child had words for soldiers or guns, Kate didn't want to hear them—or more to the point, she didn't want anyone else to hear them. She counted on the malleability of a toddler's brain.

The girl was remarkably compliant, not fussing, never crying, and yet the lack of sound, the complete absence of her voice continued to worry Kate. Of course it was the soul-searing trauma of the massacre; it could burn the voice out of anyone. The girl held up her arms for Kate to pull off her shirt and her skirt. She wore no underclothing. As soon as she was naked, the child took a few steps and squatted. A watery slew of diarrhea shot out and the girl winced as she voided her bowels. Dysentery. A health worker had said that nearly all the villagers had dysentery at one time or another. It was a disease that saps the energy of people, feeding the parasites and not the hosts. Children fared the worst, many dying from dehydration before they passed their fifth year.

Kate wrapped her in a warm T-shirt and a jacket. The two of

them sat together until more of their clothing dried. The land along the lake was steep and rippled accordion style. Fifty square miles of water, ringed by dormant volcanos. The rocks were dark gray volcanic and frequently loose to the touch, ready to come tumbling down the steep terrain. They were clearly far from the road, but in the distance Kate could hear the occasional rumble of a truck or car as it motored into San Marcos. Sofia pointed to the lake with her hand, palm up, as if asking a question. "We are going up the mountain," said Kate, pointing upward, "not back to the lake."

From their vantage point, the lake looked far too beautiful for so much death. White clouds billowed around the volcanic peaks of San Pedro, Tolimán, and Atitlán. Sun filtered along a strip of the long lake, slicing it with a silver band of light.

By midday, she tied the child to her back and then laced her arms through her day pack so that it hung from the front of her body. Her calf muscles tightened with each step, forming metal cables that made her wince. Her thigh muscles were not used to a steady steep incline and they felt like they were bleeding. Was this possible? Was there a tipping point for muscles when they began to tear?

"Here we go, little one. You get the express ride on the gringo donkey," she said, gasping for breath.

The child would hear English words but smell the indelible scent of her mother on the cloth. What strange mixture would this produce?

Lake Atitlán rested in a caldera at five thousand feet altitude. Kate had been accustomed to the sea level altitude at Davis when she first arrived. She had gradually acclimated, but her ability to hike for long distances was still minuscule compared to the Maya. Their lungs had to be absolute bellows compared to her puny lowland organs.

To get to Sololá, she'd have to climb an additional two thousand feet in altitude. She estimated that she had gone one-fourth of the way up. Estimating distances in the rugged highlands was deceptive.

"We'll be in Sololá in time to eat a plate of beans and tortillas tonight. It's going to be all right," she said with her head turned as far back to the child as possible. She reached one hand back and patted the girl in the pouch.

How much can one diminutive child weigh? The Maya were a small people, but Sofia's weight felt condensed, like granite. The extra weight on Kate's back multiplied with each step. Kate's sporadic running, three days a week at Davis, at sea level, felt inadequate to power her along. Whatever hopefulness she had mustered to talk brightly to Sofia withered as she dragged one foot after the other.

She stayed in the deeply vegetated areas, thick with scrambles of smooth-barked trees and tangles of brush. Small lizards trying to sun themselves after the cold night skittered out of her path. When she needed to catch her breath, she stopped and looked down on the lake. She could no longer see Santiago because it was tucked behind a turn in the shore, but she saw no plumes of smoke rising from it. The vast lake shone brightly. At least the entire town had not been torched. But what was happening? Had more people been massacred? Had more military arrived? What about Kirkland?

Kate emerged into an open area and chanced a rest stop. She let the pack fall off the front of her body and swung the child around and untied the knot. Both of them needed a breather from their tight connection. The girl stepped over the sharp rocks gingerly. By the time she was five, she would have soles tough enough to run over any of the hillsides. But even at her tender age and with her novice walking experience, her feet were still more hardened than Kate's, not so easily stuck and stabbed by thorns and rocks. Kate wanted nothing more than stillness, her legs craved a rest and her chest burned with the extra effort of pulling in enough oxygen. She wanted the remaining bottle of water to last for the rest of the afternoon.

The whop-whop-whop sound arrived just as Kate finished a sip of water. Helicopters? She hadn't considered them. What direction were they coming from? They had to be military helicopters; she'd never seen any other sort since she'd been in Guatemala. She and the child were in the open, unprotected.

Kate dropped the water bottle and dove for the child. She scooped her under one arm. They weren't safe anywhere!

The water bottle had landed on its side, and water poured from it. Kate bent deeply, grabbed the water bottle, and ran for the cover of thick brush. She stashed the girl under a bush and went back for the pack and the cloth. The sound of the helicopters grew louder; a giant drumbeat in the sky.

The cloth was impossibly long and it caught on something, a stick that protruded from the ground. At the last second, Kate let it go when the helicopters crested the hill. She slid into the gulley as if she was sliding into first base. She pushed the child farther under the brush and lay over her. She turned her head and watched with horror as the red cloth flapped like a flag, thirty feet away.

If there is a soldier on the copter who knows the fabric designs of the villages, they will know that this cloth is from Santa Teresa. Mayan boys had been conscripted for years, when they were twelve, even ten years old. Please not this time, not now, she prayed. Then her fears multiplied: It was two helicopters, not just one.

One helicopter flew straight across the lake, straight for Santiago. What were they doing? She pulled her knees up and around Sofia, her arms wrapped around her. She tried to say something to the girl but if she did, even she could not hear it. Her ears vibrated as if they were being struck. The second helicopter was directly over the flapping red cloth with an ear-splitting hammer of helicopter blades. Kate pulled the pack against her face. Dirt and pebbles flew into the air from the powerful machine.

The helicopter hovered, pulled up, and turned facing the steep hillside. Suddenly the air exploded in machine gun fire. Dirt and rocks flew through the air and screamed with the assault. It was over in seconds. The helicopter swooped and turned and followed its partner across the lake. Adrenaline surged anew, exploding throughout her system. A deep guttural sound rose up from her belly. More than a scream, deeper, darker.

Kate waited for nearly an hour, soothing the shaking girl, holding her as she rocked. She sang a Beatles song that her mother said was popular when Kate was a little girl, "All You Need Is Love," forgetting half the words, making up new verses. Then she crept out and found the cloth, pockmarked with bullet holes. Part of the long cloth was still serviceable and she could use it to carry the child, but they were not going to budge from this spot until night. The assault had drained her last reserves of energy.

She suspected that the decision to shoot at the cloth was a lark for the soldiers, a practice moment. Would killing a child be as easy for them? Were the soldiers looking for them, a white woman with a Mayan child? Would the soldier on the helicopter have killed them? Any doubts that she had about this possibility had evaporated. She had to get to Antigua.

This is what had been happening right under her nose. If you were Maya, the wrong color cloth on a mountainside meant death. Kate's universe shuffled and rearranged. She had not seen beneath the thin veneer of village life, even after Kirkland's stern warnings, even after Manuela said, *They take what they want from us.*

Did Sofia know that they were lost? Kate had been lost once when she had ventured too far from a campground with her parents. She had been six, lured from the tent by a path that disappeared when she tried to retrace her steps. Her voice had been swallowed whole by the forest when she yelled for her parents, coming out in thin strands of sound. When panic overwhelmed her and the late afternoon sun gave way to dark, she heard her mother. "Katie! Katie!" Her mother emerged wearing her tie-dyed T-shirt and cutoff shorts, her legs strong and tanned. She picked her up, patting and rubbing her back, swaying in time to a heartbeat. "I will always find you, Katydid."

Kate knelt in front of Sofia. "I promise, I will take care of you. I promise Manuela. I promise my mother."

Kate slept under the bushes whenever the child napped, curled in next to her. They waited until night and she prayed for clear skies with a generous moon. She was not disappointed. Kate loaded up as before, the child on her back, her day pack hanging from the front of her body. She could not straighten up entirely, feeling more like a cartoon version of an upright turtle. The child sipped the last of the water. Dehydration was far worse on children than on adults; that much Kate did know about kids. As night fell, Kate began again, picking her way along her own trail, ever upward.

The temperature dropped, and a new danger loomed: hypothermia. The only defense was to keep moving. But the child was not generating any heat from movement and she would suffer. She had the heat from Kate's back, true, but it was not enough. Kate felt Sofia's hands grow colder.

They made two major stops during the night. First Kate stopped to stuff most of her clothes around the girl. Then when her throat turned to sandpaper and her head pounded, they stopped at a stream to fill the water bottles. There was the slightest chance that the water might be clean and free of parasites, and it was a chance that Kate held on to. It was better to have water, contaminated or not, than dehydration.

She remembered an outdoor training workshop that she took when the instructor said that every person they'd ever had to rescue suffered more from dehydration than hypothermia. She could deal with amoebas or giardia later. Kate tipped the bottle of water to her lips and drank. "Well, Professor Clemson, I don't have Italian shoes or even my running shoes and I've never owned a cashmere sweater. But I've got water. You were right, there's nothing like it in the entire world."

She'd already had one bout of the intestinal assault since coming to Guatemala and she knew how to deal with it. The *farmacia* in Antigua would write her a script for the powerful drug Flagyl. She wasn't sure what the child would require, but she'd find out.

The temperature continued to drop during the night, the result of the cloudless sky. She walked for hours until the predawn time of despair. The smell of humanity reached out to her through the smoke of hearth fires. Dogs barked, and roosters announced the dawn. They were alive and she had put two thousand feet of altitude between them and the lake. Her head pounded and her throat felt like it was swelling from lack of moisture. She'd been breathing through her mouth for the last hour to suck in as much oxygen as possible in the thin atmosphere.

Kate and the little girl spent the last few hours of darkness on the edge of the mountain town, Sololá, too afraid to ask anyone for help, too afraid that the black-booted militia would come here also. What would the villagers do if they saw the deranged looking white woman with a Mayan child?

The first ray of sunlight struck her sandals and highlighted a dark blotch. She rubbed it with her hand. Something had soaked into the leather straps and made a home between the fat cells of the cowhide. Was it blood from Santiago? It had soaked in before the torrential rains. Did she have blood on her sandals from stepping into the pile of bodies? She rubbed her stained sandals with dirt, sickened at the thought and afraid that the stain would scream and betray her.

This is how a coyote lives, dodging among the shadows on the outskirts of town, looking for a vulnerablc morsel to eat. Unlike a coyote, she had to take a chance on someone. She and the child needed water and food. Kate once again wrapped the child carefully with the long fabric and hoisted her on her back. She was tiny, small-boned with little birdlike features. The child looked frozen, stunned into her state of speechlessness. Kate imagined the intestinal cramping that the girl must have, and yet she had not whimpered or cried in pain, only from the roar of the helicopters.

Kate smelled the welcoming smoke of a hearth fire and longed for the polluting billows. She wrapped her hair tightly and stuffed it under the hat, not that it would hide her whiteness, her otherness, but the shock value of her blond hair could at least be shuttered. She had to ask for help.

Kate picked the house on the farthest edge of the village, hoping to cause the least amount of commotion. She stepped on a brittle stick and village dogs began to howl. She approached the house, cinder blocks covered with stucco, and announced herself.

"*Buenos días,*" she said, not realizing how dry her throat was until the words emerged like dust-coated gravel from her throat.

An old woman rose up from a darkened corner. There were no electrical wires running to this house to bring lights, refrigerators, no hum of North America at all. The roof was corrugated metal.

In her best present tense Spanish, Kate said, "I want to buy tortillas and beans, please."

The woman's face was creased heavily, her eyes hooded by the weight of her eyelids pressing down. She came only to Kate's shoulder and did not respond.

"Please, for the baby and me."

The old woman disappeared into the house. Should Kate follow her? No, she had not been invited and she was certain that she should stay outside. She swayed slightly and sank to her knees to keep from falling. She had walked two days with the child, her quadriceps were on fire and the muscles along her shoulders screamed. If she sat down, she wasn't sure if she could get up again.

Before she left California, if anyone had told her that the nights in Guatemala were anything but tropical, she would not have believed it. It was December and the altitude made the nights bone-chilling. She longed to be indoors with a door that could be shut.

The old woman returned with a small sack of flour. She nudged a fire into flame near the pathway to the house, brought a heavy frying pan out and put it on the fire. She dug her hand into the sack and extracted a fist full of flour and put it in a bowl. To this she added water, and she formed a ball. She patted and patted, slapped the ball and slammed it from hand to hand until the perfect tortilla emerged, the size of her palm, which she dropped into the skillet. With one hand she motioned to Kate to sit on the ground.

Kate tried to sit in exactly the same way as the Mayan woman, with her legs tucked modestly to one side. The old woman took a wooden scoop and dipped it into a plastic jug of water and handed it to Kate, who drank without hesitation. Then she brought the scoop to the girl's lips. Sofia drank more delicately than Kate could have imagined, placing her small brown fingers along the edge.

Kirkland had told her to go to Antigua and she had no other plan following Kirkland's directive. What would she do with Sofia in Antigua? She only knew that both of them had survived.

CHAPTER 14

The local bus, aptly called the chicken bus, offered a jarring and arduous ride from Sololá to Antigua the next day. Kate kept a scarf wrapped around her head and huddled with the child in the last row for the four-hour trip. Wooden bench seats held six across, with no aisle, so people moved to the back to let others on more easily.

This was one of the Higueros buses, named after the family who owned them. This particular bus had a large image of Mighty Mouse painted on the hood with the grill painted white for teeth. As the bus filled to capacity, stopping at every village and in between, the mix of warmth and the smells from people and chickens lulled Kate into memories of the farmyards near her home in Massachusetts. And home always smelled like her mother, before she smelled like medicine and death.

Kate offered Sofia the tortillas that she had wrapped in paper. Could she ever tell the girl about not having a mother, about the cliff of beer and marijuana that she had tumbled off in high school, how no one spoke of her mother for fear of hurting her and how much more that hurt her? How her father feared that he would lose Kate too, and how she finally surfaced again in her second year of college when she peered through a microscope and looked at water?

We are surrounded by things we can't see, she had thought, stunned by the world of organisms that live beyond our sorrows and our love. If she could look at her present life from above, in a familiar microscope, she'd see a woman with an orphan on a Mighty Mouse bus.

Climbing up the steps of the vehicle had reawakened the muscles in her legs that now felt damaged, beaten and bloodied like a boxer on the losing end of a fight. She had only been able to take one step at a time. Not only her muscles screamed, but her hip joints and her knees. Once seated, she did not plan on getting up until Antigua.

She longed to know more about Manuela; she saw the image of the young mother with her dead child every time she closed her eyes.

Kate wanted Manuela and her mother to speak from the land where dead mothers went. What should she do with this child?

The bus arrived in Antigua. The streets of the small city were paved with rough cobblestones and the bus shook so hard that she feared the axles would snap and the sides would fall off. Despite the clattering arrival, Antigua was a regal, colonial city that always made Kate feel like she had stepped into a museum of an ancient, yet ruined civilization. They passed the Arch of Santa Catalina, her favorite landmark, gleaming egg-yolk yellow, that allowed cloistered nuns to pass unseen from one building to another. Other Spanish churches had fallen prey to a series of earthquakes that left piles of stone rubble still in place, frozen in time.

The bus stopped at the large market on the edge of town, filled with stalls of fruits and vegetables. Kate made her way to a guesthouse that was somehow stuck in her brain. Kate had heard of the Casa Candelaria Guesthouse when she'd been through Pana. She'd been told that it was recently opened and cheap, a good place to stay in Antigua.

She hoisted Sofia into the rebozo, hung the pack on the front of her body, and left the bustle of the marketplace. Two blocks to the left of the market and one block right, toward the center of town. The uneven cobblestones sent sparks of pain along her strained calf muscles. She nearly missed the name, a humble three-inch-tall sign, freshly carved in wood: CASA CANDELARIA. Kate gripped the iron ring and knocked against the thick wood door. Someone opened the sliding peephole and peered out.

The door swung open and a young woman stood in the entryway, a child clutching her knee. "Hello! Are you looking for a room?"

An Aussie accent. Hair braided and piled on her head, held with a clip. Freckles. Jeans. A crooked smile. And young, maybe not as young as Kate.

"Yes."

"Come in, come in. I'm Marta," she said with an expansive sweep of one arm.

Behind Marta, a courtyard billowed with orchids, orange and purple bird of paradise, and one banana tree. To the right was a long table with a basket of skeleton keys. Room keys. This was the reception desk.

"This is our first venture at running a guesthouse," said Marta. "The rooms are upstairs. Have you just arrived in town?"

Of course there would be questions and Kate was prepared.

"Yes, today."

Kate climbed the terra-cotta-tiled stairs as if she had gained sixty years; her calf muscles were pulled as tight as steel cables, and her thighs weren't much better.

"Are you injured?" asked Marta, watching Kate's snail's pace up the wide curving stairway, holding on to the wood banister.

Kate paused to catch her breath, wincing. "No, I mean yes. I went on a long hike. Too long. I wasn't prepared for the level of difficulty." As if it had been a black diamond ski slope and not an escape through the hardest terrain she had ever hiked.

The young Aussie woman picked up her thumb-sucking child and stood in the doorway as Kate inspected the small bedroom with two beds. The woman pulled the clip out of her hair and released a dark thick braid that reached between her shoulder blades. The child tried unsuccessfully to grab it. The room was on the second floor and faced the inner courtyard. The bathroom was next door with a shower and a toilet. The idea of hot water almost brought Kate to tears.

Kate looked at the beds and felt the sense of protection offered by the thick walls and filtered water. She had not bathed or slept in three days.

"My husband is still in Australia but he'll be joining us soon. He had to go back to handle the sale of our house. We always wanted to come to this part of the world. Our families think we're daft, coming so far away when our son is so young," said Marta.

Australians were known throughout the area as the greatest of travelers, letting their high school graduates take a gap year to roam worldwide.

She wanted only to collapse on the bed, but it was soothing to hear Marta's voice, to hear about families whose worst troubles had to do with moving too far from home.

"Are you here to adopt?" asked Marta.

"What?" Kate couldn't imagine what she must look like or smell like. Adopt who? Kate lowered herself to the bed.

"I was wondering if you were here to adopt a child. I just assumed—a white woman with a small Mayan child. Or have you already adopted? She's a beautiful little girl." Marta tilted her head toward Kate's passenger on her back.

She was doing exactly what Kirkland had told her, which was to get out of the area, as far away from the massacre as she could. What made Marta assume that she was adopting? Of course Kate knew about adoption. It was hard not to notice the white couples with their new babies sitting on the park benches in Antigua.

It was easier and less expensive to get a child in Guatemala than in Asia. The market was booming. But adoption for Kate?

Ridiculous. She was too young, too much of a graduate student. What could she possibly know about mothering a child? She only wanted to bring the child to safety. Marta's blond child, now hugging Marta's knees once again, popped his thumb out of his mouth long enough to say "Baby," pointing at Sofia. Kate looked down and the dark stain on her sandal shimmered with a grisly mandala.

"I'm just here to get some medical help for her. Her village was very far into the highlands. You can't imagine how tired we are. We'll take the room." She tucked one foot under the bed.

Marta put her hands on her hips in approval. "Oh, I knew you would. I had a feeling about you. How long will you be staying with us?"

"I don't know yet. The medical process can be lengthy. Can I leave it open-ended with the rental?"

"Of course. And what do we call the beautiful girl?"

"Sofia. Her name is Sofia," said Kate, knowing that this was the name Manuela gave for the outside world, not her true Mayan name. She had never learned her true name and the lack of it stabbed at her.

CHAPTER 15

By the next morning, Kate's intestines were boiling with activity. She took the girl to the local clinic and had both of them treated. As long as she didn't try to climb steps, or step off the curb, her legs didn't bellow in protest. Walking on flat surfaces worked. She was positive that Sofia's intestines were compromised by parasites, amoebas, or any of the other troublemakers that could have hitched a ride. Kate wasn't absolutely sure if the child was ill or if everything in her intestines had turned to water from terror, but she decided to err on the side of pharmacology. At least Kate had the power to fix basic digestive distress.

Were all two-year-olds this small? The girl wore the traditional skirt, a piece of handwoven cloth wrapped around her waist and held with a cloth belt. The highly embroidered *huipil* that was worn as a blouse was essentially a piece of fabric folded in half with a hole cut out for her head. If the child wore this outfit in Antigua, every indigenous person would know exactly where she was from and Kate didn't want the location of the massacre, or her connection, broadcasted.

Kate had to venture out once with the child in her brilliantly colored cloth, woven by Manuela, because she had nothing else for the child to wear. She went to one of the two stores in Antigua that sold western clothing for kids. Western meaning non-Mayan, but made in Guatemala. Kate bought a white peasant blouse with puffy sleeves, a skirt, a wool sweater, and some amazingly small underpants. The only available shoes looked like they would fall apart within the week. She bought two pairs of shoes, sandals and little sneakers, and several pair of socks.

Then she went to the central square of Antigua, a city that retained the colonial architecture of the seventeenth century despite massive damage from an earthquake fourteen years ago. The small city was impossibly beautiful. The central park was dominated by a fountain that, even now, flowed and calmed whoever paused along the park benches. Water poured from the breasts of four statues, graceful hands supporting each breast, water cascading from them into the large pool. Water, like breast milk.

The street on one side of the square was dotted with a handful of shops, prepared to sell ice cream, coffee, and cold beer to the tourists. Kate headed directly to the café with the bookstore in the entry room. Casa del Sol Café. She pushed the dark wooden doors, opening them like a fan. The notion of finding Fernando and his café had beamed like the North Star.

She asked a waitress for the owner. A Guatemalan man approached her. Was he a ladino, the Guatemalans who are a mix of Spanish heritage and indigenous bloodlines? Or stranger yet, Mayas who have abandoned their indigenous heritage. Until this moment, it hadn't mattered to her to understand this.

He was thin, older than Kate, and wore a white shirt, sleeves rolled up, dark pants. The man gave away nothing in his attire, no hint of who he might be. It looked as if he had decided to reveal nothing about himself, to strive for a kind of neutrality. He pulled out a chair and nodded to her.

She came to the point. "Is there a message here from Kirkland for me? I'm Kate."

His eyes held something familiar, a weary kindness that reminded her of her father. "Yes, I know who you are. I am Fernando. Kirkland said you would look earnest and afraid." He smiled. "And blond. She said to give you this." His English was flawless. He handed her a sealed envelope. If she were not feeling the pull of illness and fatigue, she might have noticed how beautiful his hands were. Kate took the envelope and unfolded the slip of lined paper.

Story phoned in. You can trust F.

She folded the note and slid it into her pocket and trembled with a sigh of relief. Would Kirkland have been as terrified as she had been, bushwhacking through the dark with helicopters spraying gunfire? The child on her back stirred and poked an eager arm out to Fernando.

The man was slight, dark hair combed neatly. "Sit and have something to drink. You do not look well. Your travels have been difficult." He had chosen a table in the inner courtyard. He signaled to the waitress for a bottle of Coke and pulled a chair close to hers.

"I've known Kirkland since she started reporting in Guatemala. If there is something that I can do to help you, I will."

The sweet darkness of the Coke mingled with her saliva, then etched her throat with the explosion of bubbles. Kate had never been a fan of soda, not for health reasons, but because carbonation of any kind gave her the hiccups. But in Guatemala it was easier to find soda than it was to find clean water. There had been a massacre just five hours from Antigua, helicopters had shot at flapping cloth on the hillside; at the end of the world, would we all be sipping Coca-Cola?

"For now it's enough to know that Kirkland is okay. I was worried about her. When I left her—"

Fernando held up a hand. "I know what happened and it is better for you not to say it." One of his feet tapped on the tile floor, a fluttering heartbeat, belying his motionless hands folded on the table.

Kate's head pounded. "I'm probably sick from drinking the water." How long would the medication take to work its magic?

Fernando reached out his palm to her forehead and said, "May I?"

Kate nodded.

His hand was cool, amplifying how hot she was. "You have a fever. I will walk you back to your hotel. Do you have medicine?"

His gentleness was dissolving her. This felt like the end of her first half marathon that she had run as an undergrad. What do you do at the end?

She placed both hands on the table and pushed hard to stand up. She could not remember ever having to concentrate so intently on her leg muscles and she could not remember someone placing a hand on her forehead since her mother had died. Was that possible? She was shocked by his tactile expression of concern, as if she was a small girl who needed to stay home from school. They both stood up. Terrible groaning sounds came from her intestines.

"Are you injured?" he asked.

"I hiked with the child from San Marcos to Sololá. I may have gotten lost several times."

Fernando's eyebrows squeezed toward each other. "May I carry the child?" he asked, nodding toward Sofia. "You are exhausted."

"No!" Kate swung around with fevered awkwardness, knocking the empty Coke bottle to the tiled floor. The bottle hit the tile and spun, echoing on the earthen tiles.

Kate was stunned at her response, and at the silence that filled the café. Fernando bent down to pick up the bottle and set it upright on another table.

"The bottles are deceptively thick and strong. We use them in building materials. Have you seen them, stuck into concrete walls? I will walk with you and you will carry the child." He motioned to the door with his arm. He lowered his voice. "Trust no longer comes easily once you have tasted savagery. Kirkland told me of the massacre. She thought you would have had an easier time of it getting to Sololá."

She was too sick to apologize, to thank him, to do anything

but walk by his side as she carried Sofia, stumbling along the rough cobblestones. His kindness was a foreign language that she could not entirely decipher. When she stepped off an uneven curb, she nearly fell, saved by his well-placed touch along her elbow.

At the door to the Casa Candelaria, he said, "Please rest with the child. You have been dropped into our troubles too abruptly." He smiled at her and left. She put her forehead against the massive door, breathing deeply, until the weight of Sofia burned in her arms. Miraculously the child had fallen asleep. How was this possible? Had Kate ever fallen asleep in her mother's arms? She wrapped her hand around the iron knocker, raised it, and knocked twice, each time fearing that her head would explode.

Marta opened the door, took one look at Kate, and said, "Off you go now, the both of you. Sleep will do you wonders. I swear by it."

She climbed the stairs to her room, feeling that at any moment her strength would give out. She placed Sofia on the bed, curled in next to her, and fell asleep.

Later, Kate bathed the child in the shared bathroom on the second floor. How did women take care of children when they themselves were sick? It seemed impossible. She used part of a T-shirt for a washcloth, noticing the scrapes and scratches that Sofia had suffered as a result of their exodus from Santiago. She enunciated each noun that they encountered.

"Soap, water, sink, faucet, floor, water . . ." she said, smiling at the girl as she wrapped her in a large towel.

"Wahdur," said the child. "Wahdur." The child trilled the *r* at the end and it sounded crystalline, like music. Her first words since the massacre. No, not her first. She had cried for her mother, the memory of which tore at Kate. The child had not become mute. Kate was filled with images of Sofia and her brother playing at Manuela's feet in the church, in the marketplace, as she sang songs to them.

Kate had never heard anything as beautiful as the sound of

her voice. So this is what Sofia's voice sounds like in English. Kate turned on the faucet again, letting the water cascade over her fingers. "Yes! Water. Wonderful water."

She held Sofia on one hip and let the girl lean forward and mimic Kate's water play. Then Kate took the child's old clothing and dunked them in the sink. The soiled skirt, *huipil,* and belt sank into the water. Sofia's forehead drew into troubled lines when she saw her clothing in the sink. Her lip trembled. She turned her dark eyes to Kate, as if to say, *This is not right. My clothes should not be drowned in this strange sink.*

Kate pulled a chair into the bathroom and let Sofia stand on it. Together they gently washed the clothing, wrung it out, and hung it over the rusted shower rod. Kate longed to sleep again, to let the medicine do its work with the parasites in her system. It had never occurred to her that there must have been days that her mother had the flu or a miserable cold and yet she had still taken care of a young child. How could she not have known this? In her fevered state, the idea seemed revelatory.

Kate paused and wondered what to do with the cloth. Should she burn it? The bullets had shredded a section of it. She would ask Marta for a scissor and cut off the destroyed bits. For now, letting it dry and folding it up would be enough. Then she helped Sofia on with the new clothes. Kate sank to her bed and held her head in her hands. Simply bathing and dressing Sofia left her exhausted.

The medicine took several days to fully work. Sofia had tremendous powers of recuperation while Kate spent the best part of two days in a cycle of sleeping for several hours and then waking in a lurch, not knowing where Sofia was. She woke once and scanned the room for the child and nearly fell out the door when she couldn't find her. Kate leaned over the courtyard balcony and yelled, "Sofia!" Even as she did, she saw Marta, her child, Felix, and Sofia, digging in the dirt of the raised flower garden. The blaring sensation from her legs had calmed down a few notches.

"Go back to bed. We are busy with gardening here and the

children are helping me. Go," said Marta, with a flutter of her hand.

Kate returned to their room and sank into her bed. In the gray light of early morning, she awoke to Sofia's body pressed to hers. The child's eyes were open, Kate was certain, but they were such dark pools that it was like looking into sunglasses.

Sofia sat up and pressed closer to Kate, her back against Kate's hip. She began to sway, moving to a song that she hummed. Kate did not want to move for fear of closing this window into the child. Sofia held her arms up and let her small hands flutter staccato style down to the bed. She opened her arms wide and looked up and hummed and spoke in either Kaqchikel or the universal babble of toddlers.

Kate's throat constricted and her lips began to quiver. Sofia knew all the hand motions to "Itsy-Bitsy Spider"; she remembered the day that Kate sang to them, when Manuela was too sad to learn English. Kate lay on her side and hot tears ran off the ridge of her nose. When she had to sniffle or else stop breathing all together, Sofia turned her head mid-song and patted Kate along her bottom ribs, just two pats, the touch of which was unlike anything Kate had ever felt before. Kate sat up and sang the song with Sofia.

CHAPTER 16

Two full days passed before Kate emerged from her delirium, abdominal cramps, and bouts of sleeping. Her head cleared and she ate a welcomed breakfast of tortillas with Marta.

"So now that you've gotten medical treatment for the little tyke, will you be returning to her village?" asked Marta as she dipped her warm tortilla into refried beans. They sat at a small wood table topped with ceramic tiles.

What? Kate had almost forgotten what she told Marta when she first appeared at her door. Of course, she had said that Sofia needed medical treatment. What could she tell her now? She liked Marta; couldn't she just tell her the truth?

"Turns out that she might have to see a specialist in Guatemala City. A cardiac specialist," said Kate, hoping to move on.

Marta put her hand on her chest. "Oh no! It's horrible when innocent children are faced with illnesses meant for adults."

It's horrible when innocent children are killed, when women are gunned down, when boys wear automatic weapons across their chests.

"Yes. Um, you'd never know it to look at her. . . . I couldn't tell until she saw a doctor," said Kate, pushing away from the table. "Can Sofia stay here for a bit while I run down to the plaza?"

Marta's eyes welled up. "Don't even think twice about asking me! Of course she can."

Prior to running for her life in Guatemala, lies had been only a social lubricant in Kate's world, like the lies she told friends: your hair looks beautiful, your butt doesn't look big in those pants, no really, this turkey is not the least bit dry, in fact, it's the best I've ever tasted. But there had been the lies of omission, the unspoken agreement between Kate and her father after her mother died. "Are you doing okay, Katie?" he had asked her through the remainder of high school. Everything that she thought he couldn't bear to hear had gone unsaid.

In the underbelly of Guatemala, the lie of omission was the ticket to survival. She saw that now. Say nothing. Do not respond. Don't blink, don't flinch when a seventeen-year-old soldier walks by with his automatic weapon dangling from his hand, ammo strapped from shoulder to hip. Swallow the sound that threatens to erupt from your throat. Don't let it out.

Today she'd go to Fernando's again, to the one place where she did not have to lie. He knew she had the child and why. She wore a denim skirt, sweater, and sandals. The December mornings were cool, even in Antigua. She pushed open the heavy door to his café bookstore, ready to feel the tender caring that he offered with the palm of his hand on her forehead.

Seated to the right were five soldiers, each with a plate of tortillas, beans, and fresh cheese. Their guns leaned against the wall like lazy bicycles back at UC Davis. Kate could not shift quickly enough, rearrange her face, or shrink her lips down to the neutral zone. She froze in place, unable to breathe. Fernando appeared in the doorway to the kitchen. With a nearly imperceptible movement, not even an entire shake of his head, he answered her unspoken question.

"Your book is not here," he said in Spanish so that the soldiers could hear everything. "Come back tomorrow," he said sternly. All his warmth from yesterday was stripped from his voice.

She sighed and feigned annoyance while blood pounded in her eardrums. Kate turned and left the café, walking with exaggerated slowness along the covered walkway in front of the shops. At the end of the street, she crossed diagonally and walked along the front of a Guatemalan bank, stopping to catch her breath. She looked back to see if she could see the entrance to the bookstore. Thick wood pillars lined the walkway around the park and Kate stood behind one, waiting for the soldiers to leave, waiting for her heart to stop pounding like a crazed drum.

"Here are your options," said Fernando, after the soldiers left and Kate returned. They sat in the small courtyard where empty tables waited for customers. The first room of the café was heavy with two walls of books, for loan or purchase, giving the room a scent of molding paper. The courtyard was bright and filled with fat terra-cotta pots of flowers.

Fernando's voice was smooth and round, soft. "The child is now an orphan. Her mother, father, and brother were killed. Most men from that village have either been conscripted into the army or killed. But there could well be aunts, uncles, or grandparents nearby."

Kate waited for the spasm of hiccups to arrive with the Coke. Does a constant state of fear preclude hiccups? If she had allergies, would they have also fled in the face of the massacre? She nodded to Fernando so that he would continue.

"We don't know yet exactly who else was killed in the massacre. We can find out, but it will take time. The military uses mass graves to hide their crimes."

Kate thought back to the English lessons in the church with Manuela. They had worked on English words for mother, father, grandmother, grandfather, aunt, and uncle. They had learned the word for *dead.*

"Dead," Manuela had said when they came to *father.*

"Your father is dead?" asked Kate.

Manuela had lowered her head, then looked up with the slightest movement. It had taken weeks of the lessons for Kate to learn that Manuela's father and her father-in-law were both "missing." Both men had traveled along the Mayan trade routes to northern villages and they had not returned.

"Dead," said Manuela when they came to her mother.

Now Kate wished she had asked about every single relative that Manuela and her husband had. *Tell me what you want me to do with your daughter*; that's what she wanted to know more than anything.

"And here is the other issue," continued Fernando. "The child is a witness, a terribly young witness, but that may not matter to the soldiers. And Kate, you are a witness. You may think that being white and North American will protect you, but I am long past believing that any of us are protected. You could not go back to Santiago. It would not be safe. It would be much easier for the government if you disappeared also. Do you understand?"

The massacre cut a moat in her memory. She remembered everything except the sound of the gunfire and walking over the bodies to get to the child. Surely it had been louder than the popping of marbles, which is all that she remembered.

"If Sofia has a relative, taking her back might endanger them," said Fernando. His voice hovered in the sacred octave of unbearable truth. "And yet if they exist, they will want nothing more than the return of the child. Family ties are powerful."

"She has no living grandparents; Manuela told me this."

Kate pictured Sofia back at the guesthouse with Marta's son, Felix. She might be toddling after the boy, nibbling on food that Marta provided. Surely Sofia wondered where her mother was, the familiar smell of the lake, the flight of the blue heron over the water. How did a two-year-old contain the ache of death? Was sending Sofia back the right thing to do? But these were her people.

"I don't pretend to come from the heralded, pure Spanish lineage. I am mixed, part Spanish, part indigenous, part who knows what? But I know enough about the life in the villages to understand that there has been no childhood since the war began, not as you know it. The government has been at war for thirty years with the Maya and age makes no difference to them."

Kate took a sip from the bottle of soda. She immediately hiccupped. Maybe these would be the sorts of hiccups that went away quickly; she never knew.

"There is something else to consider. If Sofia goes back to the remains of her village and if she does not have family to protect her, she could be kidnapped or sold into the *casa de engordes.*"

The house of fat? Kate's rough translation made no sense. "What is that?"

Fernando placed both palms on the table and took a large breath. "They are the fattening houses for stolen babies. They are sold into the adoption system. The international demand for young children is strong and war breeds orphans. The black market for orphans looks for unprotected children."

Kate felt the soft pat of Sofia's hands on her ribs.

"But who would adopt a child from the black market?" She hiccupped with a powerful convulsion in her throat.

Fernando glanced at the door, constantly checking.

"There are many routes for a black market child, but by the time that a North American or European came face-to-face with a young child, they would see all the papers in order, and they could believe that everything was legal." He paused. "Or the child could be sold as a servant in Guatemala City. Or the military could take the child for other purposes. . . ."

"Stop," said Kate, hiccupping madly.

Kate pictured Sofia's dark eyes, her small hands, and her sleek black hair. The child's scent filled her, as if she was sitting in her lap at that very moment. A fear gripped her that was unlike anything she had felt before, unlike helicopters or soldiers, or the pain of carrying a child up a mountain.

"What if I adopt her?" she said, for the first time. "Many people come to Guatemala to adopt children and surely there are legal routes and not from the *casa de engordes.*"

Fernando pushed back in his chair. "This is something you should spend a long time considering. But you do not have a long time before your presence here is noticed by the wrong people."

She left Fernando with the mandate to make a choice. Should she adopt Sofia to save her? She walked into the side-street open markets, filled with color, fabric, fresh coconuts, and a dense cloud of food aromas.

She had seen the face of evil in Santiago and it would never wash off her. The tiniest bits of it had crawled under her skin and gripped her bones. But she could stand between Sofia and the bits of evil.

Were there other Maya selling goods in Antigua who knew of the massacre? The question more likely was who would not know of a massacre? If she told them that she had rescued the girl from the massacre, would they understand, or would they insist that the girl stay among the Maya? Would the temptation of getting money for an orphaned girl prove too great for someone if she returned the girl?

If she told any of the gringos, could she trust them? There had been talk of infiltrators, even Americans, who gave information to the military government. Kirkland had sounded so outlandish when she suggested that the CIA were involved, too much like a conspiracy theorist. Now she wondered if Kirkland was right. And maybe, just maybe, Kirkland could help her.

CHAPTER 17

The western sky turned dark in the sudden advance of the storm. The thick roll of clouds looked like an army thundering into the town. The active volcanoes on the outskirts of Antigua glowed and sent up a steady snake of smoke against the indigo bank of clouds.

When Kate was in sixth grade, her parents had taken up using a pressure cooker after friends returning from a trip to France brought them a gift. "Everyone uses them in France," they said. The back-and-forth motion of the rocker, clicking away with regulated shots of steam, made all of them uneasy, especially the family dog, Ben, who had panted in anxious time to the pressure-release rocker. The following year, the pressure cooker was sold at their annual yard sale, to everyone's relief.

The volcanoes that squatted at the edge of Antigua continued to relieve the gas and heat boiling beneath the cone, ticking away with shots of fiery heat, much like the family's old pressure cooker. Kate longed for the simple fears of childhood—would the pressure cooker explode with lentils, splattering them on the ceiling? As a geologic metaphor, the active volcanoes of this small city were perfect. Guatemala boiled and glowed red with the syrup of molten rock and at any minute, all hell could break loose. Earthquakes and molten explosions rocked in syncopation to the instability of both land and politics.

Kate hadn't felt earthquakes in the highlands around the lake where the ring of volcanoes were dormant. Aside from her initial entry to the country, when she had stayed in Antigua for only a few days to catch her breath, she had spent little time in the old colonial city.

The ruins of the massive earthquake that struck Antigua in 1976 still dotted the city. The cathedrals remained only partially repaired, walls were in tumbled disarray, cracks in buildings went untouched, and the narrow streets still tilted at precarious angles. And yet the beauty of the city was undaunted, still dappled with flowers in every courtyard, still serenaded by flocks of brightly colored birds.

She slept with Sofia snuggled next to her despite the second twin bed in their room. Mayan children slept with their mothers, never more than an arm's length away. One look of fear in Sofia's eyes as she lay in the strange bed alone had been enough for Kate. She put the child into her own bed with her.

At first Kate tried not to move at all with the small girl pressed against her. After a few more days, they had found a rhythm, a dance, with Kate eventually getting more sleep. When she woke now, it was to stare at the child, watching the tiny movements of her eyelids as REM sleep visited her dreams.

Kate was asleep when the bed shook, jumping in a strange side-to-side jig that matched the sway of the walls, the door frame, and the cloth that hung over the door. Everything in the guesthouse clattered and tapped, the massive adobe walls groaned. Earthquake.

Kate scooped up the girl in a blanket. She had not accounted for the dizziness, her own equilibrium rolling with the room. The urge to run was overwhelming, compounded by the fear of going to the wrong place, being crushed in the street by falling roof tiles or entire walls.

She lunged for the staircase, which rolled like liquid. She had nothing with her except for Sofia: no shoes, no money, nothing. And then, suddenly, stillness and silence. She was in the center of the interior courtyard, both arms wrapped around Sofia, panting like a terrified dog.

Marta stumbled out of her apartment on the ground level, her brown hair tousled, wearing only her husband's T-shirt.

"Are you all right?" she said. "That was big. I've not felt a tumbler that big before. They'll be aftershocks. I'd better go check my boy; he's a deep sleeper, but something might have tipped over in his room."

Kate didn't move, frozen in her island of safety, nearly crushing the wiggling child. Sofia was fully awake, eyes wide, drinking in all of Kate's terror.

Marta started for her son's room, then stopped, looking back at Kate.

"I said, are you all right?"

Kate's teeth chattered and her body shook. She wanted to reassure Marta, to say something, but when she tried, she got to the letter *g*, and could not get past it. "G-g-g-."

Marta crossed the distance between them and pulled her arm around Kate. "Here, come over here, you two. If the gas lines are still connected, I'll make us some tea. But even a devoted tea drinker will check on the kiddos first," she said with a wink. "You need a blanket. You're okay. Sh, sh, shush. It's going to be okay."

No one had said that to Kate since the massacre, and the words sounded like crystals illuminating the night. Whatever she imagined for Sofia was shaken into clarity by the earthquake. She would adopt Sofia. She would protect her from earthquakes, amoebas, and men with automatic weapons. All the missing parts to her decision were knocked into place by the trembling earth.

Marta brought a pot of strong tea to the courtyard. "I can't sit with you, although you look like you need a companion. I've got breakfast to make. Can you manage?" said Marta, pausing to put her hand on Kate's shoulder.

"We're already better," said Kate. There it was, she already said *we.* They were a pair.

But there would be a cost, and it was little Sofia who would pay the price. Until now she had not allowed herself to consider the full impact that Sofia would endure. If there were extended family, then yes, that cord would be severed. The subtle richness of the culture, gone. Language, gone.

There was a list of more precious things that Kate couldn't know, that Sofia held in her two-year-old body, in the secret chambers of her nose and the folds of her lungs where the warm scent of her mother and brother lingered. Would there be a day when a miraculous combination of scents merged, when Sofia was a sulky thirteen? Would all the elements of her mother, the warm corn scent of her breath, the oil of her dark silken hair combine to bring Sofia to a screeching halt and shatter her from incomprehensible longing?

Kate didn't know when memory began; she was just a scientist who studied water. She had been looking for some essential element in its creation, its use, the way we craved it, the way we can't live longer than seven days without it, the way her mother loved to float along a wide river. She had come to the deepest lake in Central America to see if the answer would rise up like a giant sea creature and quench her.

But here is what Sofia will never see again—the night sky over Lake Atitlán.

Kate had arrived in August when the rainy season still drenched the land. It was not until a night in October that she looked up and saw the red glow of Mars, twinkling like a ruby. Was it a plane, a satellite? No, she was told, she was simply seeing the sky for the first time over Lake Atitlán, where a paucity of electricity revealed the clarity of the stars without the gauze of ambient light. It was filled with a brilliant light show unlike anything she had seen before.

The universe unfolded over the lake, shining with outlandish abundance. The reflection in the lake magnified the show. Other stars had colors as well. Who could have known this? Blues, greens, and yellows. She watched satellites scuttle across the sky as clearly as headlights on the California freeway.

It had taken her weeks to find a fisherman from the village who understood enough Spanish to agree to Kate's request. She hired the man to take her out at night during the dark of the moon, in his *cayuco,* to the center of the lake. She brought a blanket and she lay down on the bottom of the small dugout canoe and watched the stars until she became dizzy with the feeling that she could touch them and float away. She could almost feel her mother with her, arms folded under her head as she embraced the night sky.

This is what Sofia will yearn for in the hidden world of preverbal memories, the complete wonder of a sky thick with stars, bouncing off the still waters of the lake, held snug by a ring of volcanoes, and the cocoon of Manuela's arms as she held her. There was no denying the depth of what Kate would take away from Sofia.

Kate's mother told her once that a parent's love for a child was unlike anything else she had ever known. So unlike romantic love. When Kate was fourteen, before the cancer exploded into their lives, her mother told her, "When you were five and played with your friend Hannah on the porch, I lay in the hammock and watched you. And I realized that I had never loved anyone as much as I loved you. There was nothing like it in the universe."

Kate had listened with discomfort. Now, her mother's words lanced her heart. How can she be a thief of all things that Sofia loved? How could she not?

CHAPTER 18

The next day, Kate headed to Fernando's, the only other haven in Antigua. Nothing in her life prepared her for what she needed to do next. If she was going to get the child out of the country, she needed help.

She pushed open the door to the café and found a corner table. Fernando was not there; a young boy served her a tepid cup of *café con leche.* Without Fernando's steady grace, she felt like the ground was once again moving beneath her. Sofia was under Marta's generous wings back at Casa Candelaria.

A man emerged from the inner garden when she came in. He walked through the door that separated the two rooms. He was a young gringo, probably an American hitchhiking through. He stopped the young boy, placing a hand on his arm, and spoke in a low musical voice, unhesitant in his Spanish. He ordered a plate of beans, tortillas, and rice.

He picked a table near a window, closer to the front door, and settled in with a Guatemalan newspaper. He looked like every other traveler in this difficult country; well-worn running shoes, jeans, a small day pack, an extra layer of grit over his skin. Where was Fernando?

Kate felt the young man watching her and caught his expression in a reflection from a faded glassed print hanging on the wall of the café bookstore. She glimpsed a three-quarter profile, darkened by shadows, giving him an air of sadness, the part that he might not want to show. He dipped his tortillas into the beans with local expertise. Maybe he'd been here longer than the average traveler.

Kate dropped her eyes so that he wouldn't catch her looking at the glass. She stood up and walked across the room and picked another picture on the wall to examine, this time a painting of the Agua Volcano on the outskirts of Antigua spewing a dragon's spiral of steam. Maybe he wasn't North American; perhaps he was Australian, French.

She longed for home and wanted to feel only grass and sky and clean water, to take Sofia to a park where other children would squeal and laugh. She wanted to talk about the earthquake because it was astounding, but here in a land of daily carnage, danger, and massacre, an earthquake was hardly worth mentioning. She felt like a bomb ready to go off. If Fernando wasn't in, she'd come back later. She returned to her table to finish the coffee.

Kate tipped her cup to her lips, taking in the last drops. She closed the book that she'd purchased the last time from Fernando's slim supply of English books, a worn copy of Steinbeck's *Of Mice and Men,* slid out of her chair, and slung her string bag over her shoulder. The room was dim and the glaring sunlight streaming in the door disoriented her.

She passed the man and glanced at him, tipping her head a fraction of an inch. Gringos tended to acknowledge each other; the tribe of travelers assumed something about others who looked like them, who had time to idle in a shop, drink coffee in the middle of the day. She smiled. Kate was one step away from the outer world with all its bright light when something desperate reflected in his eyes, something tied down with boulders. Like the eyes of the man who had pulled her down to safety before the massacre.

She turned, as if a gravitational field caught her, and in doing so, her knee caught the edge of his table, connecting with a jagged piece of wood, a splinter ready to pierce whoever came too near. The sharp stab to her knee shocked her.

"Shit," she said, grabbing her knee.

"Hang on there," he said, springing from his seat. "What happened?"

He stood between her and the door and his silhouette against the sun forced her to put her hand over her eyes, shading them from the light that framed his body. Kate looked down at her knee and saw the first few layers of skin buckled up accordion style. Dots of blood emerged, ballooning out.

"God, this hurts. I can't believe that kids do this kind of thing all the time. Scrape their knees, I mean. No wonder they cry." Tears had sprung to her eyes.

He reached out his hand. "Come on. Let's take a look at that."

His hand was warm, lightly callused, with nails in a clean, squared-off style, but still subject to slight variations. And he was American, his accent was clear enough.

"You broke the skin. You should get antiseptic on that right away. Or get bottled water and wash your knee off. Don't let it get infected, not here."

He was late twenties, or even in his thirties, but she sensed an elemental difference that she couldn't put her finger on. The red bubbles of blood rose to the surface and flowed down her shin.

He'd been in the tropics long enough that his hair was lightened by the sun, a mix of gold and brown; parts of his hair were so curly and stiffened by sweat and dust that she imagined grabbing on to it like a handle. They stepped out to the sidewalk with its wide slabs of stone, facing the large park in the center of town.

"Did you feel the earthquake last night?" she said. Then she froze. A jeep filled with young soldiers rumbled along the side of the park toward them. The air buzzed around her in charged particles. She stumbled backward with an unbearable urge to hide. She couldn't keep responding like this every time she saw soldiers, but panic overwhelmed her.

The gringo glanced over his shoulder in the direction of the sound. Without thinking, she stepped forward, so that his body covered her from the street view, and embraced him, wrapping one arm around him in an iron grip. He hesitated and then placed his hand on the back of her head, pulling her closer. When she turned her head away, he pressed his lips to her ear and whispered, "Don't run." As if she wanted to, as if he knew.

Kate registered a full-body shock. The instinct to run still blasted through her and all of her urgency pushed hard against this man who smelled like black beans and cheese with a hint of coffee. A column of ribs pressed into her. The jeep slowed as it neared them; the soldiers hooted and whistled in unmistakable male camaraderie. What if they stopped? What if they got out of the jeep, guns slung over their arms?

The driver accelerated, squealing around the corner. The man released her and backed up, hands palm up.

"I take it that you didn't want to see those guys, but don't you think you might have taken unfair advantage of me?" he asked with a smile.

Kate leaned against the outside of the café, her face hot. Had she just grabbed this man and wrapped her arms around him? Had this man just held her and nuzzled her neck?

"Your knee," he said. "Let's get it cleaned up. The soldiers are gone. You're okay."

Fernando said to be careful, not to trust anyone. But this man had just helped her, had shielded her from the militia. She needed to tell Fernando that she had decided she would take Sofia with her. She licked her dry lips. "I'm Kate. I think I should thank you but I'm not sure. Should I apologize?"

His shoulders softened and he smiled. "Nope. I just took the kind of liberties with you that would have gotten me into all kinds of trouble in Brooklyn. But it was all I could think of. I'm Will."

"Should I call you William?" she asked him.

"We'd be off to a terrible start if you did. I'm a one-syllable guy, despite what my parents must have thought."

His smile was dazzling and almost erased the pull of sadness from his eyes. When he smiled, he looked like everything he touched turned clean. She was sure that his mouth would taste like ice cream.

The mutual question begged to be asked and answered by them; it always did with travelers, but especially here. They couldn't take another step until it was broached. Why was she here in a country riddled with civil war? Why was he here?

"You first," he said, before she could start.

"I'm adopting a child." She jutted her chin forward a notch. This is the first time she had said the words and her voice sounded unlike anything she'd ever said before.

"Oh. You're here with your husband. Now I really am in trouble. Is your husband large and uncontrollably possessive?"

A red string of blood traveled down her shin. "I'm not married. It makes adoption more complicated." Lies of omission were easier than she had imagined. She had never practiced lying before; there had been no reason to do so. Even after her mother died and her father emerged from his grief long enough to see that she was drinking his beer and spending all of her time with the boys.

Will stepped back into the café and returned with a paper napkin and handed it to her. Kate spat on the paper and then wiped the punctured skin.

"I wasn't in Antigua last night. If there was an earthquake, I somehow slept through it," he said. "I was in Guatemala City."

Why would she need to nudge him to find out what he's doing here? People emerged on the street again, a clear sign that the soldiers were gone. The smell of hot tortillas traveled on the breeze and Kate suddenly wanted to know if the tortilla lady from Santiago was among the dead. Who else had died in the carnage?

"Why are you in Guatemala?" she asked.

A muscle along his cheekbone pulled up, a twitch of sorts.

"I'm just a guy from Brooklyn out to see the world," he said. "Do you know your way around here? Is there a *farmacia* in Antigua where we can get you some Band-Aids?"

They walked together to the *farmacia* that Kate had gone to when she and Sofia arrived the week before. The pocket-sized store held an astonishing amount of medicine, all stacked in bottles and small boxes on the back wall. Will's Spanish was flawless, or at least it seemed so to Kate. He told a joke to the man behind the counter, something about music and medicine and the Pope. The man behind the counter tossed his head back in helpless laughter.

Kate sat down while she cleaned her leg and bandaged her knee, feeling that all the attention for such a tiny wound was unwarranted compared to the true catastrophe that had happened along the lake. They left the shop and before Kate could think of a way to say good-bye, Will said, "Why were you so afraid of the soldiers?"

Her heart beat faster.

"Boys with automatic weapons are unpredictable," she said.

Will arranged his day pack on his shoulders. "The whole damned country can be scarier than the worst nights in New York City. But they're gone, and we're here and I need to find the local market. Would you be my guide to get me started?"

Kate doubted that Will needed help getting anywhere. But she could bring back some fresh food for Sofia. "I can be your guide for just a little while."

They pushed through the open-air market, past the mountains of brilliant handwoven fabric and the women who sold them. Kate's neck contracted when she saw the women, seated on the ground, weaving, moving the shuttle back and forth until their particular pattern emerged. No women were here from the villages dotting the lake, but it was only a matter of time. Kate worried that the women in the marketplace could see through her, see her running off through the jungle hillsides with the child who did not belong to her.

They walked into the food section of the outside market and Will stopped to buy a sack of avocados. "Here's the best thing to eat," he said, gently guiding the green globes into his string shopping bag. "Avocados, tortillas, and fresh squeaky cheese. That's my Guatemalan diet and I'm sticking to it. Also, hard-boiled eggs and bananas."

"I have a short list of things I'd rather not tell you," said Kate suddenly.

He didn't ask her what was on her short list. She wanted to release the steam that demanded release in her chest.

"I am going to adopt a child and I don't know how to get the papers."

She'd been so careful with the men she had let closer to her, at least when she was in college. She had to be sure that they wanted her, that they had more of a need for her. What was different about Will?

Will peeled a small banana about the size of his thumb and ate it in two bites.

"Best damn bananas I've ever tasted. This will ruin you for bananas back in the States." He folded up the banana peel and put it into his bag. "What's the matter with the adoption agency? Are they asking for a payment that you hadn't expected? Did they want a bribe?"

Kate stiffened. A bribe, as if all Guatemalans were devious, despite the fact that yes, she expected the topic of bribes to be discussed. As if Sofia was tainted. Already, everything flowed back to Sofia. Who was this man anyhow? Would she go out with him if they were back at UC Davis, or would they see each other and keep walking?

"I haven't exactly gone through an official adoption agency. Yet. So far, it's been an informal process." She had said too much, but what could it matter if a wanderer from Brooklyn knew she wanted to adopt?

They turned down another street. Marta's guesthouse was only two blocks away.

"What exactly does informal mean?" he asked. They crossed

the street. A shadow washed over his face, a two-muscle twitch of his eyes, and then just as quickly, the tanned skin around his eyes relaxed, as if he had said to himself, *Relax the face.*

What would it hurt to tell Will? He'd probably go back to wherever he came from in a week. Come to think of it, he hadn't told her why he was here, not really.

"Informal means that I already have a child but I don't have any documentation." She regretted saying this. She sounded like a criminal.

They stopped in front of the large door to the guesthouse.

"Let me even things up a little. I was in the Peace Corps; that's why I'm here. I'm headed home soon. There's nothing mysterious about me, but you shouldn't tell a guy who you just met about not having documentation for the child." He put his hand into his bag and extracted some bananas. "Here. All kids like bananas."

He'd been in the Peace Corps and now he was staying in Antigua before going home. He was a great big Boy Scout. The muscles along her neck softened.

He put his hand on hers, the one that rested on the iron knocker.

"Do you know any knock-knock jokes?" he said.

Kate shook her head. "Not a one."

"Me either. Knock, knock, knock," he said. He lifted her hand with his and together they moved the hinged knocker. The sound of it echoed through her chest. When Marta pulled open the massive wood door, he walked off.

Inside the shelter of Casa Candelaria with its thick adobe walls, she smelled something delicious.

"What are you cooking?" asked Kate. At the sound of her voice, Sofia looked up from playing under the banana tree with Felix.

"Soup, with every kind of vegetable I could find. I needed something that felt like home," said Marta.

Home. How could Kate find her way with Sofia? Had she said too much to Will?

CHAPTER 19

Will

"Do not engage with people who want to put a straw through your brain and suck your energy," said Will's mother. She taught English to newly arrived immigrants.

"Where did you learn that?" Will asked when he was twelve and still in love with his beautiful mother, although even he knew he should begin the transition to disdain as some of his friends had done with their parents.

"It's from one of my Ethiopian students. It's a rough translation. It's more poetic than saying, *Don't hang around with overly needy people.* I like it."

By the time he was thirteen, he could still be dazzled and sometimes embarrassed by his golden-haired mother. Cesar Stefano Ramirez, his best friend growing up in the Williamsburg nook of Brooklyn, had said, "Face it, Will, your mother is hot. Why do you think we're all here every Saturday? Because you're so irresistible? Sorry to be the one to break it to you."

But as his mother taught new immigrants, he somehow absorbed the melody of language from her students. He had accompanied her to the evening classes since he was five, on those evenings when his father worked late.

His parents held hands when they walked or watched a movie. "The secret to a happy life is to marry a woman who is interesting," said his father as they jiggled along in a subway to Manhattan. "And beautiful, it's a bonus if she's beautiful."

He grew up around Puerto Rican kids in Brooklyn and was bilingual by age five. Speaking in two languages was as natural to him as breathing. Language poured into Will like music. Once he got the melody and the rhythm, the words fell into place.

His mother shopped at the markets where the old women spoke to him in Polish, offering him juicy bits of warm pastries and sausages. Will inhaled the sounds that came from deep within the chests of the round women, their throats rising like the muffins. They sang a different song than the Puerto Rican kids with their rapid-fire trills of hot streets and memories of trees. His mother hired a young Polish babysitter when she taught during the day. Within weeks young Will could keep up with the babysitter and was the darling of the Polish stores.

The Romance languages followed. Italian was just another variation on the tune; smoother, more like the Motown music his mother played when she vacuumed. Turkish was the first leap from round sounds to the muffled clatter of consonants, bumping against each other. The flood of people from the Saharan region of Africa opened the door of full-out world beat, symphonic variation. Multiple chambers in his brain popped open to make room for new languages.

Will joined the Peace Corps after several years of jobs that left him in free fall. Right after college graduation there had been the Outward Bound job in Wyoming with a small tribe of teenagers who were not half as dangerous as the kids he grew up with in Brooklyn. Affairs with the athletic, earnest young women who worked with him, slipping into each other's sleeping bags at night, was the unofficial benefits program. No employee stayed longer than two years and Will was not an exception.

Outward Bound was followed by one year as a bike courier in Manhattan. *Bike courier* was less accurate than bike warrior, flowing between cars and trucks, pumping hard, tucking his arms close to his body, until he had felt a strange unity with all the other drivers, flowing like water. His bike warrior career ended with a fractured collarbone and a mangled bike. But the last weeks of delivering documents by bicycle led him to the office of a public defender, Richard Curtis, who needed a translator for his Spanish-speaking clients.

"Why not hire a native speaker?" Will asked.

"Manhattan is a lot smaller than it looks," said the lawyer. "I got burned once when my translator was overly involved with the outcome of a criminal case."

Will didn't like the lawyer, didn't like the scent of bigotry that lingered on him. When Will advised two Spanish-speaking women to find a different lawyer, Mr. Curtis got wind of Will's advice and fired him.

"Didn't I tell you this was a small town? Try the Peace Corps, if you want to save the world."

The throwaway advice stayed with him. He started in the Peace Corps in 1987; by 1989 he considered signing up for a second term. The high mountains of the Chiapas region of Mexico suited him. The area bordered Guatemala and was heavily populated by the Maya, the indigenous people of the region.

By the time Will was in the Peace Corps, he was already the envy of all the other PCVs who struggled with Spanish. When he heard a Mayan woman speak for the first time in the open market, everything else stopped. Suddenly there was velvet and birdsong, the snap of a branch, cooing in the background, followed by something crisp that lasted only a second.

He wanted to know this language, wanted to let it glide off his tongue. He changed his assignment so that he worked right on the border of Guatemala and Mexico in the light, cool mountain air, building a school with the Mayan men. He had known nothing about building schools and so he became a student of the local masons. He worked alongside the small men, carrying stacks of adobe bricks that dried in the sun. He learned to put just the right amount of mortar between the bricks and how to space them. He kept his head down and worked, clear that his manual labor counted more than anything.

While he stacked and mortared, Will learned their language. The method was always the same: First listen, find the tune, let it settle in, picture the shapes and colors, the taste of a language, then let the words roll through you and sink in. By the time the sod bricks were formed, dried, put in place, and the tile roof added, Will could tell a joke in the northern Mayan dialect, tease his dark-skinned coworkers and tell them about his mother who taught English to the immigrants who moved to Brooklyn.

"You're a language savant," said Amy, the Peace Corps volunteer closest to him geographically in Mexico. They were traveling by bus into the Peace Corps headquarters in Mexico City for the annual Christmas party where, for one evening, they were wined and dined by the diplomatic corps.

"Not so. If I were a language savant, then I'd be piss poor at everything else and languages would be my only talent. Check out my adobe building technique if you want to see true skill. I think they might hire me as a laborer when I'm out of the Peace Corps. I can see my future at last."

Amy wrapped her sweater around her shoulders.

"How's that present tense Spanish coming along?" he asked her. Amy was the only one he teased because he liked her. Her boyfriend was due to visit in a few weeks. "Shall I teach you some lovely dirty words in Spanish for your conjugal visit?"

Will knew lots of dirty words from Brooklyn. The bus trip lasted six hours and he whispered each dirty word he knew in Spanish, punctuated by Amy's squealed protest.

"No, I could never say that!" Then, "Tell me another one."

* * *

He met the American ambassador, David Markman, and his wife, Helen, at last year's Christmas party, surrounded by a small circle of earnest PCVs, all vying for the diplomat's attention. This would be the last big gathering that Will would attend before his term was over and he would have to decide where to go and what to do. The American ambassador worked his way across the room and approached Will, separating him from the herd.

"You can continue to be a big help to Central America and to your own country," said David, a tall man whose facial flesh had loosened into mounds from his cheekbones and jaw. Will guessed that he was from Texas by the accent and boots. The embassy was thickly walled with massive cuts of stone, making it nearly impenetrable, and acoustically disastrous. The crescendo of voices that reverberated in the formal hall was painful.

"What do you mean?" said Will, shouting to be heard.

David ran his hand over his belt buckle as if checking to see that all his parts were still tucked into place.

"We have an agency that needs Mayan speakers. They asked me to select a Peace Corps volunteer who has a sharp ear. Your ability with languages is your main selling point, young man. I can't say more than *please* and *thank you* in Spanish and I've been here three years."

The ambassador's lack of effort with Spanish made Will wince. "Which agency are you talking about?"

He took Will's arm and led him to a balcony overlooking the inner courtyard. "Don't ever say anything too specific inside an embassy," he said. "You probably think I'm some politically appointed good old boy who doesn't know Jorge from Jesus. Speaking in mind-numbing generalities of politico talk takes more practice than you might think. I hear you can learn any language in existence. That true?"

"I haven't tried every language in existence, sir."

"Relax. Let me get you another drink." He pulled a dark plastic rectangle out of his pocket about the size of a credit card and pressed a button. A waiter with a white jacket appeared.

"Roberto, please bring two beers to the courtyard. Mr. Buchanan and I need to find a quiet spot to talk." David slid the device back into his jacket pocket. "I love techno toys. They're the future."

The waiter turned and left.

Will followed the ambassador down the balcony steps to the courtyard and they settled into uncomfortable wrought iron chairs near a fountain that gurgled erratically.

"It's not uncommon for various agencies and private industry to recruit among the Peace Corps. You're heading into the end of your time here. You must know the drill. We're selective. We don't let any yahoo come in here and recruit. We've got laws about who can and who can't. For example, it's against the law for the CIA to recruit. Do you understand?"

"So far. We can be recruited by some organizations and not others. Got it."

The waiter brought two beers on a serving tray. Will took a tentative sip from his. He had a feeling that this was a good time to stay sober.

"The Mayan languages have us pretty stumped in parts of Central America. I hear that you can speak several of the languages from Chiapas. Few Mexicans have ever bothered to learn it. Odd, don't you think?" The ambassador leaned back in his chair and stretched out his long legs.

Will tried to lean back in the chair but an iron bar hit him squarely on a vertebra. "It's a class issue. The Mexicans prefer to claim only Spanish heritage and the Maya are on the lowest rung of the ladder. Not too many people in the States study Navaho. It's the same thing," said Will.

The ambassador tipped his beer up and downed it in two gulps. Will guessed that he had learned that in college. "Interesting that you should mention Navaho. In World War Two, we counted on the obscurity of their language. We used it as a code. The Germans couldn't crack it."

Everyone knew this. Where was this guy going? Will looked longingly at a trio of Peace Corps workers who had stepped out on the balcony and were hooting with laughter.

"Do you know how many Mayan languages there are?" asked the ambassador.

"Twenty-two, if you count the ones in Guatemala, sir. But some are dialects of a main branch while others are distinct."

"That's correct." He crossed one leg over the other and leaned forward. "We have an agency that would like you to learn all twenty-two languages. They're called Department Thirty Seven. Do you think you could do that?"

The idea of learning twenty-two languages was better than sex, food, or clean tap water. Maybe not sex, but it was a very close second. He already knew two of the Mayan languages from Chiapas. The thought of learning all of them was like a shot of liquid euphoria injected into his arm.

"What else would I need to do?"

"The job description is called Language Specialist. The group in question knows that the Peace Corps has one of the best language training programs around, better than the goddamned Rosetta Stone. As I understand it, they need a man to learn Mayan languages so that Department Thirty Seven can communicate with them. Communication is the key. See, once you learn a few languages, you could teach it to the Department boys. I guess you'd say the job is like being a college professor without the fuss of academic meetings and ass-kissing."

Will looked ahead to his future, moving back to Brooklyn with the meager stipend from the Peace Corps, applying to graduate schools, studying one language or two, enduring a slow path to a degree that might enable him to teach if he was very lucky. He was being offered a deal that had never come his way before. Was there a feral scent of deception on the ambassador's breath? His high school friend Cesar had said, "When someone is trying to get over on you, they stink like cat piss."

"I know I could do it," said Will. He was sure no cats had passed this way.

"I know you can too, son. Where Thirty Seven needs you is in Guatemala. They've had a terrible civil war and we have business interests in the region. Not to mention putting an end to the pain and suffering of the people—we are interested in that of course."

"What exactly is Department Thirty Seven?"

"It's a conglomerate of sorts. Part State Department, part private enterprise, and part investigative. A company of sorts. International relations."

"Is this vague politico speak?"

"You do learn languages quickly."

"Yes, sir. And my boss would be who, specifically?"

"You'll meet him in two months when you're finished with your Peace Corps tour."

"I'm not finished for another four months."

"No, you're finished in two months. With full benefits and an appreciative letter from me in your file. You're about to become a language specialist consultant. Congratulations."

CHAPTER 20

Fernando lowered his voice although no one else was in the café.

"So you have decided," he said.

"Yes."

Kate had known Fernando for only a week and yet she felt comforted by his steady warmth, his lack of embellishment. Her father would have called him a straight talker.

Fernando closed his eyes. "If you are successful, if you can get adoption papers for the little girl, then it will still be a hard life for both of you. You will save her from our war weary country, but there will come a day when she will long for the land of her birth, for the sight of people who look like her, and for a hint of those who came before her. Ancestors. But you are right; she will be alive."

Did he think that she didn't know this? This wasn't the resounding validation that Kate hoped for, but it would do. It was only two in the afternoon, but she was already exhausted. She had started having nightmares in which she walked across bodies of murdered people.

"I've seen gringos here to adopt children. There are agencies in Antigua and I'm going to start with them. Today."

"Are you going to tell them that you have a Mayan child, who is a war orphan?" He tilted his head and spread his hands on the table and then grasped the base of the Coke bottle. "We have been at war for thirty years. Our beautiful country has been the battleground of the military and large corporations that want our land. Some of us can't remember a time when there was peace. It has made all of us desperate in good or bad ways. If you walk into an adoption agency and announce that you have a child, you will arouse more attention than you want."

"Okay, I'll be circumspect. But I need to find out what I need to do to get adoption under way."

"You do your asking and I will do mine. And I will get word to Kirkland that you need help. She is a resourceful woman."

"Wait, how do you get in touch with Kirkland?" The idea of phoning Kirkland, or anyone in the States, felt like a quantum leap in technology. She had thought of calling her father hundreds of times, but concerned about terrifying him, she had held off, knowing that this was a situation where he couldn't help.

"It is better if you don't know. The reaction to every totalitarian regime creates an intricate underground and Kirkland is one of us."

Wasn't she just a foreign correspondent? What did it mean that she was one of them? A chill moved through Kate.

"I need to know something," she said. "Why is the military killing the villagers? What could possibly be the point?"

"In order to eradicate the resistance, the government believes they must wipe out the support in the countryside for the rebels. If the villagers feed the rebels, they are subject to death. Or worse yet, if they are simply suspected of feeding or hiding the rebels, they are punished, burned out of their homes, sent to relocation camps. It is a masterful plan of terror and cruelty."

"Who is supplying the army with weapons? The Guatemalan

government? This is their army, but they've got to be buying weapons somewhere."

Fernando passed her a bottle of soda and gave it a bumpy ride across the roughly hewn wood of the table. "Are you sure you want to know?" He tilted his head back to expose the tight tendons along his throat, highlighted by a band of sunlight in the courtyard.

"I'm a scientist," she said. "Or a scientist in training. I'm apolitical. I forgot to vote in the last presidential election. I was taking my qualifying exams."

An American man might have swaggered here, rocked back in his chair. Fernando leaned forward so that he could lower his voice. Somewhere on the street, music rose up, a man's voice tangled with a stringed instrument.

Kate pulled her sweater closer and tried to pull the sleeves down over her fingers.

"Knowledge can change you painfully," he said.

"People change all the time. Tell me." The image of the massacre had imbedded in her, lodged along her ribs.

"The weapons come from your government. The guns that killed the people of Santa Teresa? They have come, perhaps not directly, who would be so stupid? They wandered briefly through other hands, other countries, but their destination was the military government of Guatemala, put in place by your country over thirty years ago."

Kate felt a rush of denial rise up like a flock of black birds.

"How do you know that? Excuse me, but no one in Kansas City has even heard of Guatemala. I might be apolitical, but I would know if we had declared war."

Even as she said it, a thick sludge of oil crept down her back.

"There are many ways to start a war," he said. What would her father say if he knew that North America had financed a war against Manuela and her family?

"Be very careful who you talk with. I saw you talking with the *norteamericano*. Had you met him before you came to Antigua?"

"You mean Will? No, I never saw him before. I'm not worried about him."

"I have learned to worry about everyone. I will ask about him. Until then, please, do not talk with him about the massacre. Will you do that? It is important."

Kate pictured Sofia back in the patio of the guesthouse, her dark eyes, the way the child woke in the night crying *Mamá, Mamá.* When Kate had picked her up to comfort her, the child shook her head and said, *Mamá, Mamá,* wanting Manuela.

"Will is just a guy, a Peace Corps type. I'll keep it at that," said Kate.

As soon as she said it, her skin tingled along her palm, a place where she had touched him last.

"I can't wait for Kirkland," she said, pushing back her chair, changing the subject. "What if the adoption agencies in town can help? My mother always said that you'll never know unless you ask."

Kate had the clear feeling that Fernando's inquiries would glean more results than hers, but even so, she had to try.

The adoption pipeline from Guatemala to North America was deeply grooved and there were two adoption agencies in Antigua. Kate planned to approach them both with what-if questions. *What if I happened to have a Guatemalan orphan and wanted to adopt her? You know, let's say I found her. Where? Hypothetically speaking, just a village. Yes, a Mayan village. Could you help me get adoption papers for her so that I could take her home? I mean, if I had found an orphan.*

The first agency was run by a woman from Wisconsin. Erika. Surely this was a completely legitimate agency. But was Kate legitimate? Two dark-haired children emerged from another room. A little girl put her hands on her hips and said in perfect English, "He said I can't play with the headphones. I want them."

A fat headset dangled from the boy's shoulders. "I had it first."

Erika swung around in her chair and held out her hand to the boy. He understood her immediately and turned over the headset. "Ask Maria if she will make you hot chocolate. Politely, say please," said Erika. The children scattered and Erika sighed. "Sorry, this is a school holiday." Erika was a large woman, in her forties, a cotton skirt of handwoven cloth pressed against her rotund belly.

"Hypothetically speaking, it would take more than six months to get the paperwork rolling through the Guatemalan government and they would need to know exactly where the child came from. It would cost six thousand dollars to us and because this would be an unusual strategy, you would be looking at a substantial bribe to get the paperwork through. We would need documentation that the parents are indeed deceased and that no other relatives exist who are willing to take the child."

Money aside, Kate doubted that she could get evidence that the parents were deceased. How could she obtain papers if the military would deny the massacre? She noted the scent of onions clinging to Erika, the blunt cut of her fingernails, the crayon drawings that were taped to the wall behind her desk, the tinkling sound of children's voices from several rooms away, the sudden blast of diesel exhaust that found its way into the building.

The warning voice of Fernando, so quickly implanted within her, whispered, *You've said enough, perhaps too much. Get out.*

"I understand. Your job must be difficult. I'll pass along the information," said Kate, standing up.

Erika turned her head toward the kitchen where the children were drinking hot chocolate. "Circumstances in the highlands can be difficult for the Maya. They love their children and will do anything to save them. Sometimes a mother will make the ultimate sacrifice and offer a child to an outsider if they know that imminent danger is coming. The military can be severe if they are trying to eradicate the guerillas," said Erika.

"How long have you been here?" Kate stood behind the chair, keeping the thick slabs of carved wood between her and the woman.

"I've been here for six years. But I want to take my kids back to the States permanently. The adoption pipeline will be closing down in a few years."

Kate raised one eyebrow.

"Insider information," said Erika. "Trust me."

If Erika had been here for six years, she fully understood the need to be circumspect. But Kate was now dealing with an adoption system that was closing down. As she left the office and stepped out to the narrow side street, she was struck by the sense of dropping beneath the top layer of the country, even after the massacre and the terror of escaping through the rugged highlands. This terrain of fear and distrust held the tinge of disease, spread under the rocky topsoil, infecting everyone. Now that Kate had fallen through to the subterranean level, she longed for the bliss of ignorance.

The second office was staffed by a Guatemalan man who stopped Kate before she went through her introduction of hypothetical questions.

"We do adoptions one way. We meet with married couples who have the means and the patience to go through a lengthy process. We cooperate fully with the government. Are you married?"

"Me? I wasn't asking about me. I was thinking about some friends in the States, really great people who can't have children. Married friends. I'll let them know."

This time Kate remembered to smile. She acted like the ground beneath her feet wasn't thick with the infection of distrust. She had all but broadcasted that she had a Mayan child to two people in Antigua and she regretted it.

What if word got out that she had a child and she couldn't legally adopt her? Sofia was a commodity. Could she be kidnapped?

Kids learn early on that if they run, they look guilty. Kate learned when she was eight years old and had joined forces with her best friend, Buddy. For reasons that seemed vague even then, they decided to throw rotten pumpkins into Mrs.

Dashell's yard. When they walked to school the next morning, Mrs. Dashell stood in her yard with her hands on her hips and looked at the two of them. Kate and Buddy sprinted away as if the living dead were after them. Mrs. Dashell was no dope. One phone call to Kate's parents and Kate was called out of school in a flash. She confessed immediately.

From now on, she would walk nonchalantly when she was with Sofia in Antigua. If she saw the militia, she would make certain that she picked up Sofia and faced the child away from the soldiers and their black guns. She could not be sure how the girl would respond, but giving in to the demand to run was no longer a possibility.

Kate was gatekeeping at the guesthouse while Marta was out for the night. If there was a checklist of options for adopting Sofia, she would have just crossed out "adoption agencies in Antigua" and circled "Kirkland, calling in favors." That's what Fernando said his friend could do, whatever calling in favors meant. She had stopped by to give him the bad news about the agencies. Relief had flooded over Kate. She had someone helping in the States. Someone smart and brave. She pictured Kirkland hauling her in by a bright cord.

Now she watched Sofia and Felix, scanning her memory for little-kid songs when someone knocked on the massive door. Kate pulled her sweater tight across her chest, glancing at the two toddlers, who stopped their play.

Kate slid open the viewing slat to look out and saw Fernando looking back at her with his slender brown face.

"Let me in quickly. Something has happened," he said.

Kate realized she had not taken a breath since she heard the knock. She inhaled, unbolted the door and heaved it open. Fernando slid in like a sleek otter and she threw the bolt behind him.

"Kirkland's story about the massacre has been picked up in Mexico and Europe. The military has lost its invisibility."

Why was Fernando frowning?

"Isn't this exactly what you wanted?"

Kate felt a hand on her leg. Sofia clung to her. Something about Fernando's tone alerted the girl.

"Kirkland will not be allowed back into the country. She told the world what was happening here. If she comes back, she'll go missing."

The rescue rope that connected her to Kirkland snapped and Kate winced as it whipped across her face.

CHAPTER 21

Will
June 1990

"Fourteen Mayan languages and still counting. Impressive. I wish I knew how you did it. I think translators have brains that are wired differently," said Will's new boss, Ron Blackburn.

They were in a mostly empty office building in Guatemala City, not far from the airport. Ron's office had a set of heavy, hand-carved chairs in front of an equally weighted desk. Aside from a few newspapers, there was no evidence of reading material. One travel poster of Kauai relieved the otherwise blank wall in back of Ron.

Will spent February through April traveling through the country picking up Mayan languages. When he returned to Guatemala City, his job had been to teach Kaqchikel to a group of government workers from the United States. Blackburn called him into his office after Will spent two weeks trawling through the flatlined brains of his students.

"I wish the class had gone better. People can get discouraged when they're first learning a new language," said Will.

The day before, he left his class in despair, unable to break through the most rudimentary linguistic barrier of teaching Kaqchikel to a dozen meticulously groomed men. They were clearly not Peace Corps types who took it as a badge of courage to dress down as far as possible and to make clothing last until the fabric was translucent. One of the guys, Emerson, turned out to be a good candidate for a beer drinking buddy, but he was a terrible student.

"Don't be too hard on yourself," said Blackburn. "You did a fine job. But we're going to scrap our previous plan and consolidate our efforts. We are never going to be as fluent with these languages as you are."

His students were hopeless. Will waited for the words that would announce the regretful firing of his incompetent ass. After trekking through Guatemala for months learning the strange pockets of languages, his one moment of glory demonstrating his accumulated knowledge had been a colossal flop. His students left the class unable to grasp even the tone of the language, how the words flowed from the land through the people, how the language had, in some areas, blended with animal sounds to express a nuance that was so subtle, Will had stayed for six weeks in the coastal area to be sure that he truly understood. Now he was going to be sacked.

"We don't have the same kind of manpower that we had a few years back. International security is a whimsical thing and we've got troubles in other places in the world. So, like I said, we need to consolidate and you're the most talented translator we have. Excuse me, Language Specialist. We don't have time for a roomful of guys to spend three months learning how to say *please* and *thank you*."

The Department guys marked every major event with a cigar. Cuban cigars were sold freely in Guatemala; political embargoes did not interfere with luxury items. Ron held out a box to Will.

"Thanks. Do you mind if I save it for later?" Will selected a large cigar, just in case they were involved in some kind of contest about whose was bigger.

"Instead of teaching languages in the Department, we're asking you to give us direct translations about some basic day-today things that could help us and help the Maya." The end of Ron's cigar glowed like a torch.

Will wasn't sure if he heard him right. It was the rainy season and the sheets of rain pounded everything: the balcony, the planters—every horizontal surface. A gust of wind shifted the angle of the rain and it slammed the windows with a metallic shriek.

"You're not sending me home?" asked Will. He wished he didn't sound so young, so much in need of whatever his boss might offer him.

Blackburn smiled. "Just the opposite. I've pulled together a job that is tailor-made for you. I've read your PC file again. The local people were always comfortable with you, back in Mexico and here in Guatemala. We'd like you to assess the agricultural commerce of the northern areas. You know—what they're growing, what they keep and how much they sell. And how far they travel to sell it."

Blackburn paused, rolling the cigar between thumb and forefinger. "Very much like the Peace Corps," he added, looking at the cigar.

"The Peace Corps goes into an area because the community requests it. I know you guys aren't the Peace Corps, but have they requested assistance?" The hair along the back of Will's neck flickered and he moved back in his seat.

What if the villages didn't want assistance? Although, who could turn down the occasional tractor or water pumps that might come with governmental help?

Ron smiled indulgently. "You've seen the squalor that they live in. Of course they need our assistance. This would be right up your alley. For example, we want you to go to Dos Erres and see approximately how many people live in the village, what they grow, and, if they sell their produce, where they take it. They've set up some sort of collective out there. We're not sure what that means. Agriculture is the key to this country. If we don't understand their system of agriculture, we can't help them, can we?"

"This doesn't have anything to do with their internal war? The military takes a pretty heavy-handed approach to the Maya."

"Do we look like the Guatemalan army? We're not. This is a country in transition and it's to our advantage that the direction doesn't turn into another Havana. We'd like to win the hearts and minds of the people," Blackburn said. "Once we understand more about their agriculture, then we can figure out what to offer. I thought this might interest you."

Will agreed to an agricultural report of the region. At least he wouldn't have to teach the language-impaired frat boys anymore, and the information might do some good. A few months should do it. With his first paycheck, he had enough to buy a motorcycle, and because his Spanish was impeccable, bargaining brought him a price that was nearly Guatemalan.

Will spent July, August, and September in the northern highlands. His approach was to arrive with his backpack, rent a room, and then set out to donate his labor, sometimes as an adobe carrier, or as the guy who formed adobe, invariably working his way into the men of the community.

The northern dialects reflected the harsher environment, as if stones caught in everyone's throat and the sounds came out in dry explosions. When the first round of corn was loaded onto wagons, mules, and one truck, he offered to go along. They drew maps in the dirt for him. He played soccer with the little boys who had a ball that was hardly a ball at all, more of a round wad of paper held together with tape. He made a note to always carry tape and to always bring a soccer ball to each village that he visited.

The young women in the villages were beautiful with their broad cheekbones, full lips, tightly belted traditional skirts, but he was polite and formal with them. He had seen the wreckage that had resulted from a romance between a young Mayan woman and a PC guy.

* * *

He was delirious with the abundance of language and sometimes had to pinch himself to ensure that this was real. He had been asked to learn languages, to spend time in the separate villages, absorbing key phrases, the different way that one group might hold their tongue for emphasis or vibrate their throats. While learning the languages, he could also learn about their agricultural economy.

What would his mother think of the Mayan languages? He longed to share the common thread of linguistics with her. He caught himself thinking of his father while he was hauling bags of stone for the wall foundations, remembering with affection his father's failure at building a stone BBQ in their patch of yard behind their apartment in Brooklyn.

He had not missed his parents with this intensity while he had been in Wyoming. Now, he had a cinematic recall of the way his father had taken him to the local YMCA for swim lessons, even though his father never learned to swim. He felt his father's love in a different way, wider and deeper, the way his father stood at the shore along Coney Island watching Will swim. Why was he discovering these things now, so far away from his parents? He felt guilty and self-centered for not thanking his father.

Maybe it had something to do with the affection that he saw in the families, who had so few possessions, slept on the ground, and sometimes ate only tortillas and coffee for breakfast before a day of intense labor. Yet fathers hugged their sons, women took time to laugh at the antics of children, and couples haggled in companionable patter.

Village life wasn't perfect; girls married far too young, children suffered from illnesses that would have been easily cured in the States, and older people lost teeth at an astounding rate. Yet, the physical closeness that people had with each other, their essential need of each other, made him long for his family in a way that he had never experienced before.

With each group, as a sign of respect, he asked to speak with the local healer, who was sometimes the shaman and sometimes not, something that not even his fleet-footed language skills could predict. He asked the same question each time. Why are the languages of the Maya different? What makes you all the same people? The answer to the second question was always the same. "We are the people of the corn. We are here to create balance between all things. We bring life into the world with our children. We dream together with our ancestors. We love the land." The answers were offered with a sense of incredulity—how could anyone not know this?

Language was the personality and the soul of a people. Will wanted to understand the Maya so that he could understand the language. Once people knew that he could speak their language, which was shocking enough because he was a white person, they would invariably ask him, *Where do you belong?* They did not ask where he was from and the difference vibrated his heart. Where did he belong? What land held him like a cradle, like a lover? Was it with his parents, his friends in Brooklyn, his friends and lovers in Wyoming? How could he explain being a wanderer? There was no such thing about the Maya. Unheard of.

Will's time in the highlands became a tonic to the weeks that he had spent teaching in the State Department. If his reluctant students in Guatemala City had tried even a little, they could have learned enough of the language to be understood. Will settled for four weeks in Dos Erres. He would not have stayed that long, but after he met Hector, he didn't want to leave.

By then, Will had met a lot of children, many of whom were inquisitive, charming, or shy. But Hector, with his skinny arms and bucked teeth, had chutzpah and persistence and more than anything, he reminded Will of the kids back home in his neighborhood growing up.

If Will had a little brother, he would have wanted him to be like Hector, with the prepubescent smell of leaves, earth, sticks, and the light stickiness of sweat with a line of dirt ringing his neck. The two of them settled on a routine of Spanish lessons for Hector after Will was done working for the day, and gossip for Will. Hector kept him informed of the girls who liked Will, which man was in trouble for getting too rough with his wife, and who was considered too lazy. Mostly they played soccer. Hector was a fleet-footed genius, running figure eights around Will.

Will's soccer ball was a prized possession. One afternoon, after a breathless game of passing the ball every which way except to Will's feet, he told Hector, "You are the official guardian of the ball. It is yours." He handed it to Hector. The boy picked up the ball and beamed. It was as if Will had anointed him Lord of the Soccer Ball.

The ultimate compliment came when Hector said his family wanted him to join them for supper in their casita. Like most houses, theirs was built of adobe, topped with a corrugated metal roof. Will spent a high school summer working with the forest service in Wyoming and his boss told him, "When you get invited to dinner, it's a big deal. Take off your hat, leave your attitude in the truck, and remember to say thank you." Will washed out a T-shirt the night before.

Hector may have tried for a state of nonchalance, but at age eight, he was incapable. After Hector introduced Will (even though he had met every person in the village many times) to his mother, father, grandmothers, two older sisters, and someone's babies, Hector and Will did the four-stage handshake that they had formulated over the past month. Grab, thumbs-up, back of the hands, slide.

Will's mastery of the local language, K'iche', had at first stunned the villagers. Now that he had crossed the threshold and was a guest in their house, they wasted no time to ask him the questions that they had wondered all along.

Where is his land?
Where is his family?
Do all white people want to steal land?
Don't they have land of their own?
Does the sun hurt his skin?
Why isn't he married?
Doesn't he want children?

What do his ancestors have to say about his travels far from home?

He told them about his mother and father. "They have a great love for each other," he said. "My mother bakes pies with peaches that come from the gods. She bakes from her heart."

About white people stealing land, he said that it was not all white people, but that yes, long ago, the Indios of Norte America had been driven from their land. At this, Hector's family solemnly bowed their heads.

About marriage, he said that all the Mayan women were so beautiful that he was nearly blind. It would be hard to find a woman in Brooklyn who could compare to the women of Dos Erres.

Will stretched out the job as long as possible until the day came when he had to head back to Guatemala City. It would take fourteen to sixteen hours of hard riding on his small motorcycle to get there. He would campaign hard with Blackburn for this village to get a pickup truck or a tractor, anything that would ease some of the physical burden that they bore constantly. But he was not eager to say good-bye to Hector. Something bright glimmered in his mind—he could return to Dos Erres and start a Spanish/English school. Nothing had ever been this clear to him before. Why hadn't he thought of it sooner?

When Hector waved good-bye to Will, he did so while bumping the soccer ball from knee to knee like a juggler. Will's throat constricted and his lip trembled. Aside from providing his physical labor to a terracing project for bean crops, the soccer ball had been the most enthusiastically received gift that Will had ever left in a village.

"*Vaya con Dios,* Hector," he yelled. Then in K'iche', "You are the sun god of soccer!" Hector's gleaming smile was the last thing he saw before he left.

On the ride to Guatemala City, he thought about all their questions, their respectful nods as he answered them, their worried looks when he told them he didn't stay in contact with his ancestors. Hector's mother, Rosa, shook her head and said, "Then they will take a bite out of your soul."

At the main office in Guatemala City, Will typed up his report on the Selectric typewriter in one of the spare offices and gave it to Ron Blackburn. In it, he outlined their crop rotations with corn and beans, their frugal use of cows for fresh cheese, and their chickens and the tiny *tienda* where goods were trekked in from the lowlands, and how little of this was transported out. In fact, only the cornmeal was sold elsewhere. He summarized that it was a successful village.

"Excellent," Blackburn said, scanning the report. "This is just the sort of thing we were looking for. You've been out in the country for months. This area is supervised by Jenkins. He'll make excellent use of this. You've accumulated ten vacation days by my count. Have yourself a good time and check back with me when you return."

As Will left Blackburn's office, he nearly collided with a man who had his hand on the outside door handle.

"Whoa, busy place," said Will. The man's receding hairline highlighted his skull, making it look larger, outlined by thin brown hair. Time and equatorial sun had etched deep lines at the top of his nose forming a perfectly inverted Y at the bridge, pulling the loose flesh of his brow down. He was a squinter, with the skin from his eyebrows draped over his eyelids. But he couldn't take his eyes off the guy's forehead, where a large lump protruded over one eyebrow. If they were in Brooklyn, this guy would definitely be called Tumor.

From his desk, Blackburn shouted, "Jenkins, this is our translator." Apparently Will didn't warrant a name. The man went into Blackburn's office, and shut the door.

Will hadn't been to the Pacific coast in months and he longed to stick his feet into the ocean. That's what he was after, sea breezes and sand. Swimming in the ocean. Dark bottles of beer and freshly caught *langosta.*

When he was on the beach, he bought a hat for Hector and

another soccer ball. A boy can't have too many soccer balls. Will pictured a place in the village for a school room. No, he had learned enough to realize that he could only suggest the idea and ask permission from the village, which he would do, with his pal Hector at his side.

CHAPTER 22

Kate invited Will for coffee in the little kitchen area available to the guests. She washed her hair in a fit of primping. She was halfway down the wide staircase when she heard the ka-thunk of the iron knocker.

Marta was first to the door and opened it. "I want a doorbell. Other guesthouses have doorbells. It's our next bit of upgrading. Come in, come in. You must be Will." She stepped forward and held out her hand for a robust handshake.

Kate's father told her once that he had recognized her mother as his true love instantly. He said that it had been the clearest thought that he'd ever had—"There's the woman I'll marry." Her mother had said the same thing.

Kate had listened, doubting every word of it. Did people become more perfect after they died? Do the dead become wiser? Would her mother know what to do with an orphan? Now, as Will tipped his head to Marta and complimented her on the courtyard, the lushness of the potted plants, and the rich scent of meat emanating from the kitchen, Kate saw him, saw how they could fit together. Is this what her father meant? Not now, oh, not now.

Marta slipped away, excusing herself, directing them to the sitting area as if they could not have found it on their own. The kitchen had one hot plate, a fridge, and a jug of filtered water. Kate directed Will to the small alcove. Will sat very still on the small, hand-carved chair. The sound of children's voices bubbled from the other end of the courtyard. Kate said, "That's Sofia."

Kate sipped the first coffee that she'd had since coming to Antigua. Her intestines no longer cramped.

The plastic shower curtain separating the kitchen from the courtyard flew open. "There you are," said Marta. "I think Sofia started to get worried. She can work up an adult-sized frown. Not much of a crier, though. Felix, now he's a bloody screamer. Takes after me."

Sofia straddled Marta's hip in her new cotton skirt and blouse. Her black hair stuck up at odd angles. Sofia stopped frowning when she saw Kate. She reached out one arm for Kate. The flesh along her small arms looked so tender, like peaches.

Marta brought out a bowl of guacamole and set it on the table. "This is the best way I know of to celebrate Kate's good news. Not only is little Sofia cleared medically, but Kate is going to adopt."

Kate flinched at the lie that she'd told Marta about the heart condition. The woman had been extraordinarily kind to her.

Will still hadn't moved since Marta brought Sofia into the room.

Kate set her coffee down and opened her arms to the girl. Is this why people can so easily kidnap children? She never thought of this before, but of course it was. Igniting trust and loyalty in a toddler could be done from love or evil. Kate shuddered at the options for a war orphan, or for any child without protection.

Once in Kate's arms, Sofia turned her head to one side and nestled into her chest, tucking her face beneath Kate's chin.

Kate kissed her and rocked slightly, murmuring, "That was a long time. Too long for you, little one." With every rhythmic sway of her hips, she wanted to wash away the horror for the child.

Marta turned to look for Felix, who appeared with an empty plastic jug that once held laundry soap, now partially filled with pebbles and clothespins. "I know I play second fiddle to Sofia, but as proprietor of this grand place, I'd like to invite you to stay for lunch."

Will did not respond. He stood up, keeping his eyes on Sofia, his face crumbling along one side of his mouth. The expected momentum of the conversation stalled and the room echoed with Kate's heartbeat.

"Will's been in the Peace Corps and now he's traveling around for a few months before he returns home. Maybe they don't do lunch or . . ." She stalled for time, giving Will time to recover from whatever was going on.

He turned to Kate. "I should be going. Thanks for the coffee. Nice to meet you, Marta." He backed out of the kitchen and left. The sound of the large front door opening and closing echoed in the entryway.

"Was it something I said?" asked Marta. "Was it the guacamole?"

"It wasn't you. I think he freaked out when he saw Sofia. He must be one of those guys who run when they see a kid."

Even as she said it, she didn't believe it. It wasn't disinterest that she saw on his face. It was fear.

Kate hadn't seen Will in two days and she wondered if he had packed up and left. Was he just a backpacker guy, post–Peace Corps worker, a vagabond? Will never told her where he was staying. She had scared him off with her seriousness and need, and with Sofia. It was better that she had not told him one thing more, better that she didn't think about him at all.

Marta's husband was having trouble selling their property in Australia and would not be returning for weeks. Marta said she longed to talk with someone and that someone was Kate. If

Kate came downstairs with Sofia, Marta was there in a flash, seeking the camaraderie of another woman, and another English speaker. Marta was a fountain of questions about the adoption process, now that Kate had confirmed that yes, she was planning on adoption.

"How long will it take? Can I help in any way? It's odd that they don't want to meet with you and Sofia together. What in blazes can take them so long? Not that I mind you being here, but surely they can't expect you to stay here forever. But come to think of it, I don't know what Felix and I would do if you and Sofia left."

While these were perfectly normal questions, life had ceased being normal. Since the massacre and finding out about the *casa de engordes* for little children like Sofia, embers of suspicion ignited in Kate, glowing hot with any inquiry about the child. She was becoming adept at nonanswers.

"Adoption is a long process," she said. "We're progressing right on schedule." Lying grated on her but she no longer felt safe announcing to the world that she had a child and that adoption was a problem. What if someone kidnapped Sofia and sold her?

Kate had already been in Antigua for ten days and she was no closer to finding a solution. Fernando would say only that he was making inquiries. She hadn't heard anything from Kirkland and she desperately hoped for a lifeline of sorts from her. And if she stayed in the guesthouse with Marta all day, she'd never clear her head enough to think. Marta's propensity for small talk far out-stripped Kate's threshold.

It was midday and the two kids collapsed on Marta's couch. This is how Sofia would have slept at her home, pressed up against her brother like two halves of a walnut, inches away from Manuela and Jorge.

"Go on," said Marta. "You have the look of a mother who needs an outing. The children are fine here."

She looked like a mother? Kate put on her jacket and headed to the street. Fernando's café would have to do as a retreat for her thoughts.

The guesthouse was five blocks from the central square. Storefronts opened directly onto the sidewalks, all the size of closets with thinly spaced stock on dusty shelves: a can of Spam, two boxes of powdered milk, bottles of orange soda, a pile of bananas, and squares of grainy chocolate wrapped in paper. The day was cloudy and cold and the volcanoes were shrouded in clouded hats. Kate had replaced the old sandals with new ones and wore thick wool socks with them. She was not a fashion statement, or if she was, it was called bedraggled gringo.

As she neared the center, something different hit her, stronger than the diesel smell of the old cars that rattled along the buckled cobblestones. It was excitement bubbling over, smiling faces under hats at each corner. By the time she got to the square, a cluster of militia huddled nervously, necks straining to look around as if they feared a sudden attack. She was still undone by the sight of soldiers, but she was becoming better at hiding it. Perhaps Antigua was far too public and open to travelers for the soldiers to do anything stupid, at least in the daylight.

Kate crossed the street so that she didn't have to walk next to the soldiers. What could they possibly be afraid of? She pushed open the doors to the café and turned her head to the table where Will had been on that first day. Empty.

"I'm not that predictable. You can't look for me at the same exact table," said a familiar voice.

Kate whirled around. Will sat with his back against the far wall, reading a newspaper. "I wasn't looking for you," she said. Too quickly, she said it too quickly.

"And I wouldn't blame you if you never looked for me. I'm a rude idiot from Brooklyn. Would you come and sit with me so that I can apologize?"

Kate could say no. She didn't have to walk across the room and join him at the table with the green plastic cloth. On top of everything else, she didn't need to get involved with a guy who told her nothing about himself and who ran away the minute he saw Sofia.

"So they didn't teach you any manners in Brooklyn?" she

said. Kate slid a chair out and sat down. Did he twitch at her rebuke? His cheek muscles jerked one side of his lips.

"They taught me manners at home, but on the streets, I learned all the best lessons from a guy named Cesar. When I wasn't getting the shit kicked out of me, he said I showed some promise as a human being. He would have been shocked at my poor behavior with you. He always said, if you find a woman who makes your heart beat faster, and your brain go slower, either run away or move in."

"Whatever happened to Cesar and his sage advice?" She placed the tips of her fingers on the edge of the table, ready either to hold on or push off. He should not say *woman* or *heart.*

"It would sound more interesting if I said he was in jail, but he's a FedEx driver."

"And his love life? Which did he choose, running away or moving in?"

"See, guys make up a lot of silly stuff in our heads that never happens. He met Ruthie and she made him wait for two years before she'd let him move in. He moved in when they got married and not before."

"What kind of silly stuff do you make up?" Kate relaxed and put her elbows on the table. Could he see her heart pounding out of her shirt?

"Me? I'm just going to keep talking so you don't get up and go away. Is it working?"

"So far. What happened when you saw Sofia? What was that all about?"

Will took a breath, then slowly exhaled. "I got close to some kids in a village. The military hammered the village pretty hard. Some of the kids got hurt. I've been avoiding getting close to kids for a few months. It was hard to see you holding the little girl."

"But surely you've seen Mayan kids since then."

The café was dark, with only two windows facing the central park, and they were heavily shaded by the wide veranda over the once majestic sidewalks. A flickering lightbulb across the room formed a yellow pool that did not extend to their table.

Kate's spine was cold and she wanted to stop pretending she was brave.

"It was the way you held her, the way she trusted you. Trust can go so wrong," he said.

Will ran his hand along one side of his neck. Had he trusted someone he shouldn't have?

"What do you mean, *hammered?* Were people killed?"

"I mean that I don't want to talk about it, not right now. Okay?"

She could press the issue, but if she did, was she ready to tell him about the massacre? A flicker of alarm fired in her about this man. "Okay."

Two Mayan men walked by the door, illuminated by a slant of light. Their shoulders were pulled up and back like they had just won the Guatemalan lottery, if they'd had one.

"Do you know what's going on today? Is it a holiday? I'm completely lost with their holy days."

Will pushed the newspaper toward her. It was the government-controlled newspaper from Guatemala City.

"Turn to page four. Then I'll fill in some of the blanks."

Kate turned to page four. She scanned the page for anything that would explain the thread of festivity that fluttered through the city. Headlines: December 20, 1990: Politicians ran for election, a photo of a military parade in Guatemala City, the president standing next to a somber-faced school child, and then there it was. She knew enough Spanish to get the nouns and verbs. *General Javier flies to Santiago Atitlán to inspect the military barracks.*

"I'm not sure what this means and what to believe," said Kate. Was there any harm in telling Will that she had been doing research at the lake? The words sank back down her throat and hovered until further notice. She folded the newspaper and handed it back to him.

Will pulled the newspaper toward his side of the table. "Here's what I know so far. There was a massacre in Santiago. Thirty-two people from Santa Teresa were killed in the village square by a bunch of bozo military guys. But here's the amazing part. The Maya from Santiago and the next village filled the square the next day. Ordinarily, it would have been standard procedure for the families to take their slaughtered loved ones and bury them. Or on days when the militia felt less generous, they'd dump the bodies into mass graves, dug by the people of the village." Will clenched his hands, and for a moment he looked like a boy who could not believe the first and worst truth of his life.

"This time the villagers refused and they stood guard over the bodies, daring the soldiers to shoot them. I'm a little hazy on this part. I didn't actually read that in the newspaper, but the market is buzzing with rumors. The villages around Santiago say they will no longer give them food or shelter. If the soldiers touch the women ever again, the women will poison them. They are done with the soldiers and they want their lives back the way they were before the military moved in. The people of Santiago don't want one more massacre, one more person killed."

Kate faced the back of the café, where an arched doorway led to the back room. The blood in her head whooshed. She pictured people standing sentinel over Manuela's body and her son, and the body of Jorge in the makeshift jail. Her eyes stung and she looked down, fussing with her hands. She pressed her lips together to gain control.

"Did anyone survive the massacre? I mean the ones who were shot, were there survivors?" What was left of her voice came out in a whisper.

"I don't know. Do you want to know the thing that tipped the balance, other than the balls-up courage of the people? There was a reporter from the *San Francisco Chronicle* in the village who witnessed the massacre and the demonstration. She wired in the story and it's all over the world. Her name is VJ Kirkland."

Kate heard the tinkling sound of a spoon against dishware and she looked up. Fernando held a tray with a *café con leche;* he shook his head slightly before he came into Will's sight.

"Hello, Kate. This is your favorite drink. For my special customers, I don't wait for them to order," he said. Fernando set the cup and saucer in front of Kate.

He'd been listening, she was sure of it. Why shouldn't she tell Will about Kirkland?

"I might have read her stuff in the States. I'm not sure." She thanked Fernando and sipped the hot drink. She pushed up from the table. "I have to get back. I don't want to leave Sofia with Marta for too long."

"How about a do-over? I mean it. I feel terrible about the last time I was there."

Something tingled in her solar plexus, all of its own volition.

Kate watched Fernando's back as he walked away, his thin torso pulsing. The cold from the adobe walls pulled out the warmth from her skin. She wouldn't say anything about Kirkland, but her desire to be with Will muffled any caution.

"Sure, let's try again. Tonight?"

Suddenly there was a light in her chest, something other than terror. Will's smile was sad and soft and the combination was unsettling.

CHAPTER 23

Kate kept her trips outdoors with Sofia to a minimum. When she did go out, she tried to take both children. With little Felix along, she was a white woman with two children, one Mayan and one white, not a gringo with a Mayan child.

The reality of taking two small children through the streets of Antigua was much harder than she could have imagined. While Sofia clung to her, Felix exploded from one spot to the next. When she ventured into the market to buy another hand-woven cloth, she went alone to the stalls on the outskirts of the city.

Kate could not use Manuela's cloth to carry Sofia; it would immediately identify the child's origins. And there were the bullet holes from the machine gun, a surprising few given the torrent. She had washed it and dried it in their room. If she were smart, she would throw it away, take it out to the base of the volcano and bury it. Any number of options had come to mind: Shred it with scissors, burn it, dye it indigo blue. But the cloth stuck to her like a spiderweb. Manuela's hands had touched every thread in the cloth. If she discarded the cloth, there would be nothing left of Manuela. She rolled it tightly and tucked it under the foot of her mattress.

Kate had on jeans and a thick sweater. She had pulled her hair back into a braid and pulled a wool cap over that. Casa Candelaria never truly got warm, but having now slept outside under the worst possible conditions, Kate was grateful for far lesser accommodations than she would have accepted only weeks ago. No rain soaked her and the child, no mudslides threatened, and they were out of the wind. Marta's place already earned four stars.

Kate walked along the network of vendors and looked casually at each one. She squatted in front of a woman and admired her fabric.

"Where do you live? What region do you come from?" Kate asked in Spanish.

"By the ocean," she answered. The woman had broad cheekbones, with fine features and skin that seemed to pull across her face and not down.

The ocean would be far enough away. Kate selected a yellow cloth to carry Sofia. She had never seen a yellow weaving around Santiago. Handwoven cloth lends itself to geometric designs, but what attracted Kate were the animals and birds that appeared along the weave. Children like animals and birds. She pictured Sofia pointing to each one, learning the word for bird, horse, jaguar, and some of the other as yet indecipherable animals.

She bought fresh cheese, eggs, and Spam. She wasn't sure what Marta intended to cook with the ingredients, but this had been the request.

That evening Marta, Will, and Kate warmed themselves by the fire after a dinner of Spam omelets and potatoes. They ate in Marta's living room, amid a collection of laundered sheets. A group of German travelers had checked in and Marta struggled to keep up with the wash. Sofia and Felix made a wonderful mess of the mashed potatoes. Both children refused the Spam.

Kate pointed to the mini-piles of the pink meat product discarded by the children. "I think they know something that we don't," said Kate.

She was on her third beer. The great salve of alcohol had entered her bloodstream as soon as her mother died and now it found the old pathways of grief once again. With each beer, Manuela's face with the black hole over her eye faded and grew hazy.

"You Americans are too finicky about your food. We ate tinned meat for Sunday supper and were glad to have it," said Marta. She patted her stomach. "Just like home."

"It was a magnificent meal of multiple meat sources," said Will. He nursed the same beer that he had started with. "Let me take care of this fire and see if I can inspire it." Will put another small stick of wood on the fire and rearranged the embers until the fire wrapped its greedy tongue around the fresh wood and sent flames upward.

"Impressive," said Marta. "You'd be right at home in the outback."

"Maybe the outback should be my next stop."

Kate set her beer down on the floor next to her chair. The idea of Will leaving gripped her throat. "Where is your next stop?"

The sound of the iron knocker clanging on the front door startled Kate.

"You're a jumpy one. That's only the German tourists coming back after their dinner." Marta scooped up a pile of towels and headed for the door. "Continue on without me, but take notes. I want to know where this fire-tender is off to."

Will's sweater smelled of fresh air and smoke, and as his body warmed, tendrils of feral spice rose from his skin. Sofia and Felix played on a rug closer to the fire. Kate got up and sat with the children, putting Sofia on her lap. The child fidgeted a bit, wanting to be near the boy. "Oh, Sofia, I know Felix is the main attraction. Be careful of the fire." Kate pointed with her finger. "Fire. Fire." She exaggerated the word, dragging it out, placing her top teeth on her bottom lip as she enunciated.

Will squatted down next to them. If sadness could have been drawn on someone's face, it would have been around Will's eyes, which had a dryness to the outer edges and eyelids that had gone heavy.

"I learned a saying about children from the Maya and I've heard it all over, in different dialects, but the meaning is the same. *Ri akkala qi wish kaj qe ri schoy.* It means—"

Sofia turned away from Felix as if the sun had just shone on her. Will stopped in mid-sentence. She stood up and walked to Will and placed a tiny hand on his cheek. Then she rocked from foot to foot and said, "*Akkala wishkaj,*" in a singsong voice. Sofia smiled and a small yelp came from her throat that Kate had not heard before.

Will said, "*Q'uel ya'? Juyu' nim?*" He was casting with a fishing rod of words, testing the water with bait until he got it right. When Sofia repeated a word back to him exactly as he said it, he smiled at her.

"Stop it! What are you doing? Stop it," said Kate. She scrambled to her knees.

Will looked over Sofia's dark head at Kate. "She's from Santiago Atitlán, isn't she? When were you in Santiago, Kate?"

She wanted to protest, but instead a new sound came out of her, not a word, but some leftover sound from the massacre, as if her ears had popped at high altitude. What came out was only air escaping from her lungs.

The door to the living room opened. "It wasn't the Germans after all. There's someone here to see you, Kate. She said she knows your friend in Oakland. She gave me this. It's for you." Marta handed her a note.

Kate jumped up and ran out the living room door. She sprinted to the front door, unbolted it, and yanked it open. "Wait." On the street, she saw the taillights of a truck two blocks away.

Kate placed her hand on the cold adobe wall. Did Kirkland have to be so dramatic, so film noir? Kate went back inside and pulled the door shut, locking out the rest of the world. She stood under one of the ceiling lamps and opened the note.

I have to leave the country for a few months. The story mattered, it truly mattered. I'm glad you're okay. Be careful of the American guy. Fernando is worried and is checking. K

Checking what? Kate squared up her shoulders and went back to Marta's living room. Marta cleared dishes. Sofia had abandoned Felix for Will, curling into his lap and gazing at him with sleepy eyes.

She crumpled the note and tossed it into the fire. "Be careful," said Kate. "She has a way of growing on you." She could tell by the look on Will's face, a deadly seriousness, that he was adding up Kirkland, Santiago Atitlán and a small Mayan child. There was no way to stop him.

"Your friend must have been in a hurry. I'll be putting Felix to bed soon. Would you like me to put Sofia in with him? The two of them sleep easier together," said Marta.

Before Kate could answer, Will said, "I'd like to hold her longer. I think she might even go to sleep right here. This doesn't happen much for me."

"Then I will put this lump of boy to bed," said Marta, scooping up the child like a large sack of rice.

"I no lump of boy," said Felix, laughing with delight. Yet he offered little resistance.

Sofia arranged herself in Will's lap so that she could look up at him. He cradled her head in the crook of his arm. She whispered to him, a question, emphasized with an imploring shrug. He smiled at her and gently shrugged, answering her.

"She wants to know where her mother is. I suspect you know the answer to that," said Will. The golden smile drained out of him. His eyes held her in a grip.

Kate slid to her knees on the cold tile floor and covered her face with her hands. Her skin stripped off her shoulders, then her torso, and fell to a puddle on the floor. She was only blood and bone.

"You're probably in way more trouble than you can imagine," he said.

CHAPTER 24

Will
October 1990

When Will was still a language specialist, he vacationed along the Pacific coast. Ten days was enough. It was late October. The beaches were sparsely dotted with tourists. The independence of his new job was intoxicating, but he longed for the familiarity of Hector and his family.

If his neighborhood in Brooklyn was ever transplanted to Guatemala, it wouldn't be all that different from Hector's village with men gossiping about imagined sex and women cooking over a fire while children tugged at them. He could fit in a side trip to Dos Erres before heading back to Guatemala City.

He bought another soccer ball for Hector, tied it to his motorcycle, and drove away from the Pacific coastline, heading north and east. Hector could hold this one in reserve for the day that the other soccer ball was beyond repair.

When he was half a kilometer from the village, he came to the last crossroad and an odd buzz resonated through him, much like walking past a dark alley in Brooklyn late at night. He pulled his motorcycle to the side of the road, flipped the key, and pushed the bike up on its kickstand. There should have been sounds from the village by now. Men and women should have been coming and going, carrying sticks for fires, coming back from the terraced gardens, their all-purpose hoes over one shoulder. What was wrong? Why weren't the dogs barking?

From the ditch on the far side of the road, two men rose up, Maya, their faces fixed and decisive, eyes burning into Will. They had guns and each man had a machete sheathed at his side. Had they been waiting for him? Machete, the agricultural tool that kept the forest at bay, cleared paths, and, at lower elevations, sliced open coconuts as if they were butter. These machetes had been transformed into weapons.

This is what hatred looked like. Will recognized it and it etched deep in the back of his throat. They had nothing to lose; they had already lost too much. They were resistance fighters and they had not bothered to hide their affiliation from Will.

"I'm going to the village," he said in K'iche'. "I have friends there. I am bringing my young friend Hector a soccer ball."

Two more men and a woman appeared, all armed. The sun bore through his shirt, peeling away his sweet expectations of Dos Erres. The woman, who, if she had lived in Brooklyn, would have been in high school, lowered her gun. Five guns were pointed at him. When the girl lowered her long, dust-covered weapon something changed; they had been ready to shoot him and now they weren't. Not now, but maybe soon. This was how he would die, not by a punk kid on angel dust in Brooklyn, but here, in the highlands where he would be food to the vultures. Who would tell his parents?

"We know who you are," said the woman. Every bit of music that was natural to their language was drained from her voice, as if her vocal cords had been torn apart and put back together in a bizarre patchwork.

All he had was his ability to speak in their dialect. Nothing mattered except getting to the village and finding the people who knew him. Was Hector in danger? Only four guns pointed at him now. He decided on formality to show respect.

"I request passage to the village to see my friends. I have no weapons," he said.

When Will had been a bike courier in Manhattan, he learned how to read drivers the way a horse reads a rider, noticing when a rider turns his head, moments before they pull on a rein. The woman driving toward him didn't have her turn signal on but he saw the rise in her right shoulder, ready to ease into the left lane, right in front of him. Or the way a man tilted his head or pressed down a forearm on an open window. The last thing that Will paid attention to were the turn signals or the brake lights. If he wanted to stay alive on his fragile bike, he had to know about a change in direction before the drivers did.

Like all languages that he decoded, driving in Manhattan was just one more language. He could not afford to be smug or cocky, which would have made him a dead bike courier, but he had known he was good. Knowing that he couldn't afford to miss any of the signs that drivers offered made him even better.

Now he needed to understand the language of resistance fighters if he hoped to stay alive.

The guerillas pointed their guns down toward the unpaved road. They had all decided something. Will missed that essential moment because he was too afraid, the scent of his sweat changed to the sharp emulsion of fear, and all he wanted to do was run. Where had they come from so suddenly?

"You want safe passage to the village?" said one man, bone thin, dark eyes. He was older than the rest with deeper lines around his eyes. "Come with us. Your friends are waiting."

The late afternoon sun was still warm, burning through the thin mountain air. Will didn't want to know their names and prayed that they weren't going to tell him. Everything that he knew before shifted and tilted.

The older armed man walked first, followed by two more,

then Will, followed by the woman with her gun slung over her chest. The last man hung back, facing the direction that Will had just come. He was barefoot, his broad feet covered in nicks and white scars, his soles as thick as leather. Will was taller than even the largest man by a foot.

The road to the village narrowed on the edge of the mountain. Two cars could not have passed each other easily. Will knew this last turn, where you could look out over the forest on the right as the road hugged the hillside on the left. Where were the short-haired village dogs with their tails curled upright into a ring? The crunch of rocky soil beneath their feet should have alarmed the dogs long ago.

When he had worked for Outward Bound, they had trained the kids to put out the campfires with water and dirt, to smother all oxygen from the fire. The smell always stayed with him and it meant the end of things; the damp, dark, acrid smell of wet charcoal.

As they turned the corner, the dead campfire smell hit him like a dark rolling cloud of a storm. He stopped walking. A monstrous dread cascaded over him. There had been a fire, then a rainstorm. The woman behind him lifted her gun and prodded the small of his back.

Two adobe houses had served as the centers of commerce; Fanta orange soda, sacks of rice, cornmeal, and tinned meat had been stacked in modest piles. Now, anything that could have burned was gone, including the shelves and the chairs that two old women used to sit on while they talked. The walls were pocked with bullet holes.

Will stopped and spun around, facing the young woman. "When?" he shouted. "What happened?" Without waiting for her to answer, he began to run to the next house. "Hector! Hector!" His muscles were alien to him, his arms heavy in dreamlike uselessness, his leg muscles refusing to go fast enough.

The first body was already swollen, skin giving way to insects and birds. A barefoot man, his striped pants cropped at mid-calf, a belly wound dark with dried blood, and his hand covered with blood from holding his abdomen together. Death made the man unrecognizable. But Will must have known him; he must have seen him before.

The village was held in a cup of land along the mountainside, a stream running down the hill to form their water supply in a large concrete container that served as the heart of the people. Women brought their laundry there and scrubbed their clothes along the concrete, children brought plastic buckets to fill for the household, people gossiped and watched their small children there. Will saw another body draped over the edge of the concrete; a woman, bent at an impossible angle, faceup, her head in the water, her feet not quite touching the ground, doing a graceful backbend in death.

Hector's family lived in a clutch of houses behind the water supply. Will could think of nothing else but to find them. He backed away from the dead woman, as if she could rise up and reach for him. Then he turned and ran for Hector's house.

Every adobe wall was dashed with bullet holes, nearly cutting one wall in half. The door to Hector's house was small for Will; he had to duck low to enter. The roof was corrugated metal and beyond that a drape of fabric, now half torn away, formed another room. This room, the kitchen, was empty. Beyond it was the doorway to the shared courtyard where Hector's mother and grandmother often sat with their back-strap looms. Will ran from room to room, to the enclosure for the chickens, looking for life or, worse yet, bodies.

When he came out, the guerilla fighters stood in a semicircle facing the doorway. He hadn't known that he was crying until he tried to talk. His words came out sloppy and wet. He sank down on the ground, falling as though he was sucker punched, landing on his butt. They waited for him to stop crying with a consideration not yet burned out of them.

The older man knelt down on one knee. He could have been a farmer, examining his crop, or a fisherman looking out over a lake before dawn. "They killed as many of the people as they could and buried them in a mass grave. The ones you see in the village are the ones who were wounded and ran into the jungle to escape. When they came back, they died from their wounds and the cloud of sorrow. But they came home to die where their families and ancestors lived," he said.

"The soldiers said they had proof that the people were supplying us with food. How could the soldiers in Guatemala City know this?" he asked. He drew a line in the dirt with his gun, a circle for the village, a line, and then a circle for the capital. "From here to the city. Tell me, how could they know anything? Who goes from here to the capital?"

The difference between a question and a statement was clear. How could he have missed the warning signs with Hector's village, with the Department guys in Guatemala City? Innuendos, silences instead of responses, the overly solicitous desire to help the Maya, all of the little bits and pieces that he hadn't paid attention to now sliced through him. For the first time in his life, he hadn't understood the signs that had been all around him. The massacre had everything to do with Will. If he hadn't been here, befriending people, learning about their meager commerce, children would still play by the water, women would continue to weave.

"Do you know Hector and his family?" he whispered. He still sat on the ground, unable to get up. "Did they survive?" Hector was a fast runner; he could have dashed through the jungle, dodging left and right as he had with soccer.

"There was no one left alive. This is what the soldiers do to punish the villages who feed us," said the young woman. "This is what the Horned Toad has done." The war made her bold and let her speak with the men.

What was she talking about? What Horned Toad? Something scratched at his brain. Will pushed up to his knees, swaying. "I was here studying agriculture, commerce, to help bring in equipment to the village . . ." He struggled to find a phrase. "I learn languages . . ." He covered his face with his hands. This had been the ruse; the seemingly benign information that he had delivered had been worked through the military intelligence and molded into something heinous. Ron Blackburn had said Jenkins oversaw this area. Would Jenkins have permitted this?

Will catapulted deeper into the nightmare. Jenkins and his disfiguring forehead lump. The Horned Toad. He had been here; the resistance fighters knew him. Will had been inches away from the man who was responsible for the carnage around him.

"Stand up," said the man who pointed his gun at him again. "We will show you where Hector is now."

This couldn't be happening. This was a nightmare and soon he'd lurch into wakefulness, sweating and crying, tangled in his own sheets. He was a bike courier, an Outward Bound counselor, a Peace Corps volunteer. He loved languages and played soccer and made children laugh.

They walked again and Will stumbled; he couldn't feel his arms or legs. They went past the remains of the houses, past bodies of dogs that had not been buried, past the cooking pots that were overturned. Will's chest clenched—there was the soccer ball, wedged between a tree and a broken back-strap loom.

The dirt was freshly turned, shaped like a trench, thirty feet long, five feet wide.

"The men of the village dug this pit at gunpoint, knowing that they would be killed. The soldiers bring shovels. That is how it is done, again and again." Birds sang and swooped in on the insects that dusk delivered. A line of ants carried bits of leaves across the freshly turned mound of earth. Beneath the insects lay the people of the village.

Will knelt on the edge of the mass grave and picked up a handful of dirt, cupped it, and brought it to his lips. He heaved with sobs, convulsing beyond his control. This was a new language for him, the elemental language of unspeakable despair. He became canine, jaguar, screech owl, howling into the jungle, eyes closed, pounding his fists into the dirt.

When he was spent, his throat raw, mucus pouring over his lips and into his mouth, eyelids swollen with tears, they lifted him from the dirt, dragging him ten feet away from the horror.

This is where they would shoot him, a marker to the mass grave. They dropped him to the ground. Killing him would be better, there was no other solution. If they could read his soul, they would see it sliced by the horror of death. He would be unable to live knowing that he had played a part in the massacre; no one could live with this.

A young man, a boy really, raised his gun. More than anything, Will wanted him to shoot. The boy settled the end of the gun into his shoulder.

"You must kill me. Shoot me. I am not human anymore." Did he speak in K'iche', English, Spanish, or some other language that he had learned through the death of Hector's village? He no longer knew.

Will stood up, exposing his chest to him, ready to pay the price for being the conduit to the military. If it weren't for Will, Hector would still be alive, tapping the soccer ball from knee to knee. If only Will hadn't stopped at this village, if only he hadn't been blinded by the chance to learn languages, if only he had read all the signs.

He reached for the end of the weapon and pulled it into his breastbone. He wanted to be shot in the heart, where the jagged pain pulsed; he wanted the gun to erase him. Will looked down at the dirt so that the boy holding the gun would not have to look into his eyes when he shot him. He wanted to spare him. He dropped his hands from the gun and leaned into the hard metal.

A flock of birds rushed through the trees, seeking shelter for the night, rattling leaves as they went. A tendril of wind rose up from the valley to the hillsides. Its soft warmth seemed to caress his chin, urging him to look up. When he raised his head, the armed group had stepped back, pointing their weapons down. They said something, brief, of sorts, but Will's languages had mixed like a deadly soup. He thought that he heard *kik'el . . . wach. . . .* Blood in his eyes? Live with the blood? They retreated in a swift choreography, an instantaneous decision to let him live.

* * *

When Will returned to the place where he had first stopped with his bike, he was not surprised that they had taken it. He would have done the same thing. He was, however, surprised that they had tossed his pack to the ground and left the new soccer ball. The white ball looked solemn, perched on top of his blue L.L. Bean day pack.

After arranging the ball on the side of the road, propped with stones, a headstone to Hector, he slipped his arms through his pack and walked. He would find another village and then he'd find someone with a truck or a motorbike who would take him to a spot where he'd he catch a bus. Jenkins would pay for this.

CHAPTER 25

After the two children were put to bed, Kate and Will stood outside Marta's guesthouse.

The cobblestones had a sheen of moisture over them as if a cloud had settled on the streets overnight, slipping past the growling volcanoes on the edge of town. The sidewalk, stones embedded hundreds of years ago, hugged a tight line between the street and the thick walls of the buildings.

"The child is an orphan," said Kate. She lifted her chin, pointing it like a scabbard. She had not wanted to talk about the massacre inside the haven of Marta's courtyard.

What was she doing? Kirkland had warned her about Will in the note. Why was she telling him anything?

"And because she's an orphan, and because there was a massacre, you ran with her. I get that part. But Kate, I've lived in the villages—their family connections run deep. There will be grandparents," said Will.

"No. Manuela told me, both sets of grandparents were gone."

Will closed his eyes. "There will be other connections—

aunts, uncles, cousins. You've just lifted this kid out of her world, her language. They keep track of their ancestors like they were in the next room. They asked me—" Will stopped and his throat caught. "They asked me, *Where do you belong, where are your people?* If someone asks Sofia where her people are, what will she say?" He kept his voice steady, every word was as important as the next.

"My world is about language. For me it's like food or music or breathing. If you take away someone's language, it gouges a hole out of them. The Maya say that if you take away an entire people's language, their souls and their ancestors' souls are left bewildered. What about Sofia?"

"Do you think that I haven't thought about this? I'm trying to keep her alive," said Kate.

Kate felt like she was in a dream without her clothes, standing at a podium ready to speak. Part of her wanted to run away, or make Will run away. But what was this new sliver of light that wanted to curl around Will like a vine?

She moved in the direction of the town center and he came with her. Walking side by side kept her from looking directly at him. Kate preferred the reprieve of furtive glances at him, then the cobblestones, and at other people on the slick walkway. Smoke from the stove fires trickled into the air, adding a rough texture to the dampness, mixed with an inadequate sewage system.

"I know what you must be thinking, that I must be a deluded gringo who thinks I can save a poor child. I know I'm not a savior and my life and culture could be vastly more destructive than hers. I don't want to extract her culture from her soul." Kate moved to the left to let two Mayan women pass. They were merchants with tightly rolled fabric in baskets held on top of their heads.

Kate and Will came to the end of the block. Two more blocks to the right and they'd be at the center of Antigua. He turned to look at her, reached out his hands and took hers. She felt the tick of his energy, not his pulse, but another urgent strumming.

"You don't know what I'm thinking." He rubbed his thumb along her palm. "You've saved a child and you are the bravest person I've ever met."

It felt like he was rubbing her torso, from breasts to the deep sea of her pelvis. Her nipples tightened.

"Did you know her mother?"

"Yes. Manuela was a student, a friend. I was teaching her English. She was teaching me how to carry a child in a long strip of fabric, how to select avocados," said Kate. It was such a relief to mention Manuela's name.

"Do you know what she would have wanted for her child? If she knew that she and her husband and her family were going to be killed, what would she have wanted for Sofia?"

Kate pulled her hands out of his warm hold. "She would have wanted Sofia to live. If I bring Sofia back to the remains of her village, a witness to the massacre, what do you think would happen? What if the soldiers came for her? What if she fell into the black market adoption world? Do you know what it's like not to have a mother?"

The wind caught Will's hair, sun-bleached and dry from the mineral-rich water. He pulled the collar of his jacket up. Kate wanted to be inside his coat, curled up like a cat.

He turned to gaze at the yellow church steeple in the next street. "If you are determined to adopt, you need documentation that she's an orphan. Do you have anything at all like that?"

A motorbike rattled by with two passengers hanging on with impossible grace.

"No. I have nothing."

"You have me," said Will. That was all she had been waiting for and she stepped closer to him, putting both hands along his face.

They went to his room in a hotel where he had to ask for his key when he came in.

"Señor," acknowledged the desk attendant, who looked like he had been sleeping on a roll of blankets.

Kate stopped, needing more. "I don't know your last name."

He held her hand as they walked along the inner courtyard. In his other hand he held a fat square of wood that anchored his room key. "I don't know yours either. Will Buchanan." He bowed. "And if there is any hope of you trusting me, you need to know what I've done."

She was fire-walking, every part of her flesh tested and alive, waiting for the scorch that would come.

"Malloy, Kate Malloy," she said, bowing in return. "And you can tell me what you've done."

The room was more sparsely outfitted than hers; the adobe walls held the same winter chill. A piece of woven fabric hung on one wall, a straw crucifix on the other. They took off their coats and lay together as Will told her about his recruitment the year before, his love of languages, about Hector and the people of Dos Erres and how he had been sure that a tractor would be given to the village. And bit by bit, he told Kate about the day he carried the new soccer ball to Hector on his motorbike, the silence of the village, and the rebel fighters who cursed him with living.

"The massacre would not have happened if it weren't for me."

A frozen glob in her chest melted. Here was someone who had dropped into the same hell that she had been living. The urge to press skin to skin took over.

She pulled at his clothing, undressing him, taking off her own sweater and shirt, sliding her pants down. She circled her hands around his chest that held the cavernous sorrow of the massacre, and let her breasts press down along his torso so that her own horrors could be relieved. How could they have been matched by massacres, each touched with the burning end of a stick in their hearts? Every movement, each groan came from the language that they now shared.

Kate placed her fingers on the center of his breastbone,

wanting his sternum to crack open, releasing the black-winged birds, scavengers who had been feasting on his heart. She wanted sweet fresh air to fill the places that were stagnant with the horrors of Hector's village.

He kissed her along the soft hinge of her jaw, sucked on her earlobe; his hand held her spine, and moved to the swell of her hips. His secrets opened the raw places in her and she swam in his sorrows. Kate wanted him closer, to let their bones and flesh braid. She had found the only man who could match her, breath by breath.

CHAPTER 26

Kirkland was inextricably linked to Kate's escape with Sofia. She had handed off enough money to Kate so that she could live in Antigua. And Kirkland witnessed the massacre and this gave her hope that they wouldn't be forgotten.

At this very minute, Kirkland was probably back in Oakland, eating cheeseburgers, tossing back whatever beer was on tap, and sketching a plan in her small notebook that included whom to call to help Kate and Sofia, which politician would be most sympathetic, and how to bring them home.

Kirkland possessed all of the international political savvy that Kate lacked. She had connections with the resistance movement that continued to surprise Kate at every turn. She could send clandestine messages through couriers, contact Fernando as if he was on a special ethereal speed-dial. There might be no end to the influence that Kirkland had.

Since the night in Atitlán, after the massacre, Kate had entered a world beneath the surface, where she had to double-check every glance, ever on the lookout for threats to her or Sofia. She might be disappeared by the military, or get hauled into a prison and never be heard of again. Sofia could be kidnapped for profit. All of which made bushwhacking through the jungle, and acquiring the worst sort of parasites, minor league problems. Kirkland had understood all of this.

Kirkland came from the stock of people who had long tibias, fingers, thighbones. When Kirkland moved she was angular and stretched beyond where her body should be. Just thinking of her gave Kate a jolt of hope.

Kate was stalled by the corrupt, bureaucratic network that surrounded adoption on a good day, never mind with an orphan without papers. With Sofia on her hip, she headed for the door to the street for mundane shopping at the nearby *tienda,* shouting good-bye to Marta.

"We'll be back before dark."

But she had gotten no farther when the iron knocker slammed against the heavy door.

"Would you mind getting that?" shouted Marta from the kitchen. Pans clattered and something metallic fell on the tile floor, reverberating through the courtyard. The woman was a cyclone of action in the small room.

Kate slid the horizontal slat of wood that gave her a peek at the visitor. It was Will. After spending part of the night with him she had not seen him in two days and she batted down an initial impulse to be angry. Where had he been? She wanted to touch him, beat him, and press against him.

She opened the door. As soon as Sofia saw him, she smiled and vibrated as though a switch had been thrown and she chattered in Kaqchikel, a floodgate opening. Will bent to Sofia's ear and greeted her, then turned to Kate.

"You need to see this," he said. He lost his strained attempt at lightheartedness and his face had a sodden look, his facial muscles pulled back in preparation.

She stood aside and motioned for him to come in with one hand. She put Sofia down and the child clung to Will, patting his pant leg with her small hand. Will pulled a piece of paper from his jacket.

"I've been in Guatemala City. Don't ask me how I got this,

but it's a State Department report about VJ Kirkland, foreign correspondent. She was killed in a one-car accident outside of Oakland."

A rush of air escaped Kate's lips as if she'd been hit hard in the back, between her shoulder blades. "That's not possible. She could have only been back for a day. . . ." Every bit of courage that she possessed now rushed for the exits, leaving a vacuum. Her bones crushed inward. The atmospheric pressure threatened to snap her.

"Fernando told me she wouldn't be able to come back here, but . . ." Kate could only start sentences; the endings fell off into mist. She shouldn't have said Fernando's name, shouldn't have connected him to Kirkland.

"I can't tell you how I know this, but it's likely her death was not an accident. It was a message sent to other journalists, retaliation for her coverage of the massacre."

This was not the world that she had known and not the world that she wanted to be in. She gasped for air, pulling it in to stem the leak that Kirkland's death had sprung.

Kate staggered against the wall. She heard the noise of Marta's machinations in the kitchen. Will pushed aside the plastic curtain.

"Would you keep Sofia for a bit? Kate has just gotten bad news from home." But what did Marta know and what could they tell her? "One of her family has passed away, a cousin."

Marta pressed her lips in a consoling grimace, tilted her head, and said, "That one has had it hard. Yes, of course. I'll assign the two little ones to stirring dried beans in the kettle. You'd think I'd taken them to a carnival when they did that yesterday. Go on now."

Kate was rooted in the same place, tailbone pressed against the wall. Will took her hand and they ascended the stairs.

"Which room is yours?" he asked.

She pointed to the last room on the right off the balcony. There were four rooms and the Germans had taken the first two.

* * *

She would remember everything about this moment, how he tried to comfort her, how the picture of Kirkland killed in a car accident left her hollowed out. She would recall in vivid sensory detail the way his shoulder pressed against the door, the warm puff of his breathing, the curve of his neck. Who knew why this, why now?

They lay with each other as if they were old and married for decades, as if this is what they did when they came home at night, stretched out on the bed, telling each other about the day. They still had their clothes on, but Kate twined one leg around him, pressing into his side, resting her head on his shoulder.

She told him everything, starting with Manuela and her two small children and ending with how she picked up Sofia and walked away after the massacre.

He rubbed a circle over her heart with his palm, the dried riverbeds of her grief. The quenching rain of his touch shocked her.

Her face was wet. "I was someone else before the massacre, before I took Sofia. Sometimes I see my old self. There's a shadow of her in the mirror."

"You did what I couldn't do—I couldn't save Hector. I don't know how you carried her across that mountain. I don't know how you did any of it."

She sat up and pulled off her sweater. Will stood up and pushed a chair against the wobbly door, and flicked off the harsh overhead light. The glow from the courtyard windows illuminated them. She had let her hair fall over the tops of her breasts. In three steps he had pulled off his shirt; his pants fell away with a whoosh and they were together in bed.

A faint voice niggled at her—she should ask how he had learned about Kirkland—and yet the smell of his skin pushed any last remnants of language away. The press of his body, soft here, sharp there, mixed with their outstretched hands pressed hard into each other. Kate's body arched and opened.

* * *

When he left, it was dark. They had warmed the room as if their bodies had been furnaces. After the door closed behind him, Kate saw his socks on the floor, thick and dark. She gathered them up and slipped them under the covers, where she pressed them between her feet.

What did Kate really know about Kirkland? Maybe she had been exhausted, or distracted and driven off the road outside Oakland. She could have fallen asleep. Did she have too much to drink? Was the life of a foreign correspondent so rugged, so ungrounded by the lack of normal, mundane certainties of family and friends that Kirkland resorted to the comfort of drugs to cope? Or was this a clear message that Kate's present situation was far more dangerous than she could have imagined?

The military government didn't want the weight of world opinion against them. They didn't want a white woman and a small Mayan girl to emerge as witnesses to a massacre. If Kirkland's death had a message for Kate, it was get the hell out of there and take Sofia with her. Don't be distracted by the love of a man, the seductive curves of the banana trees, or the hypnotic beauty of the country and the people.

Message delivered and received. Except for the part about the love of a man like Will. That was going to have to be a big exception.

CHAPTER 27

Will
October 1990

He walked for the remainder of the day, past dusk, into the night, until he came to a town that was large enough that he could inquire about a place to stay. For the first time since leaving the United States, he was struck dead-on with dysentery and a fever that threatened to fry his brain. His immune system had been incinerated along with Hector's village. Through a fevered haze, he checked into a room, the kind that Peace Corps Volunteers called a one-sheeter. The bed had one sheet and a threadbare coverlet.

By the time Will fell back onto the bed, the number of sheets didn't matter. The hallucinations of his fever dragged him back to Hector's village, where the dirt of the mass grave exploded and every man, woman, and child walked past him, condemning him with their dead stares.

For four days he voided everything possible from his body. He was disassembled; parasites and amoebas follow the same opportunistic path that thieves do, checking to see which doors had been left unlocked.

He shivered so violently that the bed springs creaked, followed by a wave of sweat that soaked through all of his clothing. He woke once and searched for his clothes. Had he stripped off his clothes when he was hot, or had someone taken off his clothes? Had he soiled his pants or was that one of the nightmares? One morning, he saw his shirt and pants washed and folded, piled on his pack. When he emerged from his room, he asked what day it was. Five days had passed.

All the spaces newly carved by the amoebas and parasites were filled with the smell of Hector's village after the soldiers had murdered them. His winding trail of intestines had been emptied to make room for the carnage that he had caused. He owned it. He carried it. There was only life before the day that the resistance fighters held him at gunpoint and showed him the scorched-earth remains, and his life after.

Life before receded like a high-speed train, a green vibrant island of language, sidewalks of Brooklyn, the way his mother's hair fell across her face when she graded papers, bicycling through Manhattan, skimming the hot streets as he glided between lumbering cars, his friend Cesar teaching him to salsa, the slick sex with Lisa in their Outward Bound–issued sleeping bags, the taste of fresh tortillas when Hector's family had invited him for a meal, the way all of his life seemed honed for the moment he was called Language Specialist by the State Department.

After the guerillas allowed him to live, a swill of dark tar dripped over his eyes, seeped into his bloodstream, and reconstructed his bones and his breath, his taste buds and his heart. His heart had surely changed shape and color. His finely tuned ear detected the change in his pulse; the heart shriveled and solidified in a jagged, lacework design. This is why they let him live, not because they didn't want to shoot him; he was sure that they wanted to, but now he understood the brilliant craft of their justice.

Will was new to the way time twisted and staggered in

drunken oblivion when an old life was destroyed and a new version born. He would not have imagined that a month could go by as he sipped boiled water and gradually added in food, then a few more weeks as he advanced to sitting in the courtyard planning his strategy. By December he paid his final quetzales to the proprietor, hoisted his pack over one shoulder, and waited outside for the bus that would jostle him unmercifully all the way to Guatemala City, back to Ron Blackburn's office.

While every cell in Will's body had changed, Ron Blackburn looked untouched. His shirt was ironed fastidiously, the photo of his family still sat angled on the right corner of his desk, and he flipped open the box of cigars as if he and Will were still in mid-conversation from two months ago.

Will had typed in his report of the massacre on the office Selectric.

"You don't look well," said Blackburn. "Have the secretary give you the name of one of our doctors. They can fix you up. We've all had Montezuma's revenge."

Revenge? Is that what Will wanted? Hector's face was engraved on his brain. He handed the report to Blackburn.

"You've got a problem with Jenkins. I gave you benign information about agricultural use in the Dos Erres village and the result was mass murder. The military came in and annihilated the village. Torched it. Babies, children, women, old men, everyone. Is that what you're about?"

Will's rage hummed beneath the surface of his skin like fire ants eating their way out.

Blackburn closed the box of cigars. He pushed back in his chair.

"What you might not understand is that the villagers offer aid to the rebels—"

"What I understand is that you used me. Jenkins is well-known in the northern regions. They've got their own name for him. The Horned Toad, that's what they call him," said Will.

Blackburn shifted, closed his eyes, and took a breath. He slid open a drawer and unplugged a wire and let it snake into a coil on his desk. "A moment of silence will throw the Agency into a fit, so I'll be brief. We have a problem with some of our employees. They are more corporate and less governmental. And I have less control of them. They arrive one day and I'm supposed to fold them into our operation. Jenkins overstepped his position and I'm fully aware of it. The multinational companies hired him and now I'm stuck with him."

"Multinationals? Who?"

"That's not your problem. Shut up and listen. He will be demoted one rank, which is going to be like poking a bear with a sharp stick, but it's the best I can do. If I were you, I'd be very careful."

Blackburn picked up the wire. "I suggest that you find a new career. You are no longer on our books. Anything else?"

"You're firing me because I'm reporting Jenkins's massacre?" asked Will. "Are you okay with killing unarmed villagers? I mean wiping out entire villages of civilians." Will wanted more from him.

Blackburn put down the wire and wiped his face with both hands, starting at his forehead and moving down to either side of his neck. "I didn't invent the system. Read your history books. Unarmed civilians are precisely the people who are killed in wars." He plugged in the wire and closed the drawer.

"Thank you for coming in. This concludes the need for your linguistic services. The Department offers sincere thanks for your efforts to make Guatemala a free and democratic state. You can pick up your final check in several days."

The price for killing everyone in a village was a demotion, one rank down the ladder? Rage churned through Will's veins as he walked along the corridors, seeking the fresh air outside.

CHAPTER 28

Will

Will rubbed his thumb along the inside of Kate's arm. A wind chime rang with a new tempo as the gusts swirled throughout the city. Finding Kate changed everything. He was not cut out for revenge. He did not have to pursue Jenkins. He deliberately left out details about Jenkins when he described Hector's village to Kate. They could leave the worst of the horrors behind and start a new life in the States. He was positive that he could find a way. He would do this for Hector, for all the people who had died senselessly. Kate and Sofia were about living.

They squeezed into one chair outside Marta's kitchen, where they could keep an eye on the kids. Kate had one leg over his and they were turned inward to each other, a kind of V shape.

Time had accelerated with Kate; he had to speak up or she might slip away as soon as she obtained adoption papers. He swallowed hard. His vast linguistic skills were on the verge of failing him—all of his words were stuck in his throat, bumping into each other in terror that Kate would reject him. How to say something simply, clearly?

"If we were in the States and you and I had just met, I would . . ." He would what? Know that Kate was exactly the woman he wanted to spend the rest of his life with? How could she ever believe him? Kate had faced down armed soldiers, protected a child from helicopter gunfire, bushwhacked across Guatemalan mountains, and now he wanted to offer himself, his dubious, multilingual self. How could he measure up?

His lips trembled. "I'm in love with you. I want to be with you wherever you are. You and Sofia."

Was she smiling, had he ever seen such a tender smile? Was it meant for him? Then her smile left as she squeezed her lips together.

"You don't know enough about me. You only know this part right now. What if you knew everything about me and then it was too awful for you and you'd leave me?" Her last words were whispered. She turned her face away as if she had dragged the words through barbed wire.

"My father saved me after my mother died. I was going down hard and he pulled me back in. Even so, the first time I felt like I had some traction beneath me was when I went to college."

"What sort of traction? I might need to know," he said. He pressed his thigh against hers.

"Biology, science, things that jump out at you from beneath a microscope. Things that we are all made of. Water. The thing that I found in the biology and botany class was like someone switching on a light," she said, shaking her body like a damp dog, changing topics.

"What was your worst?" He was prepared to take in her hard years.

"The worst? Trying to blot out my mother's death with sex, alcohol, and a few drugs thrown in. My father had to pull me out of my own way again and again. I think we saved each other."

Will tried to picture a teenaged version of Kate, motherless and inconsolable. He took her hand and kissed it.

"It was just like my mother said, except I felt it explode inside me. We're all made of the same stuff. We all need water, sunlight, and food. We all thrive if we are touched, even tomato plants. In my last big drug blowout, I mean it was 1984 after all, my two textbooks merged like strands of DNA and they wrapped around me."

He put his right arm around her and pulled her into a crushing embrace.

"That's how you got some traction going? You are a funny scientist, all wrapped up in a big postapocalyptic-psychedelic DNA strand."

A sudden wave of warmth hinted at the end of the Guatemalan winter, something bursting up from the volcanic earth, the kind of air that made bougainvillea bloom and orchids unfold. Kate placed her hands on either side of his face.

"I never thought I'd find you here, but here you are. I don't need a microscope to see you." Kate looked like she was standing on the edge of a cliff, ready to fly or drop. She was taking that much of a chance with him.

Out of all the languages that he spoke, all the nuances, the tonalities, every musical bit of Mayan, he had never heard or felt anything as beautiful as Kate's words of love.

They played with Sofia until it was time for bed. Will read one of Felix's books to the children, tucking one on either side of him, the three of them nuzzling into Marta's couch. Felix put a pirate hat on Will's head and he kept it there, perched on his thick hair, tilting to one side.

Marta raised an eyebrow at Kate, then placed both hands over her heart and stage-whispered, "If I wasn't a married woman, I would have that man for breakfast."

"I heard that," said Will. Love was stitching him back together again. "All my breakfasts are spoken for." Forever.

CHAPTER 29

Will borrowed a motorbike from complicated means that included Fernando. He looked comically oversized perched on its seat and she wondered if it would make the first hill out of town.

"I need a day, maybe two in Guatemala City. One of my former language students in the Department could help with the documents for Sofia. It's a long shot but worth a try," said Will.

"Wouldn't they have to meet us, see us?" she asked. Will sat on the bike outside the doors of Marta's guesthouse. Kate wasn't sure who "they" were but Will had said that she should not know names.

"Not yet. If I get the green light, we'll use the photo that Marta took of Sofia for a passport."

Marta had taken a roll of film to a friend who patched together a dark room. They now had a series of round-eyed photos of the child with her hair stubbornly sticking up on one side.

Kate waved him off as he bumped along the cobblestones, spewing gray smoke.

They spent the night before together at Casa Candelaria, pulled together in a tight universe, making plans for leaving Guatemala. After Sofia was asleep, they tiptoed to Will's newly rented room two doors beyond Kate's and hungrily slipped out of their clothes and into bed.

The street noise had been muffled by the two-foot-thick stone-and-adobe walls. The walls of the small bedroom strummed to the only sound that had been reverberating within them for hours, the sound of lovemaking and their matched heartbeats.

She hadn't wanted to think about Kirkland, about Manuela, about small boys with soccer balls. She had reached up, placed her hands on either side of his jaw, and tilted his face so that she looked into his eyes.

"I can't keep looking at you," he managed to say before his body took over, before a river of sex and want turned into a white-hot light igniting them where they connected, as if a switch had been thrown, a giant circuit breaker that had been off for years and was suddenly turned on. Kate held on to his face.

"Don't look away, don't close your eyes."

She had never said this to anyone before. Kate wasn't sure if it was her own voice speaking. Here is the man who wouldn't leave her; they were bound by massacres and love.

A river of light shot up her spine, blue and astounding, from her tailbone to her skull. The light spiraled upward and then she saw it in Will's eyes too, the arc of it from one to another, bodies buckling and imploding. Eyes linked, both of them responded with a shout of unbridled surprise, a round sound and for Kate, without precedence. The distance that she had held between her and her old lovers crumbled.

They sagged against each other, sweating, patting faces, shoulders, shuddering, sighing, their corporeal selves jumbled amid the collision. Will pushed off to one elbow, his eyes soft and huge, pupils dilated so that only a rim of blue remained, his eyebrows rising up in the middle.

"What just happened?" he said. His lips were soft and swollen from kisses.

Kate's bones dissolved and what used to be her spine hummed with the remnants of light. A rooster from the next courtyard crowed. The thinnest layer of gray sliced through the curtain.

"Don't tell me . . ." she started. They understood simultaneously and laughed, slowly at first, then helplessly until tears cascaded. They laughed as the sun tried to light up the cobbled streets. They had made love all night. Morning had found them.

After Will left for Guatemala City, she took Sofia to the central park, a peaceful place. Stone paths began at the four corners, leading into a broad stone-paved circle around the fountain. The water bubbling from the breasts of the four statues drew everyone in. Today, an old Mayan woman rested on one of the benches that faced the fountain, her feet not touching the ground.

She walked with Sofia, forgoing the rebozo that would tie the child to her back. The going was arduously slow with a two-year-old, but it had to be a relief for Sofia to get outside the confines of the guesthouse. Still, the ten-minute stroll took forty-five minutes due to Sofia's curiosity with every crevice in the sidewalk. By the time they reached the fountain, Kate welcomed the chance to sit down on a bench, while Sofia continued on, fascinated by the water.

As she stood up, a man appeared just a few feet from her.

"Adoption?" he said.

She took a step back. He was American, unremarkable in all ways except one. He had a lump, the size of a robin's egg, located between his left eyebrow and his hairline. She tried not to look at it. Why didn't he get something like that removed? Surely he could.

"Are *you* here to adopt? Is that why you assume that I am?" she said. Something about him grated at her. She forced herself to look at his eyes and not the protrusion.

"Am I being rude? I know in Guatemala that you can't just ever say what you want to say. There's all the inquiry about family, the food, the endless customs. But I saw another American and my old New Jersey boy came out." He smiled and squinted so much that she couldn't see his eyes. He extended his hand. "Henry Matthews."

"Kate," she said, deciding against an alias. His hand covered hers and he held it too long. The child had just stepped into a bed of flowers. Calla lilies. Kate pulled her hand out of his grip.

"Sofia, stay with me, over here."

"Oh, let her be," he said. "I haven't spoken with a gringo all week and I need to speak English every now and then. We can see her from here."

We? There was no *we*. This was a mistake.

"I have an appointment, otherwise I'd stay and talk for a bit. But I'm already late," she said.

Kate picked up Sofia, swinging her onto her hip. There was a hint of spring in the air. A few rain clouds emerged from the western sky.

"Allow me to walk you out of the park then. If you think you're late for an appointment in Guatemala, then you're early. Are you working with one of the adoption outfits in Antigua? They're all government-run, you know. Eventually you have to negotiate with them. Ghastly system."

She felt like she was eight years old and a bad man had just stopped his car to offer her a ride. She wanted to shake him off, but he stuck to her like a burr. She didn't want to go back to Marta's because she didn't want him to see where she lived. Not Fernando's café either; she didn't want to drag in an unknown.

"I have a medical appointment. Parasites," she said.

His nose twitched as if he could catch the scent. "Yes, of course. The scourge of the third world. Maybe I'll run into you again. You never know." He pivoted on one foot and turned to go. He looked at her over his shoulder. "But Kate, you don't want to jeopardize your chances with the child. I know people. I could help you."

This is where she should walk away. And if Kate had been in Massachusetts or Davis, she would have. If she had not found Will and the suddenness of his love, if she hadn't held Sofia in her arms, if she hadn't been scared senseless by Kirkland's death, if the entire landscape of her world hadn't shifted, then yes, she would have walked away. But what if this man, who made her pull her sweater closer around her chest, could help her? What if one little dip into the black market could set them free? Had she just found a black market possibility for papers?

"How could you help me?" Kate kept Sofia on the hip farthest from the man. Will said his contact in Guatemala City was a long shot. Could this man be any less of a long shot? The playing field changed on the day the soldiers shot Manuela and her son.

"I understand their system. I've worked with an adoption agency from the United States. Once you know your way around, it's quite simple. Well, it wouldn't be simple for you, but the government agencies trust me and they kindly remove roadblocks. But you shouldn't trust just anyone and you don't know me. So . . ." He turned his hands so that they opened, palms facing inward, soft and without aggression, priestly.

Kate felt like she was hiking in the White Mountains with her mother at dusk when they had to decide whether to turn back or not, straddling the option, wanting to go on, to get to a lookout that drew her mother with the promise of a sunset.

"Let's drop our packs and run," she had said, thrilling Kate. When they stumbled back into camp at dark two hours later, her father was furious.

"What were you thinking?" he shouted, still reverberating with anger.

"I was thinking that sometimes you have to break the rules. It was a magnificent sunset," said her mother.

Was this one of those times when you had to break the rules?

"Wait," said Kate. "Tell me how you could help." If ever there was a time to break the rules, it was now.

He turned around, smiled and blinked. "I know a place where we can talk, a cantina." He pointed one finger in the opposite direction from Marta's guesthouse. "Unless you'll be late for your medical appointment . . . I wouldn't want to keep you from taking care of yourself."

She didn't have to like him; she just had to get his help. He was as noxious as the gas fumes spewing from the buses.

"How far away is the cantina?"

"Three blocks. Would you like me to carry the girl?" he asked, tilting his head to the side.

"No. Let's go." This would be a time-limited encounter. If he could help them, she could tolerate him for a brief time.

The cantina was three blocks behind the cathedral, unremarkable, small and dark.

"What would you need to orchestrate the adoption?" said Kate. She tried to imagine how Kirkland would handle this.

He sat across from her at the small table. The tip of his shoe touched hers and she moved her foot away. Sofia sat on her lap, munching on a tortilla fresh from the kitchen.

"Your name, address. Passport number. And the status of the child. How did you come by her? I want to stop calling her the child. What is her name?"

Kate's heart rate was gathering speed and the sound of her own blood began to pound. "Katherine Malloy, Leverett, Massachusetts." She dug into her bag where she carried a copy of her passport. She wrote down the number on a scrap of paper. "Her name is Sofia. She is an orphan. Her parents were killed."

He pulled the paper toward him, grazing her hand. "War is a terrible thing." He slid the paper into his shirt pocket.

She waited for more. More what, she wasn't sure, but this couldn't be all the man needed. "What else?" she said.

"That will be all that I need to get this started. There will be the expense, naturally, but I am doing this mostly as a favor, to help a fellow American. But in order for this to work, I need your most solemn promise to keep this confidential. If anyone was to get wind of this, my credibility would be destroyed and I would no longer be able to help people. And I mean no one, Kate, not friends, family, or lovers. Do you have a lover?"

She pulled back from the table. "That is none of your business." She didn't like how she sounded, young and reactive. "When will you know something?"

He smiled again and Kate felt something slip away from her

grasp but she couldn't say exactly what it was. She needed to be careful of him. She couldn't shake the feeling that he had touched her where he should not.

"Oh, three days, tops. I'll meet you here in three days at noon. You'll have everything that you need," he said.

He stood up to leave, placing a hand on her shoulder as he passed. Her shoulder muscles retracted from his touch.

She waited five minutes, then yanked open the door and walked quickly back to Marta's. There was no way to contact Will, to let him know that she had dipped into the black market to get a passport and adoption papers for Sofia. She would tell him the instant that he returned.

CHAPTER 30

Will

Will shifted gears, and dust from the road curled up around him, leaving memories of dogs, the breath of skinny cows, dried dung, the leaves of the banana trees, and ground coconut shells. The smell of gas lingered on his fingers after he had filled the small tank. He shifted into low gear and bumped along the cobblestones through the center of Antigua.

He rode past the *mercado* where the dark essence of black beans rolled along the streets like a Chinese dragon, flipping its tail here and there. He didn't have time to stop; Emerson had promised to meet him. He rode up and out of the broad valley that was Antigua, pausing once at the top of the hill where the thickness of smoke thinned out.

Two active volcanoes spewed their own smoke on the outskirts of town. Will wondered if anyone would survive if either of the volcanoes erupted. Would it be like Mt. St. Helens, with everything buried in six feet of hot ash?

His former landlord, Jimenez, assured him that the daily

spewing of a few sparks and a steady plume of smoke meant that the volcano was happy and healthy. It was only when the volcano went silent and let pressure build up that he should worry.

"It is like this," Jimenez said while sipping a drink of hibiscus and fresh lime water. "We all need to let the pressure off every day. The pressure of love, anger, sadness. The volcano is the wise one. Take the advice of a wise volcano—don't let the bad vapors build up inside you."

Emerson picked a bar in Zone 10, where tourists were most likely to congregate. It wouldn't be noteworthy to see two gringos having a drink on a patio.

"I didn't think I'd be hearing from you again. You're not recruiting for language school, are you? We determined that I was a lost cause with language," said Emerson. He reminded Will of his old friend Cesar back in Brooklyn. He and Emerson had played a few games of basketball when he taught and they found an easy, joking camaraderie. "You still owe me one million quetzals from the last game."

"I need your help," said Will.

"Then that will make it two million Q. Sorry to hear that you got fired. I heard it got rough out there in the mountains. That was a bad mess." Emerson tapped his beer bottle with the fingers of his right hand as if he was playing a flute.

Will didn't want to talk about Hector's village. "I need help with adoption papers for a friend. She needs to take a child out of Guatemala and back to the States. This is what you guys are good at, right?"

Will slid the envelope of identity papers and Sofia's photo across the table. Emerson smiled at Will and didn't look down. Instead he motioned to a waiter with his left arm, pulling the envelope to his lap with the right.

"If this is all you want, it could be the easiest part of my day. New Identities R Us. We are creative with official stamps."

Will was taking a chance with him. He felt his body unclench with relief. "She's not just a friend. I'll be leaving with her for the States. I guess I had to come all the way to Guatemala to find the right woman. She's incredible. I wish you could meet her."

"No, you don't. I'm far too impressive. She'd probably dump you for me," said Emerson. The waiter brought two more beers. "Give me a full day to make sure the ink is dry." Emerson pulled out a slip of paper and wrote an address on it. "Meet me here in two days. And buddy? You should watch your back with Jenkins. He's stinking pissed and he's not a nice man. Blackburn demoted him one notch and you'd think that his world had ended."

Demoted. There was nothing equitable about being demoted for killing everyone in Hector's village. "In my world, we call people like him a gangster. But that's in Brooklyn and they die young. I can only hope the same for him," said Will. He shook off the volcano that brewed inside him. "I'll be long gone and making a new life with my family," he said, startled by the vision. His family. Kate and Sofia.

Emerson stood up. "Two million Q and counting, bro."

Two more days, and they could make plans to leave.

"Are you in town for tonight? Stick around. I'd be willing to kick your ass in basketball again."

Will had wanted to go back to Antigua if at all possible, but the thrill of Emerson helping him, a pickup game of basketball, mingled with the rocketing euphoria of new love, left him reckless. He'd return to Antigua with papers in hand.

"Prepare to lose to a superior player," Will said.

CHAPTER 31

It was late afternoon when he pulled up to the cantina where Emerson said to meet him. It was the kind of place that operatives liked to meet for serious work, not a tourist in sight. Behind the building, a field lay dormant and dry. It would have been a good spot for kids to play soccer.

He opened the door and selected a seat where he could see the door. Jenkins walked in. Will froze.

"You were expecting someone else?" said Jenkins. Will didn't know the man's first name, didn't want to.

"Where's Emerson?" said Will, his back against the wall in the small restaurant, far outside the business district of Guatemala City.

Jenkins pulled a chair out, wiped down the seat with a handkerchief, and sat down. Chickens murmured outside, and Will was sure he smelled beans and cilantro. They were the only customers in the four-table room.

"Emerson has been reassigned, but not before he shared a few tidbits with me. It seems he was bringing you a birth certificate and adoption papers for a certain . . ." Jenkins extracted a manila envelope from inside his jacket and slapped it on the table. "Here we are. Sofia Malloy, age two, orphan, now the daughter of Katherine Malloy. He did excellent work on the adoption papers."

The beer that Will downed while waiting turned sour in his stomach. He didn't want this guy anywhere near Kate or Sofia.

He allowed himself one glance at the envelope. "Where did Emerson get relocated?"

Jenkins smiled. "Did I say relocated? I meant that he's gone missing. Darndest thing. Assignments in Latin America are some of the most dangerous. Nuns and priests are gunned down. Terrible. This is a violent country." He drummed his fingers along the envelope.

Emerson was dead. No one really went missing.

Jenkins pushed the envelope toward Will. "Everything is in order. Kate, lovely Kate, is listed as guardian. She'll have no trouble at the Mexican or the American border. They make a stunning mother and daughter, don't you agree? Kate's blond hair is so disarming when she piles it on top of her head, along with the child's jet-black hair."

Will didn't take his eyes off the man. More was coming. Jenkins was only waiting for dramatic effect.

"You weren't thinking of going with them now, were you? Perhaps run home to Brooklyn and set up a little language school like your charming mother, with your new family?"

The marrow in his bones froze, starting at his pelvis and spreading out to his spine, arms, and legs.

"You'll find that your identity papers have become a bit messy. Let me speak candidly. You no longer have identity papers. You can't leave Guatemala."

Will pictured getting across the Mexican border almost effortlessly as an American. But the U.S. border was another matter.

"Your name and your photo are posted at every American border. You will be arrested and turned over to the stateside CIA if you attempt to reenter the country. Those boys are a rough bunch. We couldn't protect you, Will, and there's no telling where you might end up."

Will's muscles boiled with fear and rage, every cell preparing for battle, to reach across the table and destroy Jenkins, choke the life out of him, slit his throat with a cracked beer bottle.

Jenkins leaned back with luxury. "Tempting, isn't it? Bash my head in, leave the body behind this dump of a building? Find Kate and make a run for it. The owner of this fine establishment is on our payroll. If I am harmed, we have a fail-safe, sort of a bomb that's ready to go off in Brooklyn. Your mother teaches English at the Catholic church on Parkhurst, Mondays and Wednesdays I believe. She will get a new student, a Spanish-speaking immigrant from El Salvador. He will approach her after class and kidnap her, kill her (we give him free rein in his creativity), and dispose of her so that her body is never found."

Will dropped from rage to terror. He had no way to stop this man, this monster that even Ron Blackburn couldn't control.

"Let's say you try to warn her about bad men trying to kidnap her. Let's say you leave with your charming Kate and the child. We have plans for the child. She is a lovely girl, suitable for international adoption after a grinding stay in an orphanage." Jenkins paused. "Rather like a plot straight out of Dickens, don't you think?" He picked lint from his sleeve with languid attention.

"I didn't like being demoted as a result of your little fit in the office. You put him in a terrible place. He would have never known about your village of rebels—"

Will pounded the table with his fists. "You idiot! They weren't rebels."

"No matter. In the envelope you'll find plane tickets for Kate and the Mayan brat. The flight leaves tonight so you'd best get on your way. If they don't make the flight, the child will be picked up. Kate would never see her again. No time to dawdle. In fact, they might not make it." Jenkins looked at his watch, placing one finger under the metal band, stretching it out to let fresh air roll along his broad wrist.

"Why should I believe that you'd allow them to leave?"

"Because that's the beauty of this. Short-term suffering is nothing in my field. When I'm wronged, I go straight for long-term suffering, which is just what I've handed you." Jenkins smiled.

Will wanted to grab him around the neck and crush his throat. Every cell in his body wanted to exterminate this man. The sound of a helicopter slid through his rage.

"That's my ride," said Jenkins. He got up and walked out the back door of the cantina. A cloud of dust rose up and Jenkins ducked his head into his elbow, a handkerchief over his face. The helicopter door opened and Jenkins stepped in.

Will ran out to the miserably small bike. It would take him an hour to get back to Antigua. And he would need to make one stop before he went to Kate.

CHAPTER 32

Will

Will knocked on Fernando's door after closing time. His entire drive from Guatemala City, racing around cars, swerving in and out of traffic, was spent formulating a way to get Kate and Sofia to the airport. If he was going to take a chance with this man, no one else could know. Kate had assured Will that she trusted Fernando with her heart and her life. Will had been tangled in her legs and her soft smell. It was dawn and they had slept little.

"But you've only known him for a few weeks," he had pointed out, rolling a clump of her blond hair around his index finger. "Don't get me wrong, I think he's a straight-up guy. But I've been burned by believing the wrong people. How can you be sure of him?"

Kate ran the sole of her foot along his shinbone, cupping his leg with her foot. "Kirkland told me to find him and that I could trust him. Then I had to go with my gut." She looked beyond his shoulder. "I had to let go of science and drop my brain into my stomach and when I did that, I knew that Fernando was about goodness. If my mother had been with me, she would have loved him."

Fernando opened his door.

"I need your help. I can't leave with Kate," he told him, "and I have to make sure that she leaves with Sofia."

Fernando turned on a small lamp in the inner courtyard. What if Kate was wrong, what if Fernando was an informant? How does one drop the brain into the gut? Fernando was a slight man, compact, delicate by North American standards.

"What is it that you want me to do?" Fernando said, folding his hands on the table.

The air shifted between them from floating on the surface to a quick descent. Was it because the man was protecting Kate and the child? He needed Fernando if his plan was going to work. Will switched to Spanish.

"I have adoption papers for the child, but I can't leave Guatemala. My passport and all identity papers have been compromised. If Kate thinks that I'm staying here, I'm afraid she won't leave." Will hoped that his Spanish would help.

"Your Spanish is impeccable. I understand you are proficient in the Mayan languages as well. There is no one left in Dos Erres to appreciate your linguistic skills." Fernando kept his eyes on Will.

"So you know everything that happened. There was a boy, Hector . . ." Will hadn't been prepared to cry in front of Fernando. He turned his head to the side and fought for control of his lips, chin, and voice.

"I asked them about agriculture, where they sold their corn. I lived with them. When I left I promised Hector that I would bring him a new soccer ball. The kid was so fast with the crappy ball that he had." He swallowed. "When I returned weeks later, I was stopped by the resistance fighters. The village had been gutted, burned, the people massacred. You know that part. They let me live because they wanted me to suffer with the knowledge that I had been responsible."

Will felt time nipping at his heels. "I cannot let anything happen to Kate and Sofia. They have one chance to leave together."

Fernando gave away little in facial expression. Will wouldn't want to play poker with him.

"What do you need?"

"Can you get us to the airport?"

"When?"

"Now. There's one flight and they have to get on it."

Fernando stood up. "Get them ready. I'll pick you up in ten minutes."

"Do you have a car?" Will was doubtful.

Fernando smiled. "No. But one can be had. Ten minutes."

CHAPTER 33

She heard his footsteps, light, his body lifting and landing, the muscles in his legs so full of sureness. His running shoes lapped along the terra-cotta tiles of the courtyard. His footsteps stopped, paused at the step.

Kate knew he was there and she waited, a towel in one hand from Sofia's bathing. Then he knocked, the exact same knock he always used; he was blindingly consistent with his knocks. Kate pictured them living together in a house in Maine or Cape Cod and each day when Will came home, he'd use the knock, and her heart would leap just as it did now.

Kate opened the door as if it was a question, the way it works in Spanish with the question mark at the front of the sentence. Why the pause? She tilted her head to one side and saw only the tanned face of the man who wanted to help her, the man who saw her, really saw who she was.

He looked exactly the same; everything was going to be fine. He smiled his gorgeous toothy smile, a product of North American precision with dentistry, and stepped into the room bearing fresh palm-sized tortillas and cheese wrapped in paper. She opened her arms to him, folding him in through her skin. His left hand moved to the back of her neck. Kate felt the extra moisture on his palm, then the slightest tremble, unlike him.

"Fill your pack. We are going to the airport in Guatemala City. Here is some food for the trip."

Kate staggered back, her core collapsing, hit dead center with a bag of cement. From the corner of the room, Sofia trilled her new word. "Water, water," she said, keeping the accent sweetly on the last syllable.

"It's too soon. I thought we would have more time to get ready." Suddenly everything about the cobbled streets, their bed, bathing Sofia in the bucket was precious. What would await them in the States? Her hands grasped at the air like she was searching for a cord of time, pulling it back to her.

"It's time," he said.

She'd been bathing Sofia, singing the "Itsy-Bitsy Spider" song in a warbling duet. Sofia sat in a large metal bucket, the preferred option to the shower.

"I have a car waiting for us," he said.

"Now?" Why hadn't he warned her? It was nearly dark out; evening church bells were ringing. Should she tell him about Henry Matthews? Maybe she didn't need to.

"What—how—does this mean that you have papers for Sofia? How could you possibly have done that?" She grabbed a towel, wrapped it around the slick child, and picked her up. Sofia chirped something in Kaqchikel to Will. Kate had given up trying to stop the two of them from speaking Mayan. Sofia's full-out delight was impossible to deny with Will.

The three of them left the small bathroom and headed to Kate's room. Will placed his hand on her back, pushing slightly. "I'll wait out here while you two get ready. But Kate, you have to hurry. We have to be on the eight o'clock flight."

"Oh, Sofia," she said as she hugged the girl and whirled around. It had only taken her a few minutes to adjust to the shock of leaving. She dressed her in long pants and a small sweatshirt. She put everything she had into the same small backpack that she'd taken from Santiago; one skirt, two pairs of jeans, thick leather sandals, and lastly, Will's socks. . . . cramming all of it down hard into the dark caverns of the pack. She retrieved her passport from beneath her pillow. Sofia's underwear and skirt were tossed in. Lastly, she lifted the mattress and retrieved the cloth that Manuela had woven. She rolled it tight and rammed it beneath everything else.

Home, they were going home. Were they flying to New York or Boston? She didn't even know yet. She and Will would squeeze Sofia between them on the plane, keeping her safe from the bombardment of a new culture.

Kate slipped the pack on her back and took Sofia's hand.

"We're ready."

Will leaned against the balcony overlooking the inner courtyard. He'd been in Guatemala more than two years; leaving had to be bittersweet for him. Some part of him was resisting, the way his hand rubbed the stair rail. She couldn't blame him. He had become closer with people here than she'd ever been able to. The language specialist.

They were going home and they were going to be safe. She'd carry them all with her belief, like a rocket.

He reached out a hand to her. "The driver's waiting."

She jerked to a stop. "Marta! We've got to say good-bye to her and little Felix."

"I passed Marta on her way out. She's going to some potluck. I wish we could, but we have tickets, reservations, and we can't miss this flight. Everything is on go now, just a little faster than we had planned."

They started down the wide stairs. "And Fernando. We can drive by and say good-bye. I could never leave without thanking him." She pulled hard on Will's arm and felt an extra tautness that had not been there before.

"No need to go by his café. He's driving us to the airport. I asked for his help."

Will held a manila envelope in one hand. "I have everything here—our tickets and all the papers that you'll need for Sofia. As of today, she is adopted, with all the international stamps and passports and gold seals that you'll ever need."

A sweetness rushed into her throat. She could tell him now, absolve the weight of secrecy that had descended on her. "This means we don't have to go through the guy who was going to help me. I didn't want to tell you—"

Will stopped as if he had walked into a wall. "What guy? What are you talking about?" They were at the front door.

"Some guy who used to work with adoption, a gringo, who said he'd help me get papers. I met him two days ago."

"Where?"

"Right here. In the central park. I just bumped into him with Sofia. He made me promise not to tell anyone." Something was wrong. Will looked like he'd been struck.

"What did he look like?"

"Older gringo, squinty eyed, sort of on the make, big lump on his forehead. Don't worry, I knew what I was doing." Why did she feel like they were sinking, sliding downward?

"Oh God, what have you done?" He yanked open the door to the street. Fernando waited with the engine running.

"What do you mean?"

"Just get in, quickly." The car was a VW bug, ten years old at least, 1980. Kate's mother drove one for years. Kate and Sofia crammed into the backseat. Will jumped into the passenger seat.

Fernando smiled and turned to Kate. "It is my great pleasure to be your escort out of the country. Please pardon the bumpy ride."

Kate reached up and squeezed his shoulder.

Will turned around in his seat. "It was not an accident that you bumped into that man. His name is Jenkins," said Will.

"He told me his name was Henry Matthews."

Will curled forward with his head in his hands and a shudder ran through his torso. "You didn't do anything wrong. He was responsible for the massacre in Hector's village and I exposed him to his boss. He was demoted as a result. He's been out for blood ever since. He was here to find a way to get revenge. I should have known he'd try to get to you. You didn't know, it's not your fault."

Kate ran through the conversation with the man with the lump on his head. How had she been so oblivious? Now, with Will's added information, each word and glance seemed so obvious. And malevolent.

"But are we okay? We can still leave? You said you had adoption papers."

Will glanced over at Fernando as the man navigated along the cobblestone streets. "Everything will be okay. We're an hour from the airport and we can still make the flight."

As Kate stepped out of the car at the airport with Sofia in her arms, Fernando embraced her. "Don't leave a trail. There is a saying from the highlands—don't drop crumbs unless you want the jaguar to follow." Fernando put his palms on either side of Sofia's face and kissed the top of her head.

They came to the gate where passports and tickets were demanded. Fernando said he'd wait until they were gone, standing by the wall. Will stepped aside and nodded to Kate to go through, handing over her passport, the tickets, and Sofia's documents.

Kate's breath scalded her throat, burning with fear. The uniformed man looked at the documents, flicking his eyes to Kate's face, turning the pages of Sofia's adoption papers, eyeing them with extra scrutiny. He reached beneath the podium where he held the rights and privileges of all who passed through the border. Kate's breath stopped. But he brought out his stamp, pressed it into an inkpad and stamped both passports. Will's would of course be easier. Nothing fancy, just a guy going home. She stepped through and turned around to see Will, but the other passengers had squeezed through the checkpoint.

Will stood off to the side, still within arm's reach if she tried.

"What are you doing? Come on." Sofia was heavy on her hip, wiggling, wanting to get down. Wanting Will.

Will's eyes had the unblinking stare that her mother's had held when she was dying, the otherworldliness, the stripped skinless look that Kate did not expect to see on him.

"You have to get on the plane. Start walking, Kate. This is how it has to be. You've got to trust me." He looked over at a clock on the wall. "They're boarding and you have to get on. It must be this plane."

What had he done? Had he betrayed her, led her to love him, love Sofia, and then sent them away?

Kate stopped, put down her pack and her child. The ragged clutch of rejection mingled with shock, seeing others stare at them. They were now the epicenter of a drama. An airport guard turned to Will, his hand on the automatic weapon. She would refuse, they would talk this through, get past this last-minute panic on Will's part.

Will told the guard in Spanish, "One last embrace, please, for my frightened one," he said, winking, arms wide, palms open.

Within inches of the gate, he beckoned to Kate and she walked into his arms. His broad smile never reached his eyes. He whispered into her neck. "If you don't get on this flight, they will take Sofia and you will never see her again. They have taken my passport. You must be very brave. Do not look back. I love you."

His voice caught on the last three words. He pushed her away saying loudly for all to hear, "There now. See you stateside. Good-bye, sweetie."

In stunned slow motion, Kate reached down for Sofia's hand again, backing up, keeping Will in sight. What had she done? Why did she talk to the man in the park? The flight attendant stood near the open door leading to the plane. She gave Kate a come-along hand motion. Kate walked backward down the corridor, watching Will until she could see him no longer.

Her seat faced the airport gate. She could still see Will, his hand pressed to the window. She was crying and she couldn't stop, her chest seizing with pain. What was happening? What exactly had she done? Was this all her fault? She sat in the window seat with Sofia on her lap.

"May I join you?"

Kate looked up and saw Henry Matthews. Jenkins. She froze. He sat down and then leaned over to her, waving through the window.

"Let's wave farewell to your heroic, linguistically talented Will. Ah, he seems to recognize me."

Crushed by his body, Kate was pushed to the side of the aircraft. She kept her body between Jenkins and Sofia.

Here was the man who had something to do with another massacre, who wanted to hurt Will, who had lied to her.

"No, you can't join me," she said. She turned to look back at the airport window. Will exploded, pounded the window, and shouted, his face a grimace of agony. Two gendarmes grabbed him and he tore out of their arms. The dark silhouette of a gun rose, then smashed into Will, and he dropped.

"No, stop! Stop them!" shouted Kate.

"That boy should really settle down," said Jenkins. "Local jails are not a pleasant place. But then I don't really care about his comfort."

"What have you done?" Were they going to kill him? She prayed that Fernando had seen what had happened.

Two military jeeps pulled alongside the plane. Were they taking her too? And Sofia?

"I'll be getting off here," he said. "But here is what you will do. If you ever tell anyone about Will or his wild stories about massacres, I will have him killed." Jenkins smiled and glanced down at his hands, examining one fingernail. "If you contact a congressman, Amnesty International, perhaps an attorney specializing in international law, if we even get the slightest hint, I will have him killed. And then we will take care of your café owner."

Kate froze, wind sluicing down the corridors of her spine. Fernando?

"Say it, Kate. Say you will never speak of him again, never try to contact him, never tell anyone about his allegations in the Dos Erres village. It's up to you."

The door to the plane opened to reveal two additional men.

Jenkins put his hand on the seat back in front of him and pulled up, rising.

Kate wanted to kill him. She'd never felt that way about anyone before. Jenkins drew in hate like a black hole.

"Stop! I will never contact him. I will never tell anyone about the village. . . ." She wanted to say massacre. She wanted to say Manuela, Hector, babies, women, men. "I will never tell anyone about the allegations. I will never say his name."

Jenkins turned to face her. "Very good. Now, would you like to say his name one more time? I'm not without some feelings of tenderness for young love. One more time, Kate, for the last time, say his name."

She wanted to shout it, scream his name loud enough to be heard throughout the world. She wanted to say it in the dark, back in Antigua, close to his skin. She didn't want to say it to Jenkins, not in the demented way that he offered her. Kate's breath caught in the middle of her throat and turned solid, a tennis ball of air clutching her windpipe. She had to act like she had nothing to fear, like she was just another blond tourist on her way home.

"Will," she whispered. She touched her lips with her fingers to catch his name.

Jenkins straightened his jacket. "Good." He joined the two men at the door and the three of them disembarked. They injected a red static charge into the air. If someone lit a match, they'd all explode. The flight attendants closed the doors again and the plane rolled out on the runway.

Sofia, who had rarely cried in the terrible weeks since her mother and brother were killed, now let loose. She screamed, pointing back to where Will had been, eyes bulging. Sofia stood on the seat, grabbed Kate's hair in one tiny hand, and stomped her feet in blind fear.

The passengers in nearby seats turned and stared, possibly wondering if the child would wail all the way to Texas, which was where this flight was headed. The flight attendants, three women, all turned to look at the blond gringo with the hysterical brown-skinned toddler screaming for her life.

* * *

After an hour of crying, Sofia was exhausted. Kate made a nest of her zippered sweatshirt and a pair of jeans so that Sofia could lie down and put her head on Kate's thigh. She waited until the child shuddered into sleep and her brown hands uncurled. Kate pulled a scarf over the girl's face as far as she could without waking or suffocating her. Then Kate turned her head to one side and closed her eyes. She dipped in and out of sleep, from wakefulness to the halfway place of visions, her chest ripped open. She could never tell anyone.

Sofia stirred, her eyes opened, and Kate patted her back, hoping to rub the girl back to sleep. Kate forced down the glob of fear in her chest and took shallow breaths.

In two hours, they landed in Dallas. At the immigration gate, the agent looked at her paperwork and said, "Welcome home."

Was she home? The man she loved had been wrenched from her and she didn't know if he was alive. She wanted to smash something, kick a garbage can, howl out her rage.

She picked up Sofia and looked for the gate for Boston.

Part Three

2003

Massachusetts

CHAPTER 34

The clock ticked on the mantel of Kate's house. Her sit bones pressed against the unyielding brick of the fireplace hearth. How long had she been sitting here with Sofia and her father? Had she stopped talking? What did she tell them? Only what she knew. And what Will had told her. But what had she left out? Kate didn't know if she had told them about the way heat pumped off Will's body at night. Had she? She had not spoken his name in twelve years, even after it was safe to do so.

Sofia sat curled on their couch. *Stunned,* that would be a good word for her. Somewhere in the telling, Sofia found her soccer ball and pulled it close to her chest, the way a child does with a stuffed animal.

Sam was frozen. His glass of seltzer was still in front of him, on the coffee table, untouched.

"Did I say his name out loud?" Kate said. An old alarm ran through her body.

The question released her father. "Yes, sweetie, you said Will's name. I think you said it all. Or is there more?"

Her father knew about holding stories in; his tales of Vietnam came out only in bits that could fit on a postage stamp. There was always more, ready to launch him from his sleep as he screamed his way out of a nightmare.

"I can't tell you what it was like for Will, only what he did to help me bring Sofia out."

Her father stood up. "I should have known something was wrong when I picked you up at Logan Airport. You looked like a soldier coming back from battle, that dark-eyed, nerves-incinerated look. But it didn't make any sense. And then there was Sofia."

He turned to his granddaughter, extending his hands, palms up. "I fell in love like this," he said, snapping his fingers.

Kate had imagined only the worst scenarios if she told them what happened, that the world would crack and shatter, ghouls would descend and take Sofia away. Surely Kate had broken laws. But now she felt scraped clean of barnacles, polished, with a breeze sluicing through her lungs, something fresh, off the ocean, filled with salt air.

Sofia let the soccer ball drop to her knees, roll down her shins, and trapped it between her feet. The ball had been an extension of her body since she first began playing, back when she was just seven. What rumblings could this have stirred in her? She must have questions, accusations. What tirade would erupt about the betrayal of her elemental truth of birth, kin, and blood?

"Did Martin know?" asked Sofia. Now he was Martin, not Dad. But why that question, of all things? Was this a first-layer kind of question?

"He found out about a year after we were married. He knew as much as you saw in his letter. He disagreed vehemently about not telling you. We almost split up over this. He loved you so much. . . ." Kate's chest tightened and refused to let out anything but a shudder.

"He knew about Will?" asked Sofia.

It was strange to hear someone else say his name, first her father, now Sofia. "He knew that I had loved someone, that part of me still loved him. He knew that much."

Sofia stood up, flipped the soccer ball into the air with her foot, over her head, and it crashed into a lamp, sending it off an end table, miraculously cushioned by a rug.

"I lost everyone! It's not fair; why do I have to lose everyone?" cried Sofia. The full weight of the deaths crushed her. She spun on her heel and ran out of the room, up the stairs. The impact of the slammed bedroom door shook the glass on the living room windows.

Kate started to follow her.

"Don't," said her father. "She needs to be alone. Some kinds of grief can't be let out in front of others."

Kate sank back into a fat green chair.

Hours later, Kate emerged from the bathroom to find her father leaning against the wall.

"Is the Jenkins guy still there?" asked Sam.

"No. He was one of the last casualties of the war. About six months before the peace accord was signed, when Sofia was seven, a letter came. I didn't recognize the handwriting. The postmark was Baltimore. It said, 'The horned toad is dead.' That was it, direct and to the point. Will must have had a friend take the letter north. I don't know anyone in Baltimore."

Sam had a towel draped over one shoulder. "Good," he said, squeezing his fists. He had on a white T-shirt and plaid pajama pants that Sofia had given him for Christmas. "The bastard. The CIA must have disposed of him, that's my guess. Or whatever private corporation had used him. A guy like that was too much trouble for them."

He rubbed the stubble along his chin. "I can't wrap my head around what you must have been going through after you came home and how lonely it had to be, despite how it looked on the outside. You looked like a girl overwhelmed by being a new mother, finishing your degree, you know, all of that. When you didn't date anyone for years, I just thought, how could she have time for romance? And then there was Sofia. . . ."

Kate heard the faucet dripping. Sam turned his left ear to the sound and said, "I'll fix that tomorrow."

She knew he would fix anything for her and Sofia, anything that he could.

"What happened to him? What happened to Will?" asked Sam.

CHAPTER 35

1992, Massachusetts

In the first year, Kate woke from nightmares feeling shattered from the sound of gunfire, pummeled by the black boots of the military, and sat bolt upright in bed. Then she'd run to Sofia's room, heart pounding, to make sure the child was still asleep, still there. She'd sink to the floor next to the child's bed, sometimes sleeping on the rug or sliding in bed next to the small girl.

Her longing for Will was palpable; she imagined his arm pulling her tight, his belly pressed hard against her back. The next day would bring the balm of safety, a trip to story hour at the library or any of the things that marked the territory as beyond the reach of murder on the stone streets of Atitlán.

When she was alone with Sofia, outside, it felt like Will was right there with them. She imagined telling him, *Look how big she's getting, how she laughs, how good it is to be here, just like we wanted.* He would press his lips to the back of her neck and wrap his arms around her and she would feel his sun-drenched chest press into her spine. These were the small tortures of longing and she paid the price with each imagining. Her last picture of Will, pounding on the window of the airport, hit by the gun butt and dropping to the floor, rushed back in. Her heart was gouged out again and again.

Only Marta's letter from Australia kept her sane. The letter arrived five weeks after her return to the States.

At Fernando's urging, I closed the guesthouse and returned to Australia. The husband had been dragging his heels back in Sydney anyhow. Guatemala was my dream, not his. But what I really wanted you to know, and Fernando said I must tell you as quickly as possible, was that Will was released from jail in Guatemala City and is now recovering. I didn't see him but F swears that Will has all his parts, and his injuries were not as bad as some that he's seen.

Kate wrote back to Marta but she never heard from her again. She still cringed at the threat that Jenkins made. If she tried to contact Will (which she didn't know how to do) or Fernando, the Horned Toad would have them killed, she was sure of it.

Was this her life now, hiding her heartache, telling no one about Will, ripped from a connection that felt truer than anything else she'd ever experienced? Was it only the high drama, the danger that had drawn her to Will? No. Her body ached with sadness, her bones and muscles were in a consistent state of weeping. She would have loved him anywhere, any time.

By the time Sofia was three, a glorious age, she had taken to English just as Kate had hoped. Kate decided to take the child for a dip in the warm shallows of the Mill River. This was a perfect spot for children, where the smooth river rocks pulled in the heat from the sun. If they tried to walk barefoot for long, they were reduced to skipping and yelping.

Kate took Sofia's plastic pail and filled it with water. It was August and they were in the midst of a heat wave. She poured the water over the smoothest rocks to cool them enough for the two of them to sit. As soon as they touched the water, she pulled off Sofia's jelly sandals.

When Sofia's feet hit the water, unbridled happiness rippled through her body. Sofia tossed back her head and laughed as she kicked, sending out arcs of water. When her balance on the rocks improved, she bent over and splashed with her hands. They played in the shallows, only inches deep. Sofia rearranged rocks and handfuls of dirt, struggling, intent on her artistry, the small hands still rounded on top. Toddlers were like that, small and round everywhere, as if they were boneless. Even the bottoms of their feet looked rounded, making it a miracle that they could walk at all.

Sofia grabbed Kate's hand and said, "Lay down in the water, Mommy." They each reclined into the shallows, the round rocks at their backs, their hair set loose. Kate and the girl opened their bodies to the blue sky above and the water around them.

In the days after Kate arrived with Sofia at Logan Airport, her father seemed to catch whiffs of lies. He asked about Sofia's strange sounding language.

"Her language is an unusual form of Spanish"—not true—"but she's learning English quickly"—true. It was the first lie and each one that followed cut through a capillary in her abdomen, first one, then another.

"Tell me again where you adopted her?" Even as he asked this, Sofia was in his arms, changing him into a grandfather.

"The Chiapas region of Mexico. Remember, I told you. It was an orphanage." The next lie. Slice, nick, bleed.

"But you were in Guatemala. Why were you in Mexico at all?" Her father was a bloodhound.

"I should have written to you, but the mail might not have gone through. I had to switch research sites. It turned out that I did most of my research in Mexico," she said, remembering to look steadily at her father, to not flinch away.

"And what will you do when Sofia wants to meet her biological family? Most people want that," he said.

"She was abandoned. There was no family on record."

The first time she said Sofia had been abandoned, she felt a flutter go by her ear, a bird wing of ancient Maya who shook their heads. Inside her body, a band of tiny men armed with sharpened toothpicks stabbed along her ribs.

The length of fabric, the rebozo that had held Sofia to Manuela, had been rolled tight and stuffed into a plastic shopping bag on the top shelf of her closet. It ticked like a bomb, ready to blast all of them into oblivion.

By the time they landed in Boston, Kate had constructed the altered story of Sofia's origins. She had to keep her far from anything that would connect her with Guatemala. Her adoption papers said she was born in Mexico, adopted at an orphanage in Mexico, and Kate couldn't veer from this new creation myth.

Yet Kate knew the value of telling adopted children about their origins, the deep meaning in knowing where you come from, the irresistible pull of knowing the source of your life. Open any magazine, watch any talk show, and the pleading voices of adopted adults were there: *It is our life, we own it, do not keep birth information away from us.* Until Sofia came along, until shots had ripped through soft bodies, she would have agreed.

Kate fed Sofia a creation story of her own. She was careful and thoughtful with the story, giving Sofia the best memories that she could create. By the time that Sofia was three, she wanted to hear her story again and again.

They returned home from their Mill River water play, satiated with sunshine and the mineral smell of the river. After a dinner of rice and beans (this was a part of Sofia's diet that was not negotiable; the child could eat mountains of it) and a shower to dislodge plant matter from her hair, they settled into bed for stories.

Kate rented a house based on the proximity to the farm nearby. The farm was called Bramble. Its owners kept sheep, llamas, and one very small burro that was twenty years old. Kate wanted the comfort and nearness of the animals. She was intoxicated by the smell of hay, manure, the sound of the sheep and the braying of the burro.

Leverett was close to Amherst, where other dark-skinned children were not such an unusual sight. The university drew graduate students from around the world, from the southern hemisphere where darker skin was perfectly suited to the equatorial power of the sun. Here Sofia would be safe.

"I traveled very far to find you. I went to a town in Mexico called Chiapas and you were the tiniest little girl. You were a baby and you didn't have a family. You were waiting for me to get there. You had a birth mother but she was very sick and couldn't take care of you."

"We can find her and make her better," said the child.

Oh, of course the child would want to do that. Each lie left Kate exposed and needing to cover up another part of the trail. Leave no crumbs. Kate and the girl were nestled under a puffy quilt. The child was fresh and warm from a bath and three books. Kate took a breath. She had to do it. She didn't want Sofia imagining that a sick mother was out in the world.

"She got very sick and she died. So we can't ever make her better." One lie and one truth.

Kate wasn't sure how she felt about lying about a made-up person's death. The lie was not about Manuela, it was about the fictitious woman in Chiapas and that was different.

A sudden image of Manuela on the ground, arms stretched in death toward her son, eyes open.

"Will you ever get sick?" asked Sofia. "I take care of you. I tell you to stay in bed and I bring you toast."

Another lie needed to appear. Kate was unprepared.

"No. I am very strong. I am the strongest mommy in all of Leverett."

"Did my brother get sick too?"

No, the child did not just ask about her brother. She had never said this before. How did this happen? Kate raced to think of other playmates who had brothers. Yes, that must be it.

"No, sweetie, you never had a brother." She ran her hand along the pajama leg, patting her for emphasis.

Sofia shook her head in a dreamy way and lay back on her

pillow. "A long time ago, when I was small, I have a brother who is like me. He has brown skin like me and toes like me. He is the same size as me."

"When I found you in Mexico, there was only you, no little boy, no brother," said Kate. The lies settled in certain organs, small drips of tar, minuscule at first. The lie about the twin brother took up residence in her liver.

Kate tucked her in, kissed her goodnight. "Sweet dreams."

Kate was aware at every turn how unprepared she was for parenting, the responsibility of understanding the blossoming brains of toddlers, how telling them something too early could be devastating. How did people raise children without living in a state of panic, even under the best of circumstances?

Kate was Mommy. But there was someone else who Sofia called for in the troubled hours of sleep. *Mamá.* And sometimes the old Mayan word, *Wate.* Mother. The one word in Kaqchikel that Kate clearly understood. The first time Kate heard her, she put down her book and rushed to the child, who sat huddled against the maple headboard, a dazed look in her eyes. "I'm right here," said Kate, pressing in close, putting her arms around Sofia.

"No, I want *Mamá,*" Sofia sobbed, not fully awake, her eyes tightly closed. "*Mamá, Mamá,*" she whispered until the pull of sleep was too strong. Kate stayed with her the rest of the night as Sofia called for Manuela.

Sofia's nighttime searching for Manuela came less frequently now and Kate prayed that on this night, after a full day of sun and water and happiness, she would sleep through the night. And she prayed that the class she was taking at UMass would help her understand what she needed to know about young children.

She had transferred to UMass and just finished her last class for her doctoral degree in water management and was slogging through her dissertation. But the class in early childhood development that she audited seemed far more interesting and complicated than water management. She wanted to know when children began to remember. She wanted to know if Sofia would remember her twin brother, Mateo, the massacre, and her parents.

She gleaned plenty from the class. There was preverbal memory, before the child has spoken language, when they remember sounds, smells, colors, tastes, touches, faces, and such. But those memories have to find special compartments to live in and most often they lodge in bodily locations like the stomach or the throat, or an overactive adrenal system guarded by a vigilant switch. When a child acquires spoken language, she can associate a spoken word with an object, such as a banana or a machete. That gives the brain a place to fetch the memory, so that if someone says "banana" the child goes to the banana place in her brain and there it is, in all of its yellow splendor.

Up to a certain stage (and Kate was not one hundred percent convinced of when or if she truly believed this), the child cannot differentiate between a dream, a storybook, a song, or a dusty day in the town square, or a jaguar swimming along the reeds of the lake looking for her mewling and disorderly cubs.

Kate asked everyone, "Tell me your very first memory. How old were you?" Lots of people had nothing to say about memory prior to age five. A few recalled events that took place when they were about four, and even fewer claimed to remember something in their third year.

In Kate's class, they also talked about the best way to make a child crazy—not that anyone wanted to make a child crazy but as a way to understand childhood mental illness, they deconstructed the path of crazy-making. Deny their experience, their reality, and tell them that what they know is not true. Sounds like a recipe for making them into little freaking psychos, said one guy in class. How awful, she had thought, how cruel. She wanted to raise her hand and ask, *Even if you pull them out of a pile of dead bodies, even after running through horrors of rain and cold for days, afraid to look back, even then should you tell the truth?*

Kate wanted assurance that Sofia would not remember events when she was two, the way the moon hung ripe at the top of the volcano, and the birds that sounded like kittens that sang at the wrong time of the day. Was it stuck under her ribs, along her inner ear? Was it waiting to unzip her someday when she was brushing her teeth?

How do you keep a secret about images etched through the retina, poured into the brain, formed into thoughts, hot on the heels of felt emotions? How does this get sealed off? Kate knew the answer. One hundred years of psychology, mountains of self-help books told her how it works. The lie forms a scar tissue, woven into layers as tight as a basket. Kate felt the scars etching throughout her.

Kate had three early childhood books on her nightstand. The first one said that children of this age were struggling with the mastery of self-soothing. The second one made mention of defining boundaries between parent and child so that the sense of self-care became internalized. The third endorsed a communal bed with the parents. There was no end to theories about parenting.

The last words that Fernando said to her were, "Don't drop crumbs unless you want the jaguar to follow."

She would not be like Hansel and Gretel in the terrible fairy tale of danger and terror and abandonment of small children. Not one crumb would fall from her bag. She brushed the ground clean of them. The horrors of the village could never, never follow them. To keep the ground swept of crumbs she would need everything she'd ever learned, dreamt, tasted, or felt to save this one little girl.

After the day on the Mill River, Sofia went to sleep early and easily. The water had soothed her. Kate also felt her muscles softened by the water and she fell asleep after reading a few pages of a novel.

The apparition came in Kate's sleep. The Mayan woman appeared in her dream and Kate rushed to find Sofia; the intruder must have come to take the child. She smelled the tendrils of wood smoke and heard the patting of the lake water against a dock. The woman was from the village. Oh no. Kate would know Manuela anywhere; her broad face, her smooth skin. The deep liquid of her dark eyes.

Manuela spoke in Kaqchikel at first, or so Kate thought, until she realized that she understood what Manuela was saying. How could that be? Did she say *mocking bird? Martingale? Martin bird?* Manuela had the same look on her face as when she taught Kate to pick the best avocados, how to tie a rebozo, how to hold a child. Was she telling her something that she must do? Why wasn't her son with her? Kate swam to wakefulness, dripping with bitter sweat, her heart pounding like that of a hooked fish. She got up, opened all the windows, and let the summer night air wash away Manuela's apparition.

CHAPTER 36

1995

Kate whispered to herself, and then noticed where she was. She was on the sidelines of the soccer field. She stopped and coughed into her sleeve as if she had only been clearing her throat. She was lost in memory again, back with Will, reliving the last glance of him at the airport in Guatemala City.

Sofia was small for her age. She would never reach the average height of North American women, five foot four, but because of nearly four years of good nutrition, she would be taller than her relatives. Her ancestry was filled with short, mountain-climbing people who farmed steep terraced fields, and climbed up dormant volcanoes. Being tall was not an asset among the Maya.

Kate sat in a lawn chair on the bumpy green turf watching Sofia go from picking the wild violets in the grass to running after the ball like a heat-seeking missile. She had been approached by other coaches who had hinted that Sofia's talent needed special guidance. "We don't see that kind of player very often," said the coach of the traveling team.

Will would have been her soccer coach, running lightly over the soggy field, his life filled with the squeals of children who had never known about war orphans or how a journalist like Kirkland could die so mysteriously in a one-car accident. Kate fantasized about finding Will and bringing him home, making everything good and safe for him. Was Kate living for all of them: Manuela, Mateo, and Kirkland?

Kate wanted everything for Sofia that she could not have had in Guatemala. She wanted good health, shiny white teeth, a brain that happily churns on reading and writing. No men with automatic weapons who would scar her for a second time. Kate had to make a good family, with staunch friends so that Sofia wouldn't feel the howl of her own people deep in her soul. Would her soul end up bewildered as Will believed when one's language is stolen?

Kate imagined that life would feel safer for Sofia with each passing year. At every milepost, she expected that the fear of someone coming to get Sofia would be lessened, but it wasn't. Kate remained vigilant, on patrol. But there were merciful moments of feeling at ease, especially when she was in the river. She loved to float down the Connecticut River, bobbing along with her hands folded under her head. She had always loved the river, reveled in watching it get cleaner and cleaner over the years.

Fish and Wildlife hired her with the lowest G-rating they had when she first arrived from Guatemala. They said she had a good future if she finished her graduate degree, which she did at UMass. This disappointed her adviser at UC Davis. "Was it because of that business with the foreign correspondent, Kirkland?" Dr. Clemson asked by email. "No, absolutely not," she rushed to say, alarmed that he had edged too close to the truth. She asked only that he write her a letter of recommendation.

What she had needed was a job. The opening at Fish and Wildlife let her stay close to the Connecticut River, monitoring the toxic runoff from the streets in the heavy rains, giving the health department a call when she found old summer homes that still ran their septic straight through to the river.

Kate slid her baseball cap lower to shade her eyes and watched as Sofia scampered. She had all the makings of a forward, a left wing perhaps, a stealth position for those with a strong left kick. Sofia was healthy; her digestive system was free of parasites, her teeth free of cavities. Sam was an ardent grandfather, reading her stories, walking her proudly along the sidewalks of downtown.

Everything about them said adoption, which is exactly what Kate wanted. To all appearances, she was a mother who had traveled to another country for a perfectly legal, international adoption. Sofia's jet-black hair waved along her back, catching light like obsidian. Her skin was darker than that of nearly everyone in Leverett. Her grandfather, a devoted coffee drinker, called her skin the color of lightly roasted coffee. Somewhere between cream and brown and gold, a rich color that took Kate's breath away.

Soccer practice ended and a dozen girls raced for the sidelines to the waiting parents.

"Mom, can we give Emma a ride home? Is this our day to stop at Dairy Queen?" asked Sofia, her arm draped around Emma's shoulders. Emma was the only other girl who was Sofia's size and their mutually diminutive forms made them comrades.

Kate loved the sound of her daughter's voice. Today, Kate wanted to go through an entire day without deception; she wanted only to hear the true crystal tones of Sofia's voice. Just that.

"Today isn't the day we go to Dairy Queen, but we could change it this once. Sometimes we can change things." There were eight more hours in the day and she begged the universe to keep it simple, keep the day free from dark memories.

Kate never imagined that loving a child would illuminate her soul, because that's what it felt like. And she never imagined Martin, never thought she could find love again.

CHAPTER 37

1996

Martin taught art at the local middle schools. Art teachers were the first to go in lean times, so it took three schools to hire one art teacher. As near as Kate could tell, Martin didn't have bigger plans; he wasn't the kind of artist who said that teaching was his day job while his heart and soul longed to create his own art. No, teaching art to middle school kids who ricocheted off the walls was his heart and soul.

When people said to him, "Man, I don't know how you do it, spending all day with thirteen-year-olds," Martin replied, "I start with gratitude." Everyone would stop talking. Later, Kate said, "Gratitude is such a showstopper."

She wanted more than anything to love him, to come every time they made love, to have the deep sense that she wanted to be with him forever. She thought that being with Martin was a grown-up kind of love, that she would love him more over time. Knowing she didn't love him in the unbridled way that he loved her, she tried to hide her hesitations, because really, who wouldn't love Martin? What woman wouldn't fall on her knees to thank the perfect alignment of the universe for a man like him? And she did love him, how could she not?

Kate and Martin decided on a small wedding in the backyard to be followed by a reception in her neighbor's new barn. Sofia was giddy with excitement about dresses and flowers and food. If Sofia could have combined her blue silky dress with flowers and food in one blend, she might have imploded with bliss.

"I'm part of the wedding," she told everyone who would listen. "Martin and Mommy and I are all getting married."

The wedding was still one week away. Kate wondered if Sofia would collapse from anticipation. She whirled around the kitchen and ran into her grandfather, who had just come into the kitchen with his electric drill.

"You now have a side rail on your deck so the minister won't fall and break her neck on account of you wanting to be married in the backyard instead of inside, which would have been lots easier. And where is my helper who is going to help me attack the design problems with the barn?" He looked around as if he couldn't see Sofia spinning and whirling. Bear Cat wisely sat on the kitchen windowsill, above the fray.

"Here I am, Grandpa! I'm practicing my dancing for the wedding when we all get married."

Sam put his drill on the island counter and bent down to swoop up Sofia when she came within his orbit. She hung like a rag doll tucked under his arm and she shrieked with laughter.

"Kate, will you please explain to this child who is marrying whom and what a family means?" He feigned exasperation. He shook Sofia for emphasis.

"I know, Grandpa, I know. You and Mom and I are all family, and Grandma was family too until she died but she still counts. And now Martin will be in our family too. We're all getting married! You too, Martin is marrying all of us," said Sofia upside down.

Kate shrugged. "How can you dispute the logic?"

Grandpa planted Sofia on her feet. The last of her giggles leaked out of her like dollops of clotted pudding falling from a spoon.

"I can't argue. Martin is marrying all of us. Has anyone told Martin?"

A car door slammed. Sofia's head turned to the sound. "That's Martin, my dad." She ran to the front door and her voice carried in muted tones to the kitchen, where Kate let her heart expand.

Kate set a cup of sugared coffee in front of her father. "You're going to need this to keep up with her. I'll come by Bramble Barn in a couple of hours and pick her up to do a little shopping. This is the first time they've had a wedding reception in the barn and they're a little nervous."

They could hear Sofia showing Martin the addition to the deck.

"I never thought I'd say this, but I'm a little jealous. I've been the main man in your life, and Sofia's too, ever since I picked you up that day at Logan Airport. I'm truly happy for you, God knows you deserve happiness, we all do. And if I could have handpicked someone for you, it would be Martin. But if a tree limb falls on your house in the middle of the night, you're not going to call me anymore, are you?"

Her father had been there for fallen tree limbs, snow shoveling, battery starting, television installing, shed building, Easter egg hunting, soccer cheerleading, and was Sofia's confidant. Kate tried to find words to tell her father something that would assure him.

"Dad, you're—"

Sofia and Martin came in through the sliding glass door off the kitchen with the child's hand tucked into his large one.

"As your new father-in-law, I have just one question for you," said Sam.

Martin looked at Kate, who stood behind her father. She shrugged.

"If a tree limb falls on my house at three a.m., and if I call you, will you come over?" asked Sam.

Martin wiped his forehead in mock relief. "I'll be there with chainsaw and plastic tarp in hand."

"That's what I needed to know. I like the direction of things," Sam said, and winked at Kate. "Everybody on the barn-decorating crew, load up and head out."

The threesome departed. Kate collected dishes for the dishwasher and made a list in her head of what had to be done. The wedding was still four days away and she had to go to work on two of those days.

The phone startled her as it always did when Sofia wasn't at home. Had something happened?

She caught it on the second ring. "Hello."

Was it the quality of the connection? The silence? She heard him breathing and she saw the shape of his lips.

"Is it you?" she whispered. "Don't hang up. I have to tell you something important."

She had had other phone calls in the last six years. Silent calls that she knew could only be Will. Each time she had sat with the phone pressed to her cheek, caressing the beige plastic. Once she had cried very quietly, which might have sounded like quick intakes of breath. But he would have known. Each time, a thick muffled sound traveled across the miles and then the connection was broken.

Kate looked down and was startled to see that she was wearing Will's socks, the ones she had tossed into her pack at the last moment in Antigua, the ones that she wore as slippers. Her big toe stuck out of one.

"I have on your socks," she managed to say.

Silence. Would he speak this time? She heard an intake of breath.

"I was just looking for those," he said.

Oh God, she loved his voice, the rich velvet of it, the press of it against her skin, the way it fit inside the marrow of her bones. The tenderness of his voice stroked her hair, her eyelids, the cuticles along her nails. She sat down on the floor.

"I'm getting married in a few days," she said. Kate knew they wouldn't have much time; neither of them could bear it for long. There was a long pause.

"Is Sofia, are you—?"

"Sofia is fantastic. You should see her." Kate wanted to reach through the phone lines and touch him. It was enough that they both had phones pressed to their faces at the same time.

"I've been able to help with the peace treaty. You know about the peace and reconciliation program?"

Kate had read whatever fragments she could find at the university library.

"I've read tiny bits. Is it real?"

"I'm translating for the Maya in the talks. Those who have forgiven me, that is. I always tell them up front what I did. I think it helps. All of us are culpable."

All of us are culpable. Kate carried her culpability with her like a stone between her shoulder blades, sharp and abrasive. She heard the light thud of Bear Cat landing on the floor. The black cat was a magnet for people with upset stomachs, fevers, and misery of the spirit. She crawled into Kate's lap.

"I hear your voice sometimes . . ." Kate couldn't finish.

"I have two strands of your hair. I found them in my sweater after . . ." he said.

"Did you know? Is that why you called, did you know I was getting married?"

There was a pause, dark and smoldering. "No. I only knew I had to call you. I woke up this morning and I swear that you had just walked out of the room, that I could hear your footsteps."

"Stop. Don't say anything else or I'm going to die."

"Listen, I wanted to let you know that, well, I'm okay and there's someone in my life . . . I'm sure we'll get married." Will cleared his throat. "I want you and Sofia to be happy and live long and wonderful lives. I'm going to get off the phone now, Kate."

"Will, I—" The connection ended.

She had so much she wanted to ask him. Could he travel to the States again? Would she ever see him? She pictured him married to someone else and it felt like she was losing him all over again.

CHAPTER 38

Sofia

Sofia had once imagined a monster. Before her mother married Martin, she often slipped into bed with her mom when Monster showed up. In the warm double bed, under the safe tent of blankets and comforters, she had been safe from the seething anger of Monster.

Then Martin became part of them and for Sofia, more was better. A mother and a daughter were not enough, not quite a family. But at night when Monster came, Sofia was embarrassed to glide in along her mother's side of the bed with Martin on the other side. She had done it once and she felt the wide-awake, awkward bodies of her mother and Martin, trying not to move, all three of them laid out like logs in a summer fireplace.

The next day, Martin brought home a bag from the Guild Art Store. He always shopped there for his students at the middle schools. Sofia went to a sitter for two hours after school and then Martin picked her up.

"I've got something for you," he said. He opened up the bag

and pulled out a pad of newsprint, a box of thin-point markers, and a stack of tissue paper in about a million different colors.

"Would you like to draw a picture of Monster?" he said. "It won't be as scary if we see Monster now, in the kitchen, with all the lights on."

Her mother never asked her what Monster looked like. "I guess so," she said.

"What color do you need first?" he said, dumping the twenty-pack on the kitchen table.

Sofia wasn't sure if Martin knew what he was doing. How much did he know about monsters? If she drew a picture of Monster, would it come right off the page and grab her?

Since the day they had found Martin at the Laundromat, Sofia had liked him. And her mother was happier; she laughed more with him.

"Brown," she said. "I want brown."

What did Monster look like? She had mostly seen his shadowy parts and his eyes.

"He has brown eyes," she said, drawing two misshapen circles.

"Are they brown all over or do they have any other color in them?" asked Martin.

Sofia looked at Martin's eyes, which were brown, but speckled with bits of lighter brown. Then she looked at her reflection in the sliding glass door and saw the white part of her eyes. She came back to the table and drew eyes that were mostly brown with some white. She stopped.

"He could get very scared—I mean scary," she said.

Martin picked up a wad of multicolored tissue paper. "You could put something around Monster, like a fence. Or you could put him in a box. Here, let's rip up some strips of tissue paper and see if this makes a way to keep him so he won't be scary."

Sofia took yellow paper and rippled long strips of it. "We need a glue stick. I know where Mommy keeps it." Sofia opened a drawer beneath the phone where scissors, rubber bands, scrap paper, and other supplies lived.

Martin leaned over the paper and watched. Sofia corralled Monster.

"Do you need anything else to feel safe when Monster is around?" asked Martin.

Sofia picked up a black felt marker. She drew the head and gave him black hair, then arms, and added red claws, then a body, but he started to look more like a teddy bear and that wasn't right.

"Where does he live?" asked Martin.

Sofia hadn't thought about this before. She grabbed a green marker and drew steep hills behind Monster, peaks that looked like triangles pointing to the sky. She took a dark blue marker and made a circle around his feet. "This part is hard. I can't draw water very good."

Sofia heard her mother drive up, the familiar whine of her car. She tossed her marker down and ran for the door.

"Mommy, Martin helped me draw Monster! Wait until you see him." Sofia liked the feeling of all three of them together, the bulk of them.

"This looks like a major art project," said her mother. Kate carried a paper bag of groceries from Stop & Shop. She set the bag on the counter and leaned in to look at the drawing.

Her mother's face crumpled. Something was wrong with the drawing. Was she mad? What had Sofia done wrong? Without saying anything, her mother turned away.

"I forgot something in the car. I'll be right back."

Was she in trouble? Sofia moved to the window and looked out to the driveway. Her mother sat in the car, with her hands over her face. Martin came up behind Sofia and put his hands on her shoulders.

"Let me go talk to her. This isn't about the drawing . . . you didn't do anything wrong."

CHAPTER 39

"We have to talk, Kate," Martin said after dinner, after she apologized to both Sofia and Martin. She said she was upset about work, not them at all, and no, not the drawing, which she liked very much. After Sofia finished her spelling homework, took a bath, and after she and Sofia snuggled in bed together reading *A Wrinkle in Time,* Kate found Martin, waiting for her in the TV room. It was the farthest room from Sofia's bedroom but they still whispered.

They sat in the corner of the couch, a wedding present from her father. Martin pulled her feet into his lap and held them in his warm hands.

"This monster drawing has something to do with where Sofia comes from. Do I have that right?"

Should she tell him? Wouldn't it be better if no one here knew except for her? Wasn't it best if she contained all the horror?

"Yes," she said. "She's not from Mexico. She's from Guatemala."

Martin still had paint under his fingernails and he frequently smelled like glue and paper.

"And this is a big secret because . . ." Martin opened his hands, palms up, expectantly.

"Because she was a war orphan, and . . ." Kate's heart beat faster, and rain clattered on the windows. She remembered the way Fernando shook his head so slightly when the soldiers had been in his café. She smelled the beans and tortillas coming from Fernando's kitchen.

"Kate, stay with me. Where did you just go?"

She jumped. It was hard traveling from Guatemala to Massachusetts so abruptly. "There was a massacre, I was there, I was a witness, and Sofia was the only survivor. I took her and ran through the mountains. The picture that Sofia drew is a lake surrounded by volcanoes. The monster is a conglomeration of death, or of those who brought death to the people. I'm not an art therapist, but I'm pretty sure I'm at least in the ballpark."

Martin bounced back on the couch as if struck. "Wait, what mountains? What do you mean, you ran with her? What does Sofia know?"

Her breath was labored, as if she carried a child straight up a mountain. "Only what I've told you before this, what I've told my father, what I've told everyone. That she is adopted."

She saw the alarm in his eyes, his eyebrows squeezed toward the center. "How did you adopt her? How did that work? Were you in danger?"

She was right to tell Martin. He was her husband, her good husband. But could she tell him everything?

"She's from a village that was attacked by the military. Her mother was a student of mine, I knew her, and Sofia's brother. They were mowed down. . . ."

Slowly, she told him everything. About Kirkland's fatal one-car accident, Fernando's steadiness, Marta's friendship, and how a former Peace Corps worker helped her. She told him about the desperation she felt, the danger of places for war orphans like *casas de engordes,* and how Sofia was a witness, the documents that she was given, the race to leave with Sofia.

"What was his name?" asked Martin.

"Who?" she said, but she already knew who he meant. Martin had heard the unspoken story, the part that Kate left out.

"The Peace Corps guy, the one who helped you. I think you loved him. I think he loved you."

They were now stretched out on the broad couch, her head on his chest. She rose up on one elbow. "How did you know?"

Martin wiggled his fingers through her hair. "Guys are like elk. We can smell another bull elk long after they're gone."

A veneer of shellac crackled off Kate, bringing her closer to Martin.

"I swore that I'd never say his name because it might still be too dangerous. He's working on the peace and reconciliation program now that the war is over. They help relatives find the mass graves of their families. I know this sounds ridiculous here in Massachusetts, where our biggest worry is a bit of corruption over in Boston, but I won't say his name."

Jenkins was dead, but had he put in a plan B for Will?

"How do you know that he's working on the peace and reconciliation program?"

"Because he called once. Well, once that he spoke to me. He's with someone else now."

She left out the part that Will had called just days before the wedding.

Martin placed one hand on the small of her back. "And Mr. No Name was in love with you and you loved him. And your heart was broken. That's what I always knew about you, that your heart was pretty beat-up when we met. But what I need to know is, do you have enough space for me?"

Kate pictured all four chambers of her heart, squeezing and pumping. They'd been married for over a year. Surely her heart should be filled to the brim with love for this good man.

"Love makes the heart expand, not contract. I have a lot

more room in there than I had before I went to Guatemala," she said. And this was true, except it didn't entirely answer the question.

Martin didn't press her further and she wanted to take his silence for a kind of agreement. This must be what love is like under normal circumstances, steady and warm. With Martin, there was the everyday glue of life, the evenings spent with Sofia after dinner, her homework spread out on the table, the morning scramble for work and school, the soccer games, waking up together, warm breath on her shoulder.

Now that Martin shared the horror of her experience at the massacre, she felt closer to him. He saw her and she didn't realize how much she had longed for being seen. When they made love later that night and for the next two nights, Kate was shocked at how powerfully she responded. Part of her had been waiting, just waiting to be revealed.

The new depth of their closeness lasted for days. It was Kate who initiated lovemaking, weightless with the release of her secrets, or most of them. She had taken a chance telling Martin about Guatemala and yet he had seen her and still loved her.

She was shocked at the difference now, stunned that all this time he had been the one asking and reaching for her while a strange distance had pushed against her. Will had moved on to someone else and so had she.

She wondered how Martin could have loved her when he hadn't really known her. If truly pressed, she had heard a persistent voice that had found his love disingenuous. But no longer.

Now she raced home from her job, fueled by a euphoria of discovery, of being seen and heard, the folly of not understanding what had been right in front of her, the man sleeping in her bed. Sofia, while not privy to their conversation, still reverberated with the change. She asked to go to Emily's house a bit more, and asked for Emily to come to their house. She was no longer required to add her chemistry to Martin and Kate to keep the whole unit afloat. Everyone's muscles softened around their bones and their blood ran sweeter.

After the soccer game on Saturday, Sofia went to Emily's house for an overnight. Martin had taken over as assistant coach and he'd just returned from dropping off the girls at Emily's. When Kate heard his car pull in, every part of her welcomed him. But when he opened the door, she saw the change like the snapping of a green branch, jagged and raw.

"What is it? Is it Sofia?" She stood in the archway to the kitchen. Her heart pulsed.

Martin's body had rearranged; something rumbled beneath the surface of his skin. "I think you should be honest with Sofia. She needs to know where she's from, what Manuela was like, what language she spoke. A part of her will be bewildered unless she knows this."

Had he said bewildered? Hadn't Will said something like that about language, that stealing a people's language leaves the soul bewildered? Why did the two men she loved say exactly what she already knew to be right?

"Look, I know I'm the stepfather here and I haven't entirely found the guidebook yet. I'm trying to figure out what this means, when I get to say something parental or when to follow your lead. But this is wrong. . . ." he said. He had a tinge of rosiness on his cheeks that combined incongruously with the dark shadow of stubble from not shaving that morning.

Kate ran one hand along the tiled edge of the kitchen counter. "No, no, Sofia loves you. You're a great stepdad. Have you seen how happy she is?" She wanted to mitigate whatever was coming with a rush of assurance. Had she not told him enough that he was wonderful?

"I love her too. And I love you. But I can't pretend that I'm okay with not telling Sofia about her past, about her parents and where she's from."

All the ease left Kate; the soft places that had just unfurled called in the troops. She reached into a cabinet, grabbed a glass, ran tap water, and then, unable to bring it to her lips with her shaking hands, set it back down again.

"Do you think this was an easy decision for me, an idle, unprocessed conclusion?" She heard her voice retreating into a rarely used academic firmness that she didn't want to use. "There were lives at stake. There could still be repercussions. . . ." Why had he grabbed on to this?

"Kate, no matter how hard, how awful, she owns this history. She deserves to know. I understand that you couldn't tell her everything at once, but you knew her birth mother, her twin brother, and the people in her village. This is, in all ways that I can think of, wrong."

Martin pressed his lips together and closed his eyes. He ran his hands over his face. "I loved my mother and father. They weren't perfect, but I always knew they loved me. Except they kept something essential from me and they were wrong. They weren't protecting me from knowledge about my birth mother. I could have understood it. They were protecting themselves."

"This is not the same thing! The scope of what happened in her village kept reverberating out. They killed Kirkland, they might have killed Sofia," said Kate.

"You have also stolen something from her," he whispered.

"I love Sofia more than anything on Earth."

"We all know you love her. That isn't what I'm talking about, or maybe it is. I need to wrap my head around this, and I'm going away for a few days," he said.

"What? You're leaving! This is your solution? I knew I shouldn't have told you. Now you hate me." She felt like she was in a slow-motion car crash and it was her fault.

He stepped closer and held both of her hands. "I'm not leaving you. I'm just leaving for two days. I'll be back Sunday night. Sofia will be back here around lunchtime tomorrow. This is all too important for me to skip over and pretend that it's okay. I'm going to stay at my old roommate's cabin in Vermont."

Martin was true to his word. He returned on Sunday evening to a clamorous welcome from Sofia. Kate hadn't slept. She didn't know what he would do.

"It's okay, Kate. This is your call. I've made my peace with this."

Years later, she would learn what his peace meant. He had put a plan in place with the lawyer. He wrote the letter to Sofia that burst open their world.

CHAPTER 40

2003

Kate didn't know that the fall from grace would be like dropping headlong into Carlsbad Caverns, bouncing off unforgiving rock, slick with years of stalactite untruths, never finding a foothold, just plummeting. Yet there was no denying the twelve years with Sofia, living as mother and daughter. Kate had never imagined the kind of love that grows with a child, that you would lay down your life for a child, that the joys and agonies would be so profound. Now this letter, this rupture sent via Martin.

For two days Sofia spoke only with her grandfather, who served as ambassador, or United Nations negotiator.

"Please inform Kate that I am not going to school today and that the school needs to be called," Sofia said to Sam as he sipped his morning coffee. Kate was also in the kitchen. The lack of *mommy* or *mom* or any parental reference was noted, as intended.

"Sofia, I am right here! I can hear you—" said Kate. But before she had finished her sentence, Sofia turned her back and left the room.

Sam, caught in the minefield between his daughter and granddaughter, seemed to understand his role as the buffer zone. "She can't keep it up forever," he said. "But there are times when I wish more than anything that your mother was here. I would much prefer to claim my male status as lawn care expert."

Sofia would take no probing, no apologies, not anything from Kate. Sofia had taken a box cutter and excised Kate from her existence. Kate understood the primitive intent; she was being shunned. This was punishment.

On one level, the situation was preposterous. Sofia was fifteen, living in the family home, showering in the family shower, walking on the same floorboards and breathing the same sad air as Kate. The girl had to be exhausted by the effort and Kate longed to be the one to soothe her.

On day three, Kate waited for Sofia outside the bathroom door. The pipes clanged when Sofia turned off the shower. Kate knew Sofia's routine by heart: Rub her hair roughly with the towel, brush it out, pull on her running shorts, sports bra, and last year's soccer team shirt.

Maybe she shouldn't hijack her like this, lurking around the bathroom door. Maybe she should take the higher road and wait her out. But Kate wasn't going to last much longer. Her insides were collapsing. She felt like someone was dying, the way she felt when the police had come to her door to let her know that there had been an accident with Martin. Hadn't they lost enough loved ones already? Her heart squeezed until it hurt to breathe.

Sofia pulled open the door and jumped back a bit when faced with Kate. Her dark eyes widened in alarm, her face not yet hardened into the new version of scorn. Kate resisted the urge to step forward, to step back into their old world. She knew not to trap her any more than she already was by her own anger.

"Scream, hit, kick—go ahead," said Kate. "But I know you

want to ask me more things. I'll tell you anything. I promise not to spare you details, not the gruesome parts, not the parts where I was so afraid that I'm not even sure if I remember correctly. But I will not be shunned in my own home. And I won't let you hurt yourself by doing this."

Sofia's face crumpled and Kate reached for her. Sofia pulled back and a sound rumbled up from her throat.

"No! Don't touch me. I don't believe you. I don't believe anything you say."

Kate fell backward against the wall of the hallway and slid to the floor. Sofia raced for her bedroom. The air pressure in the house sucked outward as the front door opened and Sam announced, "Anyone home? Kate? Sofia?" He was trying to sound normal.

"Upstairs, Dad," said Kate, rubbing the bridge of her nose.

The clomp of his size-eleven shoes echoed along the hallway and up the stairs. He stopped at the top of the staircase, one hand on the banister, eyeing Kate, who still sat on the floor.

"I see the morning isn't going so well," he said. He walked to Kate, extended a hand, and pulled her up.

Kate wiped her eyes. She was surprised that any fluid remained in her tear ducts. "You might say that," she said. Sam pulled her into a hug.

"Go to work. Sometimes work is the easiest part of life. After your mother died, sorting mail at the post office was the one thing that I knew I was good at. I could count on the mail arriving and leaving. I can't tell you how soothing it was. Go to work, Kate."

She hadn't thought of going to work. For two days she had called in sick. She was torn between wanting to do something to bring Sofia back again and the relief of going to work.

Sam shook his head, as if he was reading her mind. "Don't worry. Sofia and I have a date to look for another bike. Give her some space. Go on, get dressed and go to work."

Guilt and relief washed over her as she left the house. It was not until she pulled into the parking lot of the Fish and Wildlife office that her ribs uncurled enough that she could take a full breath. It was true what every flight attendant said before takeoff: *In the event of an emergency, place the oxygen mask over your face and then attend to your child.* Kate's oxygen mask just happened to be the wide expanse of the Connecticut River. As she hopped into her green truck, she knew she could at least take care of the river, and then her daughter.

Day four.

Kate was losing her, not to an oppressive military, not to a black market adoption market, but right here in her own house. Sofia had turned away.

After another night of sleeping in jagged bits, bookended by nightmares of Jenkins returning from the dead, Kate pulled on a T-shirt and sweat pants, went downstairs, and made a pot of coffee. She waited until seven a.m.

Normally Kate loved the morning, the sun cresting the hill of the farm across the way. Not today. Today she had to turn everything inside out, pull the soles of her feet up through her torso, scramble her brain around and let it drop to the floor.

She stood up from the kitchen table and shook her body like a water dog. She walked through the living room and up the stairs to Sofia's room. She knocked the polite, one-knuckle mother knock and opened the door.

Sofia was already at her computer desk, the blue light of the screen hitting the whites of her eyes in a ghastly glow. She switched off the screen as soon as she saw her mother.

Sofia struggled to rearrange her face into the new mask of scorn. She looked as if someone said to her, *Okay, now show me your mad face.*

Kate put up her hand and said, "Don't. This is what we are going to do. We are going to Guatemala. The peace accord was signed seven years ago. I'll take you to the village where you were born."

Outside Sofia's window was a tall lilac bush, its spring flowers now just a memory. The wind took a sudden hold and screeched a branch along her windowpane. Two blue jays squabbled about territory with the neighborhood crows. The day was off to a rough start, not a soft day.

Sofia looked shocked. "How can I leave the country? I don't have a passport. What if my birth certificate isn't real?"

Sofia had been thinking about this.

"Your birth certificate is real. I mean, it's the only birth certificate you've ever had. You wouldn't have had one in Santa Teresa. No one did."

Every mention of the village or Guatemala seemed to push them farther apart. This is not what Kate wanted, and it was exactly what she knew she had to do.

"I'm calling Vincent when his office opens. He doesn't specialize in immigration law, but he has a friend who does. If he can help us, he will. And you're going to school today. And soccer practice."

This wobbly parental stand felt better, erecting some sort of boundary after the explosion of Martin's letter.

Sofia blinked hard. "What if—"

"No more what-if. You have fifteen minutes to get ready for the bus. And please eat some breakfast. I'll let you know what I find out when you come home."

"Okay," said Sofia in a small voice. Some tiny link between them was okay again, but it was as fragile as a spiderweb. Kate feared coming any closer in case she'd become entangled and destroy the filaments that hovered between them.

Day five.

Vincent's attorney buddy had trawled through every avenue of possibility. In the final analysis, she had said, "If the CIA had created documents of identity for a hypothetical child in another country and the child was legally adopted as shown on further documents, then those documents are as real as they get. These papers were created prior to the World Trade Center attacks, which also helps."

Vincent gave the green light for requesting express service for passports, which would take five to seven days at a cost that made Kate cringe. She announced the Guatemalan plan to Sam at dinner time, over a large thin-crust pizza. Sofia had taken a plate to her room.

Sam dropped his slice. "Have you lost your mind? After everything you've told me about Guatemala, now you want to go back? It's dangerous. She's a child. She's my granddaughter. Don't I get any say in this at all? Martin would blow a gasket," said Sam. He looked like a volcano ready to erupt.

"This is exactly what Martin expected me to do. If he were still alive, his bags would be packed and ready to go," said Kate.

"Then I'm going with you." Her father had not been out of the country since he returned from Vietnam. He had married, had a baby, and found a job at the post office. He often said to his family that leaving home was the last thing he ever wanted to do again. When Kate was a child, the three of them had camped in Vermont and New Hampshire and once in Acadia, off the coast of Maine. But Sam saw no reason to ever leave the United States until now.

Three passports arrived five days later. They would make an odd trio: one vet with moments of PTSD who hadn't dipped his toes beyond the border of the United States since the 1960s, a Massachusetts-raised Mayan girl, and Kate leading the group through her past.

Part Four

2003

Guatemala

CHAPTER 41

"What now?" said Sam.

The airport in Guatemala City was framed with dark corners, food vendors selling sandwiches, and a crush of men at the entrance all wanting to be their cabbie. But it also had a hum to it that Kate had not experienced. She felt the pulse of commerce, travel, freedom of movement, and something vibrant like hope.

It had been twelve years since Kate had been at this airport in 1991, and now she felt like a ghost. At any moment she'd see her younger self, gulping back tears with the small child in her arms, stunned by the image of Will in the airport window, the final threat from Jenkins.

"Now we go to Antigua," said Kate. "Sofia, we're going out into that throng and I need to do a little bargaining to get a van out of the city. Wait with Grandpa."

Had she lost her mind? Within two weeks she had gone from her isolated holding pattern, containing all the lies from long ago, to flying to Guatemala with her daughter and her father. Since Martin's letter to Sofia arrived, Kate had been buffeted by the extremes of relief and then full-out terror. A breeze might blow through her hair and she'd feel the weightless freedom of honesty lift her nearly off her feet. The burden of elaborate lies was no longer hers to hold. The next moment, she'd shatter from Sofia's icy glare, her hand brushed away from her daughter's arm.

What could they find here? For two days she had listened to Spanish tapes from the library to jumpstart what had never been a brilliant facility with the language. But she had gotten by.

Kate negotiated with a cabdriver and she waved Sam and Sofia over from the curb.

"We'll spend the night in Antigua and then head to the highlands tomorrow or the next day," she said as the driver put their luggage into the back of the van.

Two of their flights had been canceled and rescheduled and they arrived far later than Kate planned. It would be 10 p.m. by the time they pulled into Antigua. They could at least catch their breath by sleeping in. Sam stood back until Sofia stepped into the van. Sofia headed straight for the back and put on headphones. Anything to block out Kate. Kate absorbed the intended slight and slid into the bench seat, followed by Sam.

Because it was dark, they could have been anywhere sitting in the back of the van. An hour later when the van turned abruptly to the right and she felt the familiar thump of cobblestones, Kate felt dread rise up to meet her with a skeletal grip. Would she see Will and his wife strolling about Antigua? Would she be able to look at him and pretend that she was glad for him? And she was happy for him; he deserved every happiness.

The van pulled over and stopped, hoisting the right wheels on the edge of the sidewalk. It was almost midnight. Her eyes burned, her stomach curdled from too much airline coffee. The old sense of dread of being in Antigua with Sofia found an easy access point and swept in like oily fog. The driver pulled their bags out while Kate rang a buzzer on the immense door. A sleepy night clerk slid open the viewing slate.

"We have a reservation. Malloy," said Kate.

With each word that she spoke, her stale Spanish came back, jagged at first, hesitant, the language unlocked from a forbidden fortress. Sam and Sofia stood behind her as she took their room keys.

She was shocked at the relative ease of calling ahead to get a room. In 1990, finding a phone, never mind connecting to the United States, was nearly impossible. Now there were guidebooks to Guatemala. She selected a guesthouse several blocks from the central park.

Sofia insisted on separate rooms.

"We don't sleep in the same bedroom at home—why should we start now?"

After two weeks of being shunned by Sofia, Kate was still not accustomed to the hollowness of her new role. This was part of the new landscape with Sofia, part of pulling away with disdain, part of her rage. Kate felt each rejection, eye roll, and carefully aimed missile.

The rooms were on the ground floor, along a brown tile walkway, surrounding a garden. Even in the dim light, the bougainvillea stood out in their papery magenta glory. Sam walked the perimeter of the inner courtyard, an awkward show of bravado in a country that he knew nothing about, peeking into Sofia's room, then Kate's, then settling into his own like a Bernese mountain dog. Kate heard his familiar snore within minutes.

Refusing to give in to Sofia's emotional campaign, Kate said, "Goodnight. See you in the morning."

Kate stood in the doorway of her room, waiting for something, a reply, a nod, a grunt, but Sofia closed her door in wordless reply. Kate wanted to kick something, punch a wall, scream, curse. She had all but groveled, explaining what she had done years ago, cried, apologized. Kate arranged the trip so that Sofia could see her homeland, seeking a nugget of connectedness.

She rolled her suitcase into her room and sat on the bed. She was done asking for forgiveness and imploring. Inside a well-guarded cavern of her chest, a flint was struck, catching fire, warming her. Clusters of light urged her spine long again. She stretched out on the bed, relaxed for the first time since Martin's terrible letter. There was a soft knock at her door and her stomach muscles contracted.

"Mommy?"

Sofia? Kate sat up. Was Kate Mommy again?

Kate opened the door. Sofia wore her sleepwear. No one seemed to wear pajamas anymore. She had on a tank top and jersey shorts.

"Can I come in?" She sounded like her daughter again. Kate was cautious, not ready to take another strike to the heart.

"Of course you can come in."

Sofia sat on the bed, legs crossed. Kate sat next to her. "I just want you to know, I mean, thank you for bringing me here." She reached across the bed and hugged Kate.

Kate was shocked at the sudden departure from aggrieved teenager to thankful daughter. But she took the moment, having been starved for connection with Sofia. Kate inhaled her daughter's essential fresh water scent beneath the shampoo and the conditioner.

"I want to sleep in tomorrow morning. Okay? You're the big early bird. Grandpa is too. But just let me sleep, please. I haven't slept for a couple of nights."

Kate said yes, of course.

CHAPTER 42

Kate woke mid-morning, drunk with the perfume of flowers, incense, wood smoke, and coffee. She had dreamt so many times of Guatemala, had been so often startled by Manuela's ethereal visitations that she at first thought she was still home in her bed. As she swam to consciousness, she realized with a start where she was. She still struggled to keep up with the feeling of being on a high-speed train since Martin's letter catapulted all of them into the past.

Kate wasn't sure of her next move, but she knew she had to arrange for transportation to Lake Atitlán. And from there, what? How would Sofia's return to her home village affect her? What would she think being back in the Mayan Highlands? Would she be overwhelmed by preverbal memories? Or would her past knit together with her life in the States in a way that would make her whole and glorious? Or would she reject Kate forever?

She longed to see Fernando. His café was her first stop today.

She needed to see that he had survived the bad years. She stepped into the shower, barely able to turn around in the tiny space. Even these accommodations, a luxury for 90 percent of Guatemalans, would seem shocking to Sofia. Her daughter, by comparison, had been a child of adequate food, education, housing, and safety.

She dressed and stepped into the corridor to the courtyard. Tourists had discovered Antigua; the guesthouse had a steady stream of rugged-looking travelers, the kind who wanted to be far off the beaten path, but with running water and beds.

Kate knocked on her father's door. He opened it. He was dressed and freshly shaved, his cheeks still glistening. "Just waiting for you gals to wake up," he said.

She knocked on Sofia's door and then pushed to open it. Locked. Of course. "Sofia, we're going out for breakfast." No answer. Sofia was a heavy sleeper, but surely she'd hear someone pounding on her door. Something was wrong.

Kate felt a whoosh, a breath of air rush by her and she knew instantly that Sofia was gone.

Sam knocked on the door with enough force to bring a young Guatemalan man from the front desk.

"I am Pablo, the owner. The señorita checked out before dawn," he said.

"Do you mean she is gone? Did she take her suitcase?" asked Sam. Kate translated.

"She took a small backpack. She left her suitcase in the room. And she left this note for you." Pablo handed a folded note to Kate.

I have to do this alone. Love, Sofia.

Sofia had no idea how to get around in Guatemala; she'd be lost instantly. She only had high school Spanish. The crush of who Sofia was hit Kate like a body slam. A brown-skinned girl, plucked from her home and brought to a small enclave of mostly white people in New England, where she was never told about her birth family. Everything about her clothing, her bearing would scream American. She walked with the sureness of an athlete in a country where girls did not play sports. Sofia was a hybrid, a painted bird. She was going to attract attention, nearly as much as she created in the States.

The vacuum of Sofia's absence sent a shock wave through Kate. She expected her father to erupt. Instead, he said, "How can we find her?" He had switched to some other gear, an old military sense that was driven by mission.

Did she remember the way to Fernando's? She pushed open the door of the guesthouse and ran, with her father in slower pursuit. "Go, go," he said. "As long as I can see you, I'll catch up."

Three blocks south, four blocks west. Yes, that was it. There were tourists on every street, motorbikes, and cars rattled along the cobblestones. Antigua had exploded with life and businesses. A colorful parade of goods was sold along the streets. She prayed that Fernando was still doing business in his café bookstore. She rounded the corner and there was the central park and across from it, the café.

Kate stopped outside the door to catch her breath. Her father caught up with her. They went in.

The tables were filled with young travelers, backpacks at their sides. Two young Mayan women waited on the tables. Teenagers, they would have been just toddlers when Kate had last been here.

"Where is Señor Fernando?" she asked, trying to level her voice, not let the full out panic escape and fill the room.

When he appeared from the courtyard, he did not look older at first. His hair showed no graying. Something had relaxed along his jaw that she had not known was there before. Seven years of peace allowed him to breathe more deeply.

"Kate." He smiled a toothy grin, something else that she hadn't seen before. It took four steps to reach Kate and in that time, his warm smile changed to alarm. Kate knew that he read her face. This old friend still knew her.

"It is so good to see you. Welcome to my country now that we are at peace," he said. Fernando waited for Kate to initiate an embrace. He would have stood there forever if she had not opened her arms.

"Oh, my friend," she said, her voice thick with emotion. Had she slipped back in time, needing Fernando again? Was Will waiting to step into the café? Correction, Will and his wife.

She turned. "This is my father, Sam. Dad, I told you about Fernando."

Sam reached out a hand. "I am in your debt. You helped my daughter and granddaughter when I couldn't."

"Tell me what is wrong," said Fernando, urging them to a table. "I remember the way your face told a story. We have a saying that means that one's heart is drawn on their face."

The shift in adjusting to the slow pace of life in Guatemala surrounded Kate. It was the custom to move slowly, to ask about family, to eat, drink. If she did this, her head would implode.

"We came here with Sofia. She is fifteen now. She only just learned about Manuela, her father, her brother, and the massacre. We arrived last night and now she's gone." Kate knew how abrupt she sounded. She put one hand over her mouth, holding back a flood of screams that ached for release.

"And why did you tell her now?"

"I didn't. Her stepfather . . . my husband died six months ago and he left instructions with a lawyer to inform Sofia of her background."

Fernando blinked, laying his thick black eyelashes on his high cheekbones as if he bowed in sorrow.

"Do you know where she has gone?" he asked.

Sam leaned forward. "I think we all know where she's gone. She wants to go to the village where she came from."

A rivulet of sweat ran down Kate's back. This was not at all what Kate had planned. She wanted to offer Sofia's past to her, show her the lake, the night sky, the church where she taught English classes, where Manuela came with her two children.

Sofia had just changed the game. Her high school soccer coach said, "When Sofia walks on the field, she's the game changer." But this wasn't soccer. How could Sofia know what the rules were here?

Fernando reached his hand across the table, placing his fingertips along Kate's arm, as light as a dragonfly. "How can I help you?"

"Can you help us get to Lake Atitlán?" asked Kate.

"Of course. When did Sofia leave?"

"Around dawn," said Sam.

"Then she may have taken the first bus out of town. It is a very slow journey by bus. It stops in every town. . . ."

"I know," said Kate. She was yanked back in time, huddled on the bus with a small child in her arms.

"They may just be arriving in Panajachel now. It will be wise for us to drive. Let me arrange this. While I do, you can go back to your hotel and gather your things."

Something niggled at Kate. Fernando was too prepared, not surprised enough by her presence in Antigua. He hadn't asked her quite enough questions, but most importantly he hadn't asked her why Martin had left the revelatory letter with the lawyer.

They stood up and Sam turned to leave. Kate couldn't take her eyes off Fernando. She knew how his steady manner could belie his intricate web of connections, how his café had masked his support of the Maya for so long. But there was nothing more important than finding Sofia. The image of her daughter traveling alone carved out a desolate pit in Kate.

How had Sofia managed to find a bus, to know where she was going? Of course, the late night light under Sofia's bedroom door, the way she had flicked off her computer the instant that Kate walked in. She knew her daughter; Sofia had been researching everything about traveling to Santa Teresa for the past two weeks, even before Kate announced that they were going to Guatemala.

Fernando walked them to the front door. "Are you only now realizing that she is as smart as her mother, both her mothers? Go. I will pick you up at your hotel. Ask them to store your luggage and only bring what you need for a few days. We will find her."

CHAPTER 43

Sofia

Sofia had studied Spanish for two years. At first, it didn't come any easier to her than it had for the white kids. Her mother told her that she had only spoken a weird kind of Spanish for a few months after coming to the States and then adapted to English. But she had been so little then, she had to rely on what her mother told her about that time, and who knew what was true and what wasn't with her mother. By year two of Spanish, something clicked with the language classes and the pulse of Spanish felt comfortable, like old socks.

While her mother was planning their trip to Guatemala, getting time off from work, and getting assignments from her teachers, Sofia was doing a different sort of planning. She read travel guides at the library, and between the Internet and long-distance phone calls, she was able to secure a way to Lake Atitlán once they got to Antigua. And here was the important part: She wanted to go alone, without her mother or grandfather, and she knew they wouldn't let her go without them.

She packed the cloth that her birth mother had woven, which might help her find her brother. Kate had retrieved it from the top shelf in her closet and handed it to Sofia. It had been sealed in a box, wrapped in tape as if it could have escaped on its own. She slept with it every night since. She also packed a deflated soccer ball. Everyone knew that soccer was a big deal in Latin America. Maybe it would help somehow.

What was the fastest way to get from Antigua to Lake Atitlán? Helicopter, at least according to guidebook number two. And how did one pay for a helicopter ride? Cash. Her grandfather had set up a savings account in her name. She emptied it three days before they left, and reserved a dawn flight out of Antigua. Would American dollars be okay, she asked in a phone call? "*Claro,*" said the crackly voice from Guatemala.

All of the phoning and strategizing had to be done in the hours after school, before Kate got home. There would be astounding long-distance charges, but after Guatemala, she wouldn't care.

Sofia knew her mother thought she was angry and pouting, and maybe she was. But that wasn't why she spent so much time in her room. She was studying maps, calculating how long it would take to get across the lake, and how she would find the village where she had been born.

With a twin, even if it is fraternal, you're both born with the same antenna. She wanted Mateo to be alive, but she knew her mother and grandfather would never believe her if she told them. She had heard a long-distance drum beat all of her life, hammering under her skin. It had to be him.

Sofia knew it wouldn't be like they both always loved cherry ice cream even though they were separated at birth, well, not at birth, but at age two. That kind of stuff happened with identical twins. They were born with the same chemistry. He had called to her in dreams, or when she heard a bird song, or when she smelled the rich mineral scent of lake water.

Sofia slipped out of the guesthouse at 6 a.m. A taxi took her to the landing pad, a flat parcel of dry ground behind a churchyard. She handed the pilot a white envelope with a wad of dollars. He wore a baseball cap, jeans, and Nikes. He counted the dollars and helped her up the steps. Sofia feared he would ask if she was old enough and she began to wonder if she was old enough too. He didn't ask. He helped her strap in, put on his sunglasses, and they rose straight up.

A sudden panic struck her, not from acceleration, not from leaving the ground, but the sound of the whop, whop, whop beating a murderous dread into her, like an ancient war beat, a giant from the sky sent to destroy her. Her heart raced. She closed her eyes and gripped the edge of her seat. She wanted to be covered and held.

"We will be there in thirty minutes," said the pilot. "Don't worry. I haven't killed anyone yet."

She covered her eyes with her hat for most of the flight, peeking only when she felt a turn or a change in altitude. They flew over the mountains as the sun came up, blinding her. She looked at the pilot to be sure that he could see. The combination of sunglasses and baseball cap was practical. Sofia gasped when the massive lake came into view, jolting her with the force of electricity. It looked like a giant mountain had been scooped out by a melon baller, leaving a sunken bowl filled with water. Sharp peaks surrounded the lake. Volcanoes.

They landed in a schoolyard, blowing a vortex of dust into the air. "Where is the boat launch?" Sofia yelled, trying to be heard above the engine.

The pilot pointed off to the left. She grabbed her pack and slid out of the seat, dropping to the ground. She'd find it. She'd find everything. First, she'd find out where to inflate the soccer ball.

CHAPTER 44

Kate and her father walked back toward their guesthouse. Sam wiped his forehead with his palm. She could not have imagined what Sam's reaction would be to this hardscrabble, mountainous country. Would it bring out all of his long-simmering PTSD born of the war in Vietnam? Would the presence of the military in Guatemala, while massively subdued from the war years, fire up his hypervigilance? Would the throngs of impoverished indigenous women and children drag him back to his violent and guilt-infused memories of the country he had been sent to invade as a young man? And what old military know-how might he call upon now that his beloved granddaughter had skittered off?

As they turned the first corner on the long block, Sam stopped when he saw a soldier standing on the cobblestoned street corner, young and tender with his thin arms poised on an automatic weapon. Kate put her hand on his arm, thinking to anchor him into the present.

"He is just a boy," he said. "He is only beginning . . ." and then words failed him and his eyes filled with tears.

"That was me," he said. Sam's response was not what she had feared. He looked like he was being reborn, baptized into a kind of awakening, half a world away from the source of his old war traumas. Sam seemed to be looking at the alternate universe of his life as a young man, watching the calamity of war and its aftereffects as if it was a private showing just for him. A kind of stainless steel brace lifted off him and he looked younger.

"Let's see if they'll stash our luggage," he said. His voice was clear and sure in a way that Kate had never heard before.

They were on the road by noon, with Fernando at the wheel. By five, the sun was low in the sky and they had not even reached the halfway mark.

"Here is our sign of economic progress," said Fernando. "Road construction. Once this is finished, the route from Antigua to Sololá will be smooth and twice as wide as it is now. And we will move along it easily. But for now, we crawl like ants."

The traffic was thick with chicken buses, large trucks carrying concrete and stone, every sort of pickup truck, and cars. Emissions controls were not yet part of their economic growth and Kate's eyes and throat burned from the diesel exhaust. Their progress could be measured in feet, creeping along at a rate that made Kate want to jump out of her skin. She wondered if it might be quicker if she got out and ran, huffing up the steep mountain road.

The odd feeling scratched at her brain again, the too-easy way that Fernando had welcomed her. Something was off.

"You knew I was coming. How did you know?" she said. Kate sat in the backseat, giving her long-legged father a chance to stretch out in the front.

The traffic was at a standstill. Fernando pressed his palms together and took a breath. "I received a letter a few months ago. Mail delivery is still unbearably slow. It was written by your Martin, sent by his lawyer in the event of his death. He wanted me to find Will and give him an envelope. Martin knew that Will was the man you had loved long ago."

Kate grabbed the back of the front seat. Martin had put this into place after she told him about Guatemala. Their years together flew past her, ripping through time in fast-forward. He had never mentioned Guatemala again. But she never told him Will's name. How could he have known?

"Why did he do that? Will is married. I told Martin that he was with someone else."

Fernando turned his head and registered surprise with a small smile. "Will has never married. He has never loved anyone else."

Sam looked back at Kate. "Do you think Martin sent more letters? Should we be on the lookout for further communiqués from the dead? I mean that in the best way possible."

"Do you know what was in the letter?" asked Kate, ignoring her father's attempt at humor.

"Will told me only that you had lost your husband and that we should expect you and Sofia."

"And where is he?"

"He is often in Guatemala City, working with the forensic teams, identifying the remains in mass graves, always translating. Or else he spends months, sometimes years in the northern villages that were hardest hit in the war. It was not an easy thing to locate him," said Fernando.

"But you did. I know you did," she said.

Sam put his hand on the dashboard. "We need to stay focused on our girl," he said. "The rest of this can wait."

"Where is he?" said Kate.

"There is a good chance that you will find him in the remote villages outside Santa Teresa. He said that he had never been there, that he had avoided it, and now he was ready to help with translations."

Why had Martin created this avalanche? He must have known how deeply his letter would affect Sofia.

Fernando broke into her thoughts. "After we arranged for Will to be released, he needed time to recover. He lived with my wife and me for a few months. He insisted on washing dishes for the café, even with his injuries. . . ." Fernando paused. His Adam's apple slid up and down as he swallowed. "He had broken ribs, a broken arm, and other injuries that he chose not to tell me about."

The wind picked up a swirl of dust. Kate rolled up her window, picturing Will beaten and bloodied. She shuddered. He had helped them escape. He had paid the price.

"Then for several years after that, we lost track of him. We heard he was working on a coffee plantation. But wherever he went, he translated, that much I do know. As the war limped to conclusion, he was asked to translate for the peace accord. He was the only person who could translate every dialect." Fernando flexed his fingers on the steering wheel. "He's been translating ever since, helping villagers come face-to-face with the soldiers who had terrorized them."

The weight of losing those she loved bore down on her, crushing her skull. She massaged her temples. "What if Sofia hates me? What if she finds her people and wants to stay here?" she whispered.

Sam said, "First we have to find her, that's the important thing."

CHAPTER 45

Sofia

Sofia found the dock and boarded a water taxi to Santiago. She put her newly inflated soccer ball inside a string bag she'd purchased. The interior of the boat was painted a delicious sky blue, with rows of seats, enough for twenty people. She had never done anything like this before, nothing that was this important. She had been shot out into the world and everything she had known before felt distorted.

At Santiago, the boatman reached out his hand to steady the passengers as they climbed up to the edge of the boat and onto the dock. Sofia put one foot on the bright blue edge and pushed up and over, declining the man's hand. She was an athlete. Her calves were reliable springboards, her quadriceps roped in firm flesh. Years of soccer left her light on her toes, with her knees flexed, sure of her place on the field.

She always wondered how far she could run if she had to. Say, if someone dropped her off in the center of a rain forest, how long could she run if she had to? Sofia had asked her mother about this once. Was it when she first entered high school? Her mother had dropped a pan of hot water filled with potatoes and shouted, "You will never be dropped off in a jungle! Why would you ask such a thing?" She vacillated between hating her mother and wanting her to be there with her right now.

Her muscles ticked to something new. There were two North Americans with a band of high school kids on the boat. Three Mayan women seated in the back of the boat glanced at Sofia when she climbed in at Pana. After spotting the brown-skinned women, all lit with primary colors of red, yellow, and blue, she felt a pinch in her chest, hot and hard. She wanted to say, *Excuse me, but I don't know who I am. I've grown up in white Leverett my whole life running around with a soccer ball. But do you happen to know my people?*

The dock poured the passengers onto a road that led up a hill. Sofia hitched her ergonomically correct backpack to her right shoulder and started up the path. A cluster of small Mayan boys, all of whom came to her ribs, glanced at her and ran by, moving instead to the white high school kids. The little boys eagerly tried to sell small wooden flutes. A group of girls ran past her in blue *huipiles,* their little-girl hips wrapped in handwoven fabric held tight by a cloth belt. The girls held scraps of cloth for sale and they focused on the two adult North Americans.

Sofia was in a pool of people who looked like her, and yet did not. She walked up the hill, dotted with merchant booths on either side, filled with leather goods, fabric, hats, sandals, tinwork, and an unending array of crafts. She was taller than the Mayan women. Mom's home cooking, she thought with a stab of uncomfortable longing. Did she miss her mother or her birth mother? Sofia stopped and dug into her pack. She extracted the roll of fabric that Manuela had woven. She asked at the first booth, *Where is the village where the women weave this cloth? I am the daughter of Manuela and Jorge.*

The woman had a roll of cloth wrapped around the crown of her head like a rope. She said something to Sofia in a language that she didn't understand. Her mother had called it Kaqchikel. Sofia shook her head. The woman called to a little boy across the street and she bent her head near his, her finger holding him firmly. She said something to him, and they both looked at Sofia. He ran off on what looked like an errand.

Sofia continued up the street, looking at the women in front of stacks of cloth. Now she asked only about the fabric, thinking that perhaps no one here knew Manuela and Jorge. Had too much time passed for them to be remembered? Did Sofia's Spanish sound too official, too North American? Did the merchants speak only Mayan?

Sofia continued up the steep street, gripping the cloth.

The air was filled with the raw scents of onions, potatoes, open piles of ground corn, bananas, along with stacks of fabric. At several stalls, women sat on the ground weaving, passing a smooth piece of wood back and forth. The weaving rig was attached to the women's waists and at the other end, to a pole. Smoke was the background flavor, lending a charcoal seasoning to everything.

She knew she was a strange mix of American dress, schoolgirl Spanish, and indigenous face. If what her mother said was true, the village she sought was not so far from Santiago. But could she believe anything that her mother said? That was a big question right now.

She began to experiment with streets, keeping the central square in sight, walking two blocks down one direction, making a right, then two blocks right again, and she was back at the central square. By mid-afternoon she had made a grid of the town that extended four blocks in each direction from the center.

She purchased and ate fresh palm-sized tortillas. They were not at all like the tortillas that came from the grocery store at home. They were thicker and so much smaller. She wasn't sure what else she should eat and nothing looked familiar. She bought a banana.

She heard a familiar sound down one street, the noise of

children playing. She followed it and saw a group of boys outside a school. They were maybe ten or eleven, playing soccer with the most dilapidated ball she had ever seen. The ball was held together with tape. The boys played on hard-packed dirt. They were artful with the old ball, each boy dribbling it as if the ball were attached to them by an invisible band. Their control of the ball was easy and they flew from one end of the yard to the other, dancing lightly, shouting at one another.

Sofia put down her pack and dug around in the string bag until she found the new soccer ball that she had brought with her. What would they think of her, this brown girl, taller and older than them?

She dropped the ball to the ground, flipped it to one knee and then the other, while advancing toward the boys. It didn't matter if this was Guatemala or Massachusetts, she had a glistening new soccer ball, dazzling white with black lines, and they would not be able to resist. If she couldn't find the village, she could at least play soccer.

The boys saw right away that Sofia was very good. Their game slowed as Sofia came closer, and then they stopped completely. They stared at her as if she were a gazelle.

"Can anyone play?" she asked, not really a question, but an announcement. She pulled her hair back into a ponytail.

Several boys stared at her with mouths open, others stole sideways glances to each other.

"We can use this ball," she said in her best Spanish. They would not be able to resist the ball, no soccer player could. "*Me llamo Sofia,*" she said. She asked the boys to say their names and then they divided into teams in a way that Sofia did not entirely understand, but it felt good to run, to be fast, to use her body. Soon the boys shouted her name. *Sofia, Sofia, here, pass the ball!*

This is what she loved about running, about soccer; she could forget everything else. There was nothing except her body and the ball, the heavy breath of the other players, the feel of the ball beneath her shoes or on her knees, the shocking thump of it on her forehead as she headed the ball to a teammate.

The boys danced with the ball, as agile as if they had been born with it. A small lad named Roberto slid so perfectly between two opponents that he would have qualified as a shape-shifter. He made the goal, marked by two rocks. Sofia jumped in the air, pumping one arm up, and gave a whoop.

The boys stopped and looked beyond Sofia. She turned around and a white guy walked toward her. There was a kid with him. Wasn't he from the first stall where she had asked about the village?

"Sofia?" the man asked, tilting his head to one side.

She nodded, still breathing hard from the game.

"I hear that you are looking for Santa Teresa," he said in English.

Her heart thumped so loudly that everyone must hear it.

"And that you are the daughter of Manuela and Jorge."

Maybe it was the altitude. Her mother had said that they needed to drink water, that the mountain air was dry and dehydration could take them by surprise. She felt light-headed.

"Hello, Will," she said.

CHAPTER 46

They arrived in Pana hours after sunset. The wind howled, a fierce *El Norte* across the lake.

"The water taxis have closed down," said Fernando. "Even in better weather, the boats do not have lights and accidents have been deadly at night. There is no one willing to take us across the lake and for that, I am grateful."

The three of them stood on the dock as the wind whipped their hair. They looked out on the dark waters with white caps that rivaled an unruly sea. Kate tried to imagine Sofia finding her way in Santiago. She was so young, so driven by one purpose that she would be unaware of dangers, of men who would find her beautiful and offer their assistance. What did Sofia know of any of this?

Before she could speculate aloud, Sam said, "Our girl is not an idiot. She has checked into a hotel and has wedged a chair against the doorknob. She knows what she wants." He turned to Fernando. "How long do these *El Norte* weather systems last?"

"By morning, the lake will be as smooth as glass again. Allow me to help you find rooms for the night. We will take a boat in the morning."

They walked up the steep incline from the dock and several blocks to a hotel. Nothing about Pana looked the same except the lake. The streets were paved and restaurants were filled with people eating at small tables. When they walked past a storefront that said *Internet Café,* Kate stopped as if struck by an invisible wall.

"I can't believe this," she said.

Fernando smiled. "The world has found us, but more importantly, we have found the world."

Sam rubbed Kate's upper arm. "This place doesn't look anything like what you told us about Guatemala. I was expecting a tiny village with dogs and chickens running around. This must be what it feels like for vets when they travel to Saigon and see a vibrant city filled with food carts and kids running off to school." Sam stopped. "Okay, not quite the same, but I understand how disorienting this must be."

She felt more like a ghost from the past.

They checked into a small hotel. Fernando and Sam went in search of food with promises to bring back something for Kate. But she would not be able to eat, not while Sofia was out there on her own.

CHAPTER 47

Sofia

"I'm here alone," Sofia said. "I want to find the village where I was born. My mother and grandfather are back in Antigua. I wanted to do this alone. Do you know where my village is?"

Will was an older guy, she didn't know how old, but it had been twelve years since she left, so that must make him . . . She didn't know, but his hair was whitish around his temples. The rest of his hair was light, a sun-bleached kind of blond. He wore sandals and his feet were really tan, like he wore only sandals. She'd never seen such tanned feet.

She stuffed her soccer ball back in the bag, despite the groans of the boys.

"I do know where the village is, but let's get back to you being here alone. Does Kate know that you're here? Why isn't she with you?" He handed her a backpacker's bottle of water, the refillable kind. Yes, this was her mother's kind of guy.

"I want to do this alone. She will try to soften everything, protect me. Believe me, they'll know where I've gone. I'm guessing that I've got about a half-day lead on them. Will you take me to Santa Teresa?"

"What do you mean by *them?* I thought that her husband, your stepfather had . . ." For someone who was supposed to be so smart, Will looked sort of clueless.

"My grandfather is with us. And you're right, my stepfather is . . . he was killed in a bike accident. I mean a car accident. I mean he was hit by a car when he was riding his bike." It was still hard to talk about the way Martin had died. "Will you take me there?"

Will rubbed his eyes as if there was something in them. "I'm sorry about your stepfather. It's terrible to lose someone you love." He took a breath. "I've been in Santiago for about a month. The truth is, I've been waiting for you. I'll take you there only because I know Kate and I know that she'll come after you. I'm guessing that she's with Fernando. But you need to know something first and then you can be the one to decide if we should go to the village before your mother gets here."

A shiver ran up her spine.

"Your brother survived the massacre. I found him a few months ago."

Sofia's breath flew out of her, her hands pressed against her mouth, and she made a squeaking kind of noise, unintelligible, birdlike. She had a brother, a brother, someone else who was part of her first family. She was right! A balloon of loneliness that she never fully recognized before burst as if hit by a pin. Tiny stars came out of the balloon and glittered throughout her body.

"I knew it, I've always known it," she said. The day was growing later and it had a dreamy quality. The wind whipped up the dust along the playing field. "I knew he was alive, I could feel him." She had the weirdest sensation that her heart was turning inside out.

"Wait, why were you expecting us?"

Will smiled at her and the skin around the sides of his eyes crinkled. "It's a long story. I'll tell you as we walk. But I wish that I could have known Martin. I'm glad he was with you and your mother."

Sofia stole glances at Will as they walked along the road that turned to dirt as soon as they left Santiago. Three men overtook them and passed easily, short-handled hoes hanging from their belts. They wore pants that looked too short for them.

So this was the man her mother had loved. This was the man who had suffered at the hands of the military when her mother had taken her out of the country. This was the man who had known her when she was just a toddler. This was the man who was taking her to her brother, her home.

"The village is tucked behind the volcano about four miles from Santiago," he said. "But Santiago is where people come to shop, to sell their merchandise, and for those kids who can, this is where they go to school," Will said. His legs were long and Sofia had to double her speed to keep up with him. He had on cargo shorts that brushed his knees and his muscles were tight and toned.

She stopped walking. Her stomach clenched and for the first time since she had planned this, she was afraid.

Sofia blurted, "What if he doesn't want me? What if he resents me?"

Will had a tenderness around his eyes that Martin had too. "You and Mateo share ancestors, and for the Maya, that means everything. You are a missing piece in the family puzzle for them. They had extraordinary losses, deaths that were unimaginable. The fact that you are alive means they lost a little less, that life won out over the war just a little more. He's had more time to think about this than you have."

"What do you mean? My mother thought he was dead. How would he know anything about me?" Even as she spoke, she felt something growing closer to her; part of her brother was carried on the wind.

"Your stepdad, who must have been some kind of guy, arranged for a letter to be sent to me in the event of his death.

He let me know a few things, and by then, I had found Mateo. So he's had a few weeks to think about you coming here. Which, by the way, he insisted you would do."

A hint of cool air ran up the path from a shadowy gully. "When I first found Mateo, it took me months to put the picture together. I was here with a group that wanted to reunite the men who had been conscripted as boys to be soldiers with the people of the area villages. They were also trying to identify people from some of the older mass graves."

Birds rustled in the trees, rattling the leaves.

"He has an amazing affinity for languages. I could spot it right away with him. He's been learning English. And French from one of the French anthropologists."

The sun sank a little lower. "Can we keep going now?" Will asked. "Mateo isn't always in the village. Most days he's in Santiago studying, but today he's helping his grandfather. Not a blood grandfather, but the man who took care of him after the massacre."

Sofia exhaled a shuddered breath. Her head was ready to burst with old imagined images of her brother and now he was real. "I'm ready," she said.

They turned off the dirt road and walked up a partially paved road, some concrete, some stones set in place, but ever upward. Was she going home?

She heard the village before she saw it. A few dogs with tightly curled tails approached them and others barked in the distance. She smelled wood smoke, even though the day was still warm. She wondered how this would all go. Would they be shy? Run to each other in cinematic joy? She didn't know how to be with a brother. She only knew that nothing would be the same after this.

Will knelt down to the first child he saw and said something, not in Spanish so it had to be in Mayan. The child, a little girl with a red skirt exactly like the cloth that Sofia had in her pack, looked wide-eyed at Sofia and took off running up the road.

"I just rang the alarm," said Will. "Now everyone will know that you are here."

They walked into the center of the village, paved with stones, and highlighted by a small church. It was unlike any house of worship that Sofia had ever seen, and she knew what it was only because of the wood cross atop the one-story building. Next door was an adobe building. The sign outside it said *CLINICA*. A few dark-haired women washed clothing in a concrete water tank. They looked up at Will.

How much farther would they have to go? Sofia wasn't sure that she could keep breathing. Tiny paths and streets darted off the central area. She swiveled her head around, wanting to find something familiar, something that she could remember.

She felt a hand on her shoulder and there he was. He was a few inches taller than she was. She had to turn her chin up only a fraction to look into his eyes. She shivered. The dark eyes of her brother flicked a switch and she would never be a child again. She doubted that he had ever been a child after their parents were killed. She reached up with one hand and put her palm on his cheek. He was not a dream. He was solid and real. He mirrored her and did the same with his hand.

"Mateo, Mateo," she said.

"My sister," he said in English. His chin quivered and he blinked hard, just as Sofia did.

The brother and sister sat on a stucco wall outside his house on the steep hill. Mateo had not let go of the roll of fabric that Sofia pulled from her pack. He clenched it in his hands. A veranda was covered with wide palm leaves, layered like roof tiles to let the rain run off the low stone wall.

"On the day that you disappeared, chaos reigned for weeks. How could the dead be tallied, never mind the missing? Both our parents were dead, first our father, then our mother was killed in the massacre. I can show you their graves. I was taken to a hospital in Sololá and it was the start of the rainy season before I was well enough to leave. Children heal quickly, but our ancestors were searching for you and too busy to tend to my torn body."

They spoke in English and Spanish. He paused and Sofia

was too mesmerized to speak, afraid that if she made a sound, he would evaporate like the morning fog on the river. She wanted him to take his shoes off so she could look at his feet. Would they look the same as her childhood dreams of brown feet?

"The big question back then was who was going to take care of me. I was a small child without parents or grandparents. I don't remember being in the hospital. I remember something about the smell of not being touched. How does that smell, you ask? Like burned beans mixed with a drink they gave all the children. In the hospital you are touched, and kindly, when a wound needs tending, like mine, or when the women come to change the sheets, wash them and hang them from the clotheslines on the roof. You are touched for all kinds of reasons, but not the way a mother or father touches a child, not the way you are wrapped tightly on her back, surrounded by her smell."

They held Manuela's red cloth between them, each rubbing between thumb and fingers as they talked.

Sofia's foot had gone to sleep because she had tucked it beneath her. Squirming, she said, "If I move, I'm afraid you will vanish. I have dreamt of you for so long. But if I don't move, the blood will be cut off to my leg."

"Please save your leg. And watch, I will not disappear."

He wore tan pants, with a belt, and his shirt was tucked in. There was a gap between his two front teeth, spacious enough that she could easily slip a dime through. This would never happen in Leverett, where all teeth are perfectly spaced and precisely straight.

"There was a question of who would claim me. The country was filled with orphans of the war. One of the doctors wanted to send me to the orphanage in Antigua. And then Juan Ortega came for me. He was old then and he is even older now," he said. "He told them he was my grandfather, which he was not, but he became my grandfather. He came for me because he said the ancestors called to him. He saw our mother and all the others killed and saw the white woman pick you out of the pile of bodies, right in front of the soldiers. He said she was filled with courage and very stupid."

Sofia put her hands over her face. "Why didn't she take you with us?"

Mateo reached to put his hand on Sofia's arm. "Everyone thought I was dead. Do not blame her. Kate saw a dead boy. It was not until they moved the dead bodies that someone saw that I was still alive, breathing quietly."

Two little girls walked by in traditional dress, woven cloth wrapped around their thin bodies, tied at the waist. They turned their heads to stare at Sofia, who was like them, but not. What was she?

Sofia turned her head at the crunch of gravel footsteps. It was getting dark and the wind had picked up. It was Will, looking sorry to interrupt.

"Kate won't make it across the lake tonight. All the boats have stopped. We'll need to sleep here. Mateo?"

"My grandfather is already preparing hammocks and sleeping mats for you," he said, smiling.

CHAPTER 48

They took the first boat out of Pana. Kate had not slept, but waited for the first glimmer of daylight over the lake, listening to her own heartbeat, praying that nothing had happened to Sofia, that she was not stripped from her like her mother, or Martin. Like Manuela and her son. She did not want to live a life of protracted sorrow laced with guilt.

The water taxi eased out of the dock, the engine purring softly. Then, as the young boatman increased the speed, the front of the boat rose up and they sped across the lake. The boat was filled with people going to work, women with babies strapped to their backs in tightly wrapped fabric, men with their belts cinched around their slight waists, all heading for a long day of labor. Kate was bookended by her father and Fernando on the fiberglass bench. Midway across the lake, the motor sputtered and cut out. Something was wrong. No, not now, she had to find Sofia.

A sudden spray of water rose from the lake, for no apparent reason, as if they were moving—but they were dead still while the boatman fussed with the engine. The winged spray lifted up from the lake, unlike anything she had seen before, a mini-whirlpool reaching up, as tall as a woman. Where had the spray of water come from? The water droplets were velvet across her cheeks. Did no one else notice this?

She looked at her father and he wiped his face also. Had her mother caressed them both from the very thing that she had loved, water, a great body of water? How much louder does love need to shout? Was it just Kate wishing for her mother?

"Your mother would have loved this place. I never knew the lake was this beautiful—" He was interrupted by the purr of the engine.

As the boat docked, Kate wanted to fling herself onto the rough wood of the pier, but the boat was filled beyond capacity with Mayan passengers. Kate, Sam, and Fernando somehow managed to be at the end of the line to disembark. None of them had spoken since the driver had restarted the boat.

Kate had never traveled to the village where Manuela lived. Manuela said it was small and the road to it very steep. She met with Manuela only in Santiago.

Fernando asked the boatman where Santa Teresa was. There was pointing and gesturing in a mix of Spanish and Kaqchikel.

"It is beyond Santiago, about four miles," said Fernando.

Santiago was more vibrant than Kate remembered. It had been a center of commerce before, but now someone had doused the entire town with Crayola colors. Stalls of fabric and leather, pottery and jewelry lined the steep street leading to the center of town.

Every Mayan face held traces of Sofia—the delicate curve of eyelids, the straight chisel of nose, the deepest brown eyes, black hair catching shards of sunlight. Kate's father, in comparison, looked large, with unfocused features, with skin so pale and mottled that it looked like he lived underground. Here they were the oddity. What had Sofia felt when she stepped off the boat and was surrounded by Maya? Did she think she could merge with them like a bird returning to her own flock? No, living in Massachusetts for twelve years had altered her plumage.

They walked through a haze of cooking smells, small cook fires here and there, the pat, pat, pat of hands forming corn tortillas. These were the smells before the massacre. Fernando told her once that for the Maya, everything that has ever happened exists in the present moment.

It had been hard enough to let that sink in twelve years ago when she was terrified for the toddler Sofia, but now, as she stopped to catch her breath, the smell of singed tortillas caught her, and all the past moments rumbled up from the lake, from Manuela, from the gunfire, from Will finding a way to get Sofia out—all flitted by her nostrils, and she felt her skull opening in a strange way. It took only a second for all that had gone before to collect itself into the whisper of smoke from the last woman on the far side of town cooking.

Kate caught the eyes of the small, birdlike woman who smiled at her. This couldn't be the Tortilla Lady from long ago, the woman who pressed warm rounds of flattened maize into her hands after the soldiers had pushed her aside with their guns.

Fernando and Sam kept going, oblivious to the churning of time and space in Kate. She hurried to catch up with them, but she turned to look back at the woman. Did the woman tilt her head toward the road out of town? Or had she just been looking down at something?

They climbed, ever upward, on a village road trodden by feet for so long that even the surface could not count the centuries. Sam looked back at the lake, a face-saving move to disguise a desperate need to keep his lungs from bursting. "It's okay, Dad, it's the elevation. It's hard for me too," she said.

The road curled around in sharp S curves, and on one turn, a small boy sat on a boulder. He was dressed in jeans and a thin T-shirt. The boy hopped off the boulder and said in Spanish,

"Please follow me. Sofia and her brother, Mateo, are waiting." Kate stumbled and caught Fernando's arm.

Mateo? Sofia's brother? How could he be alive? Were all of the dead going to rise up? Would Martin meet them around the next turn? Would her mother lift up from her grave and paddle across the lake in her old canoe? Manuela's children had lived, both of them.

The air glittered with dust and the road beneath her feet seemed to melt and turn to wing, or bone, blood, or water. In front of her was the miracle that Mateo was alive and behind her was Sofia's childhood of longing for her brother. Kate teetered along a fulcrum point, one foot on each side, wavering, her knees ready to buckle.

Kate had never seen Fernando undone before. His face twitched as if he was reconfiguring. "You told me that the boy and the mother were dead."

"Believe me, Manuela was dead. And the boy looked dead, I was sure of it. Things happened very quickly, I had only a moment to decide what to do," she said. Her throat was dry and tight.

Sam dropped his pack on the ground, retrieved a water bottle, and handed it to Kate. "This is what everyone prays for in a war, that the dead are not really dead. I've wished back so many people from Vietnam," said Sam. "What we have here is a miracle, or as close to one as I've ever seen." He offered the bottle to Fernando, who declined, and put it back into his pack and hoisted it on one shoulder. "The war claimed one less victim. Score one for the good guys."

Someone had to go first. Kate's lungs burned from the exertion of hiking the steep path. Sofia was just ahead in the village. And Mateo. In the thin oxygen, her pounding heart was background noise to her real fear. Here were the people who could accuse her of stealing one of their people, of taking Sofia away. Her accusers had lived in her dreams, in her skin, along the back of her neck. Now they stood ready to meet her.

The worst of the lies had been about Sofia's brother. What could be more elemental than a sibling? Why had she lied to Sofia about a brother? She could have said yes, there was a brother, but he had died. She hadn't wanted one more death to weigh on Sofia.

But she was wrong.

CHAPTER 49

Will

The letter was in his pack. He read it over and over, until the paper began to shred.

Fernando knew how to find him, through the Historical Clarification Commission in Guatemala City. Will was the main translator between the Maya and all the forensic anthropologists who sought to identify bodies from the war. French, Italian, German, Norwegian, Venezuelan, and all the English speakers relied on Will to speak with the Maya, to find the thousands of indigenous people who had been killed.

The international effort to heal the war would take a long time. Will wished that he had the patience of the Maya. Even after so many years, he hadn't been able to fully step into their understanding of time, their belief that time and place were inextricably linked, that there was no compulsion to hurry.

The letter arrived two months ago, from a lawyer in Massachusetts who sent the letter to Fernando.

Dear Will,

If you are reading this, then I am dead and two things have happened in order to get this letter into your hands. First, the letter arrived intact to Fernando. Second, he found you.

Kate never told me your name. She said it was the last thing she could do to protect you. But I heard your name from time to time when nightmares would grab my love and she'd call out for you.

I was the luckiest guy in the world to find Kate and Sofia. A lot luckier than you, it seems. We disagreed on one thing, and that was about Sofia, that the kid needed to know where she came from. Six months after my death (this is weird to talk about my death, but you never know, life is temporary) a lawyer will deliver a letter to Sofia telling her everything I know. Kate is going to wonder why I would cause such a shit storm. But I do know this, I have loved Kate and she loved me more than I ever could have hoped for. And if Kate does what I think, she'll bring Sofia back to the place where she was born. I'm giving you a heads-up notice.

Don't hesitate if love comes around again.

Martin

The boy ran to Will's side, then to Mateo and Sofia to tell them that Kate was approaching. Will wanted more time to steady his heartbeat, which pounded so hard that the women washing clothes at the center of town must be able to hear it. Kate would be here in minutes. What if the years had changed them so much that only a war-torn fantasy remained?

He feared the worst, feeling as helpless as he did when he saw Jenkins next to Kate on the airplane, when what he loved was taken from him. He ran into the only building that might contain him, hide him. He pulled open the heavy doors to the church and collapsed inside, his chest heaving. He was not a religious man, but so many years among the Maya had given him the assurance that churches were a place of comfort.

CHAPTER 50

Sofia

Why did Will duck into that church? Sofia was positive that she was in a ton of trouble with her mother. And with her grandfather. This was almost like running away from home, but not quite. She had been running toward home.

Well, not home. Her old home. But when her mother walked into the center of the village with her grandfather and the other man, her mother wasn't able to stop crying. And if her mother cried, Sofia cried, which was the way it had always been. It was some kind of automatic reaction.

Something changed and she didn't know if her mother could feel it yet. Sofia had grown older; a layer of childhood slipped off her and lay crumpled like a discarded snake-skin. Sofia, even in the shuddering hug of her mother, felt whole in a way that she never imagined before. She had found her brother.

Mateo walked toward Kate. He put one hand on each of her

shoulders and faced her. Her mother wasn't a beautiful crier and her face pretty much crumpled up.

She said something to Mateo that Sofia didn't understand. "Manuela has been trying to tell me that you were alive," said Kate. "All this time I thought that your mother was angry with me. I mean, in my dreams."

"The ancestors speak in a language that needs . . ." Here Mateo's English failed him. "Translation," he said finally. Mateo and Kate were going to get along just fine.

Sam huffed his way into the scene, clearly compromised by altitude. "Don't do that again, sweetheart," he said, pulling Sofia into a hug. "I want to know how you got here."

She'd tell him about the helicopter later. She wasn't sure when, but later.

Already the family was bigger, less defined than it had been before in Leverett. But what would it mean, this family that was bigger, blended, chopped up by war, and separated by languages and countries and then thrown together into something new?

Her mother stopped crying and sniffled.

"Mom, what happens now?" asked Sofia.

Kate wiped her face with the edge of her shirt. She looked soft and fresh as if she had just stepped from a swim in the river. She nudged Sofia. "Who is that man? He looks familiar."

She pointed to Mateo's grandfather, Juan. Sofia would tell her later. Her mother looked like she was beyond absorbing any new information. This must be what it feels like to not be a kid anymore, when she could see her mother in this softer way.

"He is my adopted grandfather," said Mateo. Oh, she was going to like having a brother. Mateo smiled at her. They already had a language of their own.

"He looks familiar. But now we thank the ancestors. That's what Manuela would do. After that, I don't even know where to start," said Kate.

Mateo pointed to the church. "Will is in there. He is teaching me languages. He told me many things about you."

* * *

Kate walked across the village center toward the church. She looked back once at Sofia and Sam. Mateo smiled encouragingly. Fernando was talking with the adopted grandfather.

Kate pulled open the door and stood, letting her eyes adjust, turning her head as she scanned the building. She put her hand on her lips as if she had seen a ghost. Then she stepped in and the thick door closed behind her.

CHAPTER 51

What was left of her insides turned to water, sparkling and fresh. The damp air of the church rushed to meet her, smelling like the last days with Manuela, the cool stones in the church in Santiago, the last lessons of English and the mysteries of tying a child to one's back with a long cloth.

Could she say his name?

"Will?" she whispered.

Kate heard him before she saw him, recognizing the cadence of his footsteps. She spun her head to the right, to the sound of him. As he came closer, a shaft of light from the front of the church caught him, illuminating the side of his face. Will stopped two feet from her.

"Kate. I want one minute with you all to myself." He reached out a hand and took one of hers. A warm glow ran up her arm. She knew she was trembling and there was nothing she could do to stop it. A tremor ran through his hand, his palm rougher than she remembered. Had too much changed? Had twelve years dulled their senses?

She brought her other hand to cover his. "I thought I'd never see you again. I thought I had to live without you."

They took the small steps to close the gap between them. Kate was no longer sure she was breathing. They touched each other as if they were blind, moving their hands up each other's arms, touching shoulders, fingertips to the neck, a caress along jawlines, fingers in hair, along the tender skin of eyelids. Yes, they were both real, no mirages had tricked them.

The doors creaked open and a shock of light spilled into the church. "Mom, are you okay?" Sofia poked her head in.

The question of the day. Was Kate okay? Were they all okay? A trickle of laughter rose up from the depths of her torso, building as it traveled up and out, gathering speed. When had she laughed with this force? Will pulled his head back, a surprised look on his face, but he caught it too. "Are we okay?" Their laughter rose up into the damp church, startling the birds that had found their way in through the cracks. The strange kitten-sounding birds. Their laughter spent, Will bent his forehead to Kate's upturned face.

"Are you ready?" she asked, not needing to know what they were ready for, only that they had found each other.

"I am so ready," he said.

Hand in hand, they walked outside to those who had survived. And from those who had not survived, Kate was certain that she heard their welcoming sighs.

ACKNOWLEDGMENTS

I am grateful to my two enduring writing groups, the Great Darkness and the Manuscript Group. These writers have supported and encouraged me through all the first drafts. They include: Marianne Banks, Jeanne Borfitz, Jennifer Jacobson, Celia Jeffries, Kris Holloway, Lisa Drnec Kerr, Patricia Lee Lewis, Alan and Edie Lipp, Rita Marks, Ellie Meeropol, Lydia Nettler, Patricia Riggs, Morgan Sheehan-Bubla, and Marion VanArsdell.

In Guatemala, I am inspired by the community of friends who live along the shores of Lake Atitlán. Thanks to Jeanne Mendez for translations into Kaqchikel and thanks to Molly Molander for helping to set the tone of Guatemala in 1990.

Thank you to Alayne Heischman, who saved my computer system from a near-death experience. Again.

Thank you to those who generously offered the solitude of their homes, or summer homes, when I needed to write without interruption. They include Jennifer Jacobson and Michael Nelson, Celia Jeffries, and Jean Zimmerman.

To everyone at Kensington Publishing Corporation: Thank you for opening your arms to this story. Michaela Hamilton is an editor with sizzling intelligence, emotional insight, and a joyful approach to the world of publishing.

Thank you to Victoria Lowes of the Bent Agency for a detailed reading of the manuscript that helped me to stitch the story together.

And to my agent, Jenny Bent, thank you for making the journey with me and my stories. Your fierce support and wisdom light the way.

A READING GROUP GUIDE

THE CENTER OF THE WORLD

Jacqueline Sheehan

ABOUT THIS GUIDE

Here are some questions that may help you start a lively conversation with your book-loving friends.

DISCUSSION QUESTIONS

1. After the massacre takes place, Kate Malloy reacts instantly to protect Sofia. What influences from her past may have made her respond so dramatically?
2. Kate is a scientist and a graduate student who has little experience with children. How does she evolve in responding to Sofia as a mother while they are in Antigua?
3. Did Kate make the right decision to take Sofia out of Guatemala? Was she justified in pulling the child out of her Mayan community? Was there any other choice that Kate could have made?
4. Times of war, disaster, and the constant state of heightened senses can throw people together in the illusion of love. Is this what happened to Kate and Will? Or would they have fallen in love so deeply regardless of time?
5. How does Will's initial excitement about his job opportunity as a Language Specialist blind him to the military forces at work in Guatemala?
6. What is Jenkins's final revenge with Will? Why would a lifetime of war lead some people to cruelty, as with Jenkins, and others to kindness and bravery, as in the case of Fernando?
7. What price does Kate pay for lying about Sofia's heritage and the circumstances of her adoption? How does the lie affect Sofia, Sam, Martin, and Kate?
8. How is it possible for Kate to remain in love with Will, and yet find another man to love and marry?
9. Kate is haunted by dreams about and visitations from Manuela, Sofia's mother. Sofia has a deep inner knowledge that she has a twin brother. How does the Mayan belief of ancestors relate to this story? Who are the ancestors who influence these characters?

10. Sam, Kate's father, is a steady anchor for her, but he has also been scarred by war. How does the experience of traveling to Guatemala change him?
11. Sofia is a soccer star at her Massachusetts high school. How does soccer bind Sofia to her homeland?
12. Discuss how your perception of Martin may have changed over the course of the book.

Don't miss Jacqueline Sheehan's next compelling novel

THE TIGER IN THE HOUSE

Coming from Kensington in 2017

Keep reading to enjoy a preview excerpt. . . .

CHAPTER 1

Claire and Richard had dinner at the seafood place over in South Portland that their daughter raved about all the time. And it was as good as expected. She'd had the lobster roll and Rich had a mountain of fish and chips. It was the sort of place where you go in and order, pay, and then they give you a number, like Hannigan's grocery store when the deli crew takes your order.

The best part was the picnic table behind the seafood shack overlooking the ocean. Claire imagined how the meal would have gone if they were twenty-five years younger and still had the relentless yearning for each other, or if Rich could think of anything to say at all, even that. They ate mostly in silence. Claire liked it better when they were in the active years of parenting, working as a team, laughing so much.

When they were done eating, they each slid into the truck and buckled up. Rich turned to her and said, "Let's take the long way home, over where they're selling off the big Johnson farm." Okay, that felt good. She slipped in a CD of early Bruce Springsteen and grew a little younger, rolled her window down and tapped her fingers along the side-view mirror. They sailed past sea grass and redwing blackbirds perched on top of cattails. The houses grew smaller, more like the old days, less monstrously rich. Claire nudged her sandals off and wiggled her toes.

It was the end of August and the hint of lengthening nights had announced itself already at eight o'clock.

"Look up there," said Rich, already taking his foot off the gas and turning down Bruce Springsteen.

A cloud slid over the low-hanging sun. Up ahead, there was a small child in the road, thumb in mouth. The road turned to gravel a few miles back and they crept along, the large truck wheels crunching the gravel like Styrofoam balls.

The child wore white shorts. There wasn't another car parked along the road, no houses, just a bulldozer that had torn into the earth, making way for a new foundation.

Claire pulled her hand into the truck, getting ready for something. She slipped her sandals back on. The truck would be terrifyingly large to a child.

They pulled up close to the child, who was sucking her thumb. Claire was a small woman and she knew how to talk to kids and she wouldn't be as frightening as a man or a truck.

The child was a girl with soft brown hair. The white shorts were underwear; she had on white underpants and a T-shirt with a faded Disney princess. Claire wasn't sure which princess it was.

She tried to think of something nonthreatening to say that wouldn't alarm the child. The girl looked to be about five.

"Hey there," said Claire, five feet away. The child was barefoot. "My name is Claire. Can you show me where your Mommy and Daddy are?"

Claire took two more steps to the child and pointed back at the truck. "That's my husband, Rich." She stopped in front of the child and squatted down to be eye level with her.

The girl had been crying; her face was covered with dust and the tears had left two stripes along her cheeks.

"I'd like to help you find your family," said Claire. What was that along the kid's arm and neck? Claire stopped breathing. It was blood.

"Sweetie, are you hurt?"

The thumb stayed firmly in the girl's mouth. Claire forced a smile.

"Everything is going to be okay. You wait right here."

She turned at the sound of the truck door closing. "I've already made the call," Rich said, sliding a cell phone into the front pocket of his jeans.

He had a windbreaker in his hands. "Here, put this on her."

CHAPTER 2

"It's not that they live forever, but they should," said Delia. "Instead, dogs live in an accelerated universe, parallel to ours."

She was helping Sam, the local vet, at his annual Spay & Neuter clinic. He had called her when one of his volunteers quit. They started at six in the morning and wouldn't end until seven or eight that night. Sam made tiny stitches along the nether parts of a female terrier mix.

"You don't usually talk about parallel universes. I suspect it's the atmosphere of anesthesia talking. But in general, I know what you mean." Sam wore his special glasses, the same as reading glasses, but larger, the kind that old people wore in the eighties, large and round, circling their eyebrows and the tops of their cheeks. Thick black frames.

Delia wasn't a vet tech, but she had known Sam since junior high. He was a good friend of her father's. His last remaining friend. The best thing about Sam was that he knew the worst parts of her and she didn't have to explain anything.

Sam straightened up, rolling his shoulders back with a groan. "This girl is ready to go back to the recovery room."

This was the part that Delia liked above anything else at the S&N clinic. It was her job to carry the still-anesthetized animals in her arms. She didn't have kids of her own, never had the feel of a babe pressed against her chest, and she wouldn't claim that hoisting freshly neutered dogs and cats was the same as carrying a baby, but there was something about it that stirred her. She protected the animals when they were vulnerable and unable to care for themselves in the postsurgical moments. Sort of like her job as a caseworker with foster kids.

She slid her arms under the small dog, careful to hold up the wobbly head, and walked into the back room where other dogs in various stages of consciousness were placed in wire crates. The techs had put old towels on the bottom of the crates. Delia knelt down and edged the terrier onto the towel. She placed her hand on the warm belly and felt the strum of the heartbeat.

She retraced her steps and returned to the surgery room. Sam stretched his arms overhead, then placed both palms on his lower back and pushed his hips forward.

"My wife tells me that my posture is terrible. She says my profile looks like a question mark. She wants me to go to yoga or tai chi. I don't think that I'm old enough for tai chi. I only ever see old people moving in slow motion doing something called qi gong. Please tell me that I'm not there yet."

Sam was in his fifties, and Delia knew age had nothing to do with his reluctance to exercise. He'd been an athlete as a young man but never made the transition to sports that an older man could enjoy, not tennis or biking, never mind the more esoteric areas of tai chi. His old days as a high school football player resulted in a recent knee surgery. He was six months post knee surgery.

The next dog, a female mixed breed somewhere between beagle and boxer, was brought in and quickly anesthetized. Sam picked up the scalpel, leaned over the spread eagle patient. The scalpel clattered to the floor. He picked up another scalpel from a stainless steel tray. "Clumsy today," he said.

Delia reeled between two things that pulled at her attention. What was different about Sam? He was a stellar vet. Animals loved him. His staff, almost all young women who were vet techs, liked working with him. The staff at the animal shelters said he was their best vet, always willing to work with them on injured animals even when no owner could be found to pay for the expenses.

She didn't hesitate when he called her for help. How could she? He had been there for her and her sister, Juniper, when their parents died. She would do anything for Sam, including assisting him so that fewer animals might end up abandoned at the shelters, terrified and bewildered at the turn in their lives.

But something was different, so slight that if she hadn't known him well, it might not have registered at all. Delia, cursed with a powerful sense of smell, had sniffed an acrid overlay from his usual older man scent, as if a new chemical had been added to his molecular mix. And the way he reached for his scalpel, a premature surge of his wrist, faster than his slow, deliberate pace. Then dropping the surgical instrument. The movement lost something in the jerkiness, a bit of connection with the dog that lay anesthetized, her lower belly ready for the slice that would take away all future puppies. No, it must have been Delia's lack of sleep, her newfound restlessness since she had actually handed her resignation to Ira, with three months' notice, which was too long for Delia but not nearly long enough for Ira. She had five weeks left.

Jill, the receptionist, opened the door. "There's a phone call for you, Delia, from the foster care place over in Portland."

How could Ira possibly know that she was working at the S&N clinic? She had turned off her phone when surgery started. He must have called her sister. This was going to be bad.

Delia followed Jill back to the reception desk and picked up the phone.

"Hi, Ira," she said.

"Sorry to pull you out of the clinic," he said, "but we've just had a request for an emergency placement. We're going to need you."

CHAPTER 3

Delia sat in the parking lot of Southern Maine Foster Services. She was keenly aware that she hadn't filed her latest case notes, becoming lackadaisical as her job drew to an end. She pulled out her laptop and typed in furiously before meeting with Ira.

She hadn't typed her notes from yesterday yet. She imagined titles for her case notes, which would be frowned on by Ira, potentially viewed as minimizing a child's tragedy or mocking the disaster of parenting gone haywire by alcohol, drugs, mental illness, or general meanness.

She never kept the titles, at least not yet, although the titles remained in her head. Sometimes titles captured an entire life or just a single interview. "Transformer Joe" for a boy who changed from sweet to tyrannical in an instant. "Don't Take My Blankie Away" for a child who had traveled through the worst of times with a shredded blue blanket, now the size of a paperback. "We're Just Atoms Combining and Recombining," a title for a family of four kids who were dispersed among three foster families until one foster home campaigned hard to take all four.

Imagining the titles was part of what helped Delia remember the most important details of a person's life, like labeling a photo in an album. But so few people still had photo albums. They had photos on their phones, or in the cloud. Although she was embarrassed to ask, she didn't really understand what the cloud was. And specifically, if you put something in the cloud like a photo or a kid's placement file, could you ever get it back? She'd ask one of the interns. One of the great things about graduate interns was that you could peel the latest technology right off them.

Her last intern said, "How old are you? You seem a lot older than you look." Her comment could have been in reference to Delia's lack of cloud technology. She hoped it wasn't the way she looked, at thirty-two. But she felt older, sometimes decades older.

When Delia told her boss Ira that she was done, Ira had not accepted her resignation easily. "This is about Juniper, isn't it? You can't keep taking care of her forever."

The truth was, resigning was about Delia and starting a new life without social services.

Ira, director of Southern Maine Foster Services, had worked his way up through the ranks. He had been a kid in the foster care system by the time he was eight years old, fresh out of the burn unit at Shriner's Hospital in Boston. She never asked him for details about the abuse; the burn scars visible along his arms were all she needed to know. He was one of the survivors. He had been in only two foster homes before he landed with a family who wanted to adopt him. His remaining biological parent, who was in prison, did the best thing he'd ever done for Ira by relinquishing all parental rights. But someone like Ira saw everything, every twitch, because he had to be vigilant when he was a kid. Now he was like one of the dogs who were trained to sniff out seizures moments before they felled their owner.

"It's the accumulation," she had told him, avoiding the comment about Juniper.

Delia finished her notes and filed them, snapping her laptop shut, and headed for whatever waited for her with Ira. Even now, walking along the hallway, she could smell it, the fear and anger of children who have come through the foster care system. Sort of a steel-wool-meets-linseed-oil smell that children give off when they've been hurt by the ones they loved.

Delia did all the right things that she'd learned over the years at the professional development workshops. Most recently she had attended another workshop about establishing clear boundaries. Buzzwords for not getting traumatized by the pain of your young clients. Bystander trauma.

She exercised, had friends, took every bit of her vacation time, and listened to music on her drive to and from work rather than the news. Even so, with each child, a droplet of something had found its way into Delia, like acid rain eating up the paint on her car. The accumulation finally hit her personal high-water mark.

Delia saw this with other people in her profession who had missed the signs. She did not want to become the bitter, fatalistic curmudgeon that others had morphed into.

As of today, she had thirty-five days left. Time to sensibly close out her cases, transfer them to others, and withdraw from the world of uphill battles. But Ira had called her and she did not, absolutely did not, want to know what waited for her. The underside of her chin itched, as it always did with the worst cases. She had stopped trying to explain the telltale itch to others. It just was and she had learned to listen to it. Scritch, scratch, like little creatures rambling about along her jawbone. This meant the case was searing hot with abandoned kids and parents in a tailspin. Or worse.

She rubbed her chin, trying to rub out the familiar twitch. She paused at her desk long enough to read the new file. A gift from Ira.

She closed the file after reading it. The child was five years old and had been released from the hospital. Blood was found on the child, but it was not her own. The pediatrician noted symptoms of malnutrition, a good deal of dirt under her fingernails, and mosquito bites that had become infected. She came in at the 70th percentile for weight and about the same for height.

They had reason to believe that she lived in a house on Bakersfield Road. Because the house was a crime scene, the on-call caseworker had not been able to get into the house to check for something that might be special to the girl; a blanket or a stuffed animal.

There had been three adults at the house, all shot close range. One woman, two men. The woman had been identified by her driver's license as Emma Gilbert, twenty-six, from Virginia. The two men had no IDs on them, as if they had been stripped of IDs or maybe they never had them. There was no information about the child.

This wasn't the first time that children had arrived in emergency foster care without any records at all. Children could fly under the radar for years, never see a doctor or a dentist, and never go to daycare or preschool.

She had been found by a middle-aged couple who stayed with the child until the police arrived. They requested to be notified about the well-being of the child. When the first cop on the scene had asked the girl what her name was, she answered without hesitation. "Hayley." When asked for her last name, she had shrugged.

Delia was glad that the job of locating relatives of the girl was up to Ira and not up to her. She looked at her job as surveyor of disaster, sort of a one-woman hazmat crew. Despite the media portrayal of foster care as the devil, foster care couldn't even enter the equation unless a true shit storm happened in a family where kids were in situations that looked like war zones. Or sometimes kids were just left with nobody, dangling, free-floating on their own.

No one wanted to be the kid who had to go to foster care, because that meant something cataclysmic happened, and one of those things might be that your parents didn't care enough about you, or weren't able to care about anyone, not even themselves. If kids at school knew you were in foster care, it was a neon sign on your forehead that said you weren't worth loving.

She paused in front of Ira's door, calming herself with several breaths. It wasn't working. Thirty-five days left. Delia slid the file across Ira's desk and said, "Were there really no family members for this child to stay with?" She looked down at the file again. The child's name was written on the file tab, not a nameless girl, but Hayley.

"What's going on here and why have you called me in? Why not someone else?"

"Because you're the best. Don't you think we should give this child the best that we have?"